W9-AZA-776

McKettrick's Luck

**Center Point
Large Print**

**This Large Print Book carries the
Seal of Approval of N.A.V.H.**

McKettrick's Luck

Linda Lael Miller

CENTER POINT PUBLISHING
THORNDIKE, MAINE

To Pam and Jon Reily, with love

This Center Point Large Print edition
is published in the year 2007 by arrangement with
Harlequin Enterprises, Ltd.

Copyright © 2007 by Linda Lael Miller.

All rights reserved.

The text of this Large Print edition is unabridged. In other
aspects, this book may vary from the original edition.
Printed in the United States of America.
Set in 16-point Times New Roman type.

ISBN-10: 1-58547-914-4
ISBN-13: 978-1-58547-914-6

Library of Congress Cataloging-in-Publication Data

Miller, Linda Lael.
    McKettrick's luck / Linda Lael Miller.--Center Point large print ed.
    p. cm.
    ISBN-13: 978-1-58547-914-6 (lib. bdg. : alk. paper)
    1. Texas--Fiction. 2. Large type books. I. Title.

PS3563.I41373M555 2007
813'.54--dc22

2006035156

CHAPTER ONE

MCKETTRICK LAND, Cheyenne Bridges thought stoically, as she stood next to her rented car on a gravel pullout alongside the highway, one hand shading her eyes from the Arizona sun. A faint drumbeat throbbed in her ears, an underground river flowing beneath her pulse, and she remembered a time she *could not* have remembered. An era when only the Great Spirit could lay claim to the valleys and canyons and mesas, to the arch of the sky, blue as her grandmother's favorite sugar bowl—a cherished premium plucked from some long-ago flour sack—to the red dirt and the scattered stands of white oak and Joshua and ponderosa pine.

It had taken Angus McKettrick, and other intrepidly arrogant nineteenth-century pioneers like him, to fence in these thousands of square miles, to pen their signatures to deeds, to run cattle and dig wells and wrest a living from the rocky, thistle-strewn soil. Old Angus had passed that audacious sense of ownership on to his sons, and the sons of their sons, down through the generations.

McKettricks forever and ever, amen.

Cheyenne bit her lower lip. Her cell phone, lying on the passenger seat of the car, chimed like an arriving elevator—Nigel again. She ignored the insistent sound until it stopped, only too aware that the reprieve would be fleeting. Meanwhile, the land itself seemed to seep into her heart, rising like water finding its level in some dank, forgotten cistern.

The feeling was bittersweet, a complex tangle of loneliness and homecoming and myriad other emotions she couldn't readily identify.

She had sworn never to come back to this place.

Never to set eyes on Jesse McKettrick again.

And fate, in its inimitable way, was forcing her to do both those things.

She sighed.

An old blue pickup passed on the road, horn honking in exuberant greeting. A trail of cheerfully mournful country music thrummed in its wake, and the peeling sticker on the rear bumper read Save The Cowboys.

Cheyenne waved, self-conscious in her trim black designer suit and high heels. This was boots-and-jeans country, and she'd stand out like the proverbial sore thumb the moment she drove into town.

Welcome home, she thought ruefully.

The cell chirped again, and she picked her way through the loose gravel to reach in through the open window and grabbed it.

"It's about time you answered," Nigel Meerland snapped before she could draw a breath to say hello. "I was beginning to think you'd fallen into some manhole."

"There aren't any manholes in Indian Rock," Cheyenne replied, making her way around to the driver's side and opening the door.

"Have you contacted him yet?" Nigel didn't bother

6

with niceties like "Hi, how are you?" either in person or over the telephone. He simply demanded what he wanted—and most of the time, he got it.

"Nigel," Cheyenne said evenly, "I just got here. So, no, I have not contacted him." *Him* was Jesse McKettrick. The last person in this or any other universe she wanted to see—not that Jesse would be able to place her in the long line of adoring women strung out behind him like the cars of a derailed freight train.

"Well, you're burning daylight, kiddo," Nigel shot back. Her boss was in his late thirties and English, but he liked using colorful terms, with a liberal smattering of clichés. *Westernisms,* he called them. "Let's get this show on the road. I don't have to tell you how anxious our investors are to get that condo development underway."

No, Cheyenne thought, sitting down sideways on the car seat, constrained by her tight skirt and swinging her legs in under the steering wheel, *you* don't *have to tell me. I've heard nothing else for the last six months.*

"Jesse won't sell," she said. Realizing she'd spoken the thought aloud, she closed her eyes, braced for the inevitable response.

"He *has* to sell," Nigel countered. "Failure is not an option. Everything—and I mean *everything*—is riding on this deal. If the finance people pull out, the company will go under. You won't have a job, and I'll have to crawl back to the ancestral pile on my knees, begging for the scant privileges of a second son."

Cheyenne closed her eyes. Like Nigel, she had a lot

at stake. More than just her job. She had Mitch, her younger brother, to consider. And her mother.

The bonus Nigel had promised, in writing, would give them all a kind of security they'd never known.

The pit of her stomach clenched.

"I know," she told Nigel bleakly. "I know."

"Get cracking, Pocahontas," Nigel instructed, and hung up in her ear.

Cheyenne opened her eyes, pressed the end button with her thumb, drew a deep breath and released it slowly. Then she tossed the phone onto the other seat, started the engine and headed for Indian Rock.

The town hadn't changed much since she'd left it at seventeen, bound for college down in Tucson. There was the dry cleaners, the library, the elementary school. And the small, white-steepled church where she'd struggled to understand Commandments and arks and burning bushes, and had placed quarters, after unwrapping them carefully from a cheap cloth handkerchief, in the collection plate.

She sat a little straighter in the seat as she drove the length of Main Street, signaled and turned left at the old train depot, long since converted to an antiques minimall. The rental car bumped over the railroad tracks, past progressively seedier trailer courts, through a copse of cottonwood trees.

The narrow beams of the ancient cattle guard rattled under the tires.

Cheyenne gave a grateful sigh when the car didn't fall through and slowed to round the last bend in the

8

narrow dirt road leading to the house.

Like the single and double-wides she'd just passed, the place had gone downhill in her absence. The lawn was overgrown and coils of rusty barbed wire littered the ground. The porch sagged and the siding, scavenged and nailed to the walls without regard to color, jarred the eye.

Gram had been so proud of her house and yard. It would break her heart to see it now.

Her mother's old van, a patchwork affair like the house, stood in the driveway with the side door open.

Cheyenne had hoped for a few days to settle in before her mother and brother arrived from Phoenix, and at least put in a ramp for Mitch's wheelchair, but it wasn't to be. Her heart fluttered with anticipation, then sank.

She put the rental in Park and shut off the motor, surveying the only real home she'd ever had.

"I'll show you an ancestral *pile,* Nigel," she muttered. "Just hop in your Bentley and drive on up to Indian Rock, Arizona."

The front door swung open just then, and Ayanna Bridges appeared on the porch, wearing a faded cotton dress, high-topped sneakers and a tentative smile. Her straight ebony hair fell past her waist, loosely restrained by a tarnished silver barrette she'd probably owned since the 1960s. When her mother started toward the rickety steps, Cheyenne got out of the car.

"Look," Ayanna called, pointing. "I found some old boards out behind the shed and dragged them around

9

to make a ramp. Mitch whizzed right up to them like he was on flat ground."

Life had forced Ayanna to be resourceful. Makeshift ramps for her son's wheelchair were the least of her accomplishments. She'd waited tables, often pulling two shifts, grappled with various social-service agencies to get Mitch the medical care he needed, sold cosmetics and miracle vitamins, all without a twinge of self-pity—at least, not one she'd ever allowed her children to see.

Cheyenne scrounged up a smile. Pretended to admire the pair of teetering, weathered two-by-fours, each with one end propped on the porch floor and one disappearing into the weedy grass. Doubtless, Mitch had used them to alight from the van, too.

If—*when*—the bonus came through, Cheyenne planned to buy a new van, specially equipped with a hydraulic lift and maybe even hand controls. For now, they would have to make do, as they'd always done.

"Good work," she said.

Ayanna met her in the middle of the yard, enfolding Cheyenne in a hug that made her breath catch and her eyes burn.

She blinked a couple of times before meeting her mother's fond gaze.

"Where's Mitch?" Cheyenne asked.

"Inside," Ayanna said, her words gently hushed. "I'm afraid he's brooding again—he misses his friends in Phoenix. He'll be all right once he's had a little while to get used to being here."

Cheyenne could empathize. She thought, with poignant longing, of her one-bedroom condo in sunny San Diego, half a mile from the beach. She'd sublet it, and that was another worry. If she couldn't convince Jesse McKettrick to part with five hundred acres of prime real estate, she not only wouldn't have a job, she'd have to stay in Indian Rock, find whatever work there was to be had and stockpile pennies until she could afford to start over somewhere else.

As she stood there despairing, Nigel's cell-phone comment blew through her spirit like a cold wind scouring the walls of a lonely canyon. *Everything's riding on this deal. And I mean* everything.

"Come on inside, honey," Ayanna said, taking Cheyenne's arm when she would have turned and fled back to the rental car. "We can bring your things in later."

Cheyenne nodded, ashamed that she'd come so close, after all her preparation and effort, to fleeing the scene.

Ayanna smiled, butted her taller daughter lightly with the outside of one shoulder. "We've all come home," she said softly. "You and Mitch and me. And home is a great place to start over."

Home might be a "great place to start over," Cheyenne reflected grimly, if you were a McKettrick. If your key fit the lock of one of the several sprawling, rustically elegant houses standing sturdily on a section of the legendary Triple M Ranch.

If your name was Bridges, on the other hand, and

11

you were the daughter of a charming but compulsive gambler who'd died in jail, and a hardworking but fatally codependent dreamer like Ayanna, making a clean-slate beginning was a luxury you couldn't afford.

Ordinary people had to settle for survival.

NURLEEN GENTRY SHUFFLED and dealt the flop—a pair of sevens and a queen. Once the cards were down, lying helter-skelter on the scruffy green-felt tabletop, she folded her hands, glittering with fake diamonds ordered from the shopping channel, and waited.

Jesse leaned back in his customary chair in the card room behind Lucky's Main Street Bar and Grill and pretended to consider his options. He felt the eyes of the other poker players on him, through the stale and shifting haze of blue-gray cigarette smoke, and gave nothing away.

"Bet or fold, McKettrick," Wade Parker grumbled from the other side of the table. Jesse allowed one corner of his mouth to crook up, ever so slightly, in the go-to-hell grin he'd been perfecting since he was eleven. Wade wore a bad rug and a windbreaker emblazoned with the logo of the beer company he worked for, and his full lips twitched with impatience. The tobacco smudge rose from the cheap cigar smoldering in the ashtray beside him.

Next to Wade was Don Rogers, who owned the Laundromat. Don squirmed on the patched vinyl seat of his chair, but Jesse knew it wasn't the wait that bothered the other man. Don was a neat freak and wanted to tidy the flop so badly that a muscle under his right eye jerked. Touching anybody's cards but his own could get a man shot in some parts, though the retribution would be neither swift nor terrible in the old hometown.

Could be Don had pocket queens, Jesse thought, but that didn't seem likely. When it came to tells, Don was easier to read than the twelve-foot limestone letters set into the slope east of town, spelling out INDIAN ROCK.

Everything about Don said, WINGING IT.

Jesse made a show of pondering myriad possibilities, then accordioned four fifty-dollar chips into the pot.

"Shit," Don muttered, and put down his cards without revealing them, one precisely on top of the other.

Wade leaned forward, his bushy eyebrows raised. Nurleen, an old hand at dealing poker and a better-than-fair player herself, though her specialty was Omaha, not Texas Hold 'Em, said nothing, but simply looked on with intense disinterest.

"I think you're bluffing, McKettrick," Wade said. He rifled his chips, which had been growing steadily for the last half hour.

"Think what you like," Jesse countered, without inflection. He'd already thrown in a couple of winning hands, just to support Wade's delusion that the poker gods were lined up solidly behind him, armed for battle. Jesse had time, and he had money—a deadly combination, in poker or just about any other endeavor.

Wade plucked a pair of sunglasses from the pocket of his windbreaker and shoved them onto his face.

A little late, Jesse thought, but this time, he kept his grin on the inside, where nobody knew about it but him.

Nurleen dealt the fourth card, known in Hold 'Em parlance as the *turn.*

Jesse ruminated. Even if Wade had twin aces to go with the one on the table, three of a kind wouldn't take the pot, which meant the beer salesman was screwed. Unless the fifth card, or the *river,* turned out to be another ace, of course.

Bad beats happened—in the back rooms of small-town bars and the championship tournaments in Vegas and everywhere in between. Jesse's gut said *Risk it,* but then, it rarely said anything else.

Out of the corner of one eye, Jesse saw someone slip through the doorway from the bar. Coins clinked into the jukebox.

After a brief intro, Kenny Rogers proclaimed the wisdom of knowing when to hold 'em, and when to fold 'em. When to walk away, and when to run.

Jesse knew all about holding and folding, but walking away was anathema to him, never mind running.

Wade matched Jesse's bet and raised him three hundred.

Jesse responded in kind.

Nurleen turned the river card.

A deuce of hearts.

Jesse let his grin show again.

"Call," Wade said. He pushed his wager to the middle of the table, showed his cards. King of hearts, queen of spades. He'd been counting on the lady in his hand and the one on the table to make a hand.

Nurleen sighed almost imperceptibly and shook her head.

Jesse felt a twinge of guilt as he tossed out two sevens.

Four of a kind.

Wade swore. "Damn your dumb-ass luck, Jesse," he growled.

Nurleen gathered the cards, shuffled for a new game. "You still in, Wade? Don?"

Know when to walk away, Kenny advised. *Know when to run.*

Jesse spared a sidelong glance and saw his cousin Keegan leaning against the jukebox with his arms folded. He looked like a city lawyer, or even a banker, in his tailored slacks, vest and crisply pressed shirt.

Jesse cracked another grin, mostly because he knew what he was about to say would piss Keegan off. "I'm in," he said.

"I'd like a word with you," Keegan said, keeping his distance but looking downright implacable at the same time. "Maybe you could skip a hand."

Wade and Don looked so hopeful that Jesse exchanged glances with Nurleen and pushed back his chair to stand and cross the floor, which was littered, in true Old West style, with peanut shells and sawdust.

There might have been tobacco juice, too, if the health department hadn't been sure to kick up a fuss. Around Indian Rock, folks took their history seriously.

"What's so important that it can't wait?" he asked, in a low voice that slid in under Kenny's famous vibrato.

Keegan was the same height as Jesse, but the resemblance ended there. Keegan had reddish-brown hair, always neatly trimmed, while Jesse's was dark blond and shaggy. Keegan had the navy-blue eyes that ran in Kade McKettrick's lineage, and Jesse's were the light azure common to Jeb's descendents.

"We had a meeting, remember?" Keegan snapped.

Kenny wrapped up the song, and a silence fell. The jukebox whirred and Patsy Cline launched into "Crazy."

Jesse grinned. First, a musical treatise on gambling. Then, a comment on mental health. "That's real Freudian, Keeg," he drawled. "And I didn't know you cared."

Keegan's square jaw tightened as he set his back molars. By now, they must have been worn down to nubs, Jesse reckoned, but he kept that observation to himself.

"Goddamn it," Keegan rasped, "you've got as big a share in the Company as I do. How about showing a little responsibility?" Keegan always capitalized any reference to McKettrickCo, the family conglomerate, verbally or in writing. The man worked twelve-hour days, pored over spreadsheets and pulled down a seven-figure salary.

16

By contrast, Jesse rode horses, entered the occasional rodeo, chased women, played poker and banked his dividend checks. He considered himself one lucky son of a gun, and in his more charitable moments he felt sorry for Keegan. Now, he straightened his cousin's tasteful pin-striped tie, which had probably cost more than the newest front-loader over at Don's Laundromat.

"You think poker isn't work?" he asked and waited for the steam to shoot out of Keegan's ears. They'd grown up together on the Triple M, fishing and camping out in warm weather, snowshoeing and cross-country skiing in winter, with Rance, a third cousin, completing the unholy trio. They'd all gone to college at Northern Arizona University in Flagstaff, where Keegan had majored in business, Rance had studied high finance and Jesse had attended class between rodeo competitions and card games. Despite their differences, they'd gotten along well enough—until Rance and Keegan had both married. Everything had changed then.

They'd both turned serious.

These days Rance traveled the world, making deals for McKettrickCo.

"Smart-ass," Keegan said, struggling not to grin.

"Buy you a beer?" Jesse asked, hopeful, for a brief moment, that his cousin was back.

Keegan glanced at his Rolex. "It's my weekend with Devon," he said. "I'm supposed to pick her up at six-thirty."

Devon was Keegan's nine-year-old daughter, and since he and his wife, Shelley, had divorced a year ago, they'd been shuttling the kid back and forth between Shelley and the boyfriend's upscale condo in Flag and the main ranch house on the Triple M where Keegan remained.

Jesse hesitated, then laid a hand on Keegan's shoulder. "It's okay," he said quietly. "Another time."

Keegan sighed. "Another time," he agreed, resigned. He started to walk away, then turned back. "And, Jesse?"

"What?"

The old, familiar grin spread across Keegan's face. "Grow up, will you?"

"I'll put that on my calendar," Jesse promised, returning the grin. He loved Devon, whom he thought of as a niece rather than a cousin however many times removed, and certainly didn't begrudge her time with Keegan. Just the same, he felt a twinge of sadness, too.

Everything and everybody in the world changed—except him.

That was the reality. Best accept it.

Jesse went back to the poker table and anted up for the next hand.

"Can't this wait until tomorrow?" Ayanna had asked, somewhat plaintively, after coffee at the kitchen table, where Mitch had sat brooding in his chair, when Cheyenne had announced her intention to track down Jesse McKettrick.

With a shake of her head, Cheyenne had said no, gathered her wits, smoothed her skirt and straightened her jacket, and made for the rental car.

McKettrickCo seemed to be the logical place to start her search—she'd already discovered, via her cell phone, that Jesse's number was unlisted.

Cheyenne knew, having grown up in Indian Rock, that the company's home offices were in San Antonio. The new building housed a branch of the operation, which meant the outfit was in expansion mode. According to her research, McKettrickCo was a diverse corporation, with interests in cutting-edge technology and global investment.

Jesse's name wasn't on the reader board in the sleekly contemporary reception area, a fact that didn't surprise Cheyenne. When she'd known him, he was the original trust-fund bad boy, wild as a mustang and committed to one thing: having a good time.

She approached the desk, relieved that she didn't recognize the woman tapping away at the keyboard of a supercomputer with three large flat-screen monitors.

"May I help you?" the receptionist asked pleasantly. She was middle-aged, with a warm smile, a lacquered blond hairdo and elegant posture.

Cheyenne introduced herself, hoping her last name wouldn't ring any bells, and asked how to locate Jesse McKettrick. With luck—and she was due for some of that—she wouldn't have to drive all the way out to his house and confront him on his own turf.

Not that any part of Indian Rock was neutral ground

when it came to the McKettricks.

The receptionist assessed Cheyenne with mild interest. "Jesse could be anywhere," she said, after some length, "but if I had to make a guess, I'd say he's probably in the back room over at Lucky's, playing poker."

Cheyenne stiffened. Of course he'd be at Lucky's—fate wouldn't have it any other way. How many times, as a child, had she sneaked through the back door of that place from the alley and tried to will her father away from a game of five-card stud?

She produced a business card, bearing her name, affiliation with Meerland Real Estate Ventures, Ltd., and her cell number. "Thanks," she said. "Just in case you see Mr. McKettrick before I do, will you give him my card and ask him to please call me as soon as possible?"

The woman studied Cheyenne's information, frowned and then nodded politely. "He doesn't come in too often," she said.

Of course he didn't.

Still Jesse, after all these years.

Cheyenne left McKettrickCo, got back into her car and drove resolutely to Lucky's Main Street Bar and Grill. The gravel parking lot beside the old brick building was full, with the dinner hour fast approaching, so she parked in the alley, next to a mud-splattered black truck with both windows rolled down.

For a moment, she was a kid again, sent by her misguided mother to fetch Daddy home from the bar. She remembered propping her bike against the wall, next to the overflowing trash bin, rehearsing what she'd say once she got inside, forcing herself up the two unpainted steps and through the screened door, which always groaned on its hinges.

When the door suddenly creaked open, Cheyenne was startled. She wrenched herself out of the time warp and actually considered crouching behind the Dumpster until whoever it was had gone.

Jesse stepped out, stretched like a lazy tomcat at home in an alley and fixing to go on the prowl, and adjusted his cowboy hat. He wore old jeans, a Western shirt unbuttoned to his collarbone and the kind of boots country people called shit-kickers. Even mud and horse manure couldn't disguise the fact that they were expensive, probably custom-made.

When Cheyenne's gaze trailed back up to Jesse's face, she realized that he was looking at her. Grinning that lethal grin.

She blushed.

Someone flipped the porch light on from inside, and moths immediately gravitated to it, out of nowhere. Drawing an immediate parallel between Jesse and the bulb, she took half a step back.

He registered her suit and high-heeled shoes in a lazy sweep of his eyes. He clearly didn't recognize her, which was at once galling and a relief.

He tugged at the brim of his battered hat. "You lost?" he asked.

Cheyenne was a moment catching her breath. "No,"

she answered, fishing in her hobo bag for another card. "My name is Cheyenne Bridges, and I was hoping to talk to you about a business proposition."

She instantly regretted using the word *proposition* because it made a corner of Jesse's mouth tilt with amusement, but she was past the point of no return.

He descended the steps with that loose-limbed, supremely confident walk she remembered so well and approached her. Put out his hand. "Jesse McKettrick," he said.

There was nothing to say but "I know." She'd given herself away with the first words she'd spoken.

"Bridges," he said, reflecting. Studying the card pensively before slipping it into his shirt pocket.

Cheyenne braced herself inwardly. Glanced toward the screen door Jesse had come through a few moments before.

"Any relation to—?" He paused, stooped slightly to look into her face. Recollection dawned. "Wait a second. *Cheyenne Bridges.*" He grinned. "I remember you—Cash's daughter. We went to the movies a couple of times."

She swallowed, nodded, hiked her chin up a notch. "That's right," she said carefully. Cash's daughter, that's who she was to him. A shy teenager he'd dated twice and then lost interest in. He didn't know, she reminded herself silently, that she'd tacked every picture of him she could get to the wall of her bedroom in that shack out beyond the railroad tracks, the way most girls did photos of rock stars and film idols. He didn't know she'd loved him with the kind of desperate, hopeless adoration only a sixteen-year-old can feel.

He didn't know she'd prayed that he'd fall madly in love with her. That she'd imagined their wedding, their honeymoon and the birth of their four children so often that sometimes it felt like a memory of something that had really happened, rather than the fantasy it was.

Thank God Jesse didn't know any of those things. She wouldn't have been able to face him if he had, even with Mitch and her mom and Nigel all depending on her to persuade him to sell five hundred unspoiled acres of land to her company.

"I heard about your brother's accident," he said. "I'm sorry."

Shaken out of her reverie, Cheyenne nodded again. "Thanks."

"Your dad, too."

Her eyes stung. She tried to speak, swallowed instead.

Jesse smiled, took a light grip on her elbow. "Do you always do business in alleys?" he teased.

For a moment, she was affronted. Then she realized it was a perfectly reasonable question. "No," she said.

"I was just heading for the Roadhouse to grab some supper. Want to come along?" He gestured toward the muddy truck.

The Roadhouse, also known as the Roadkill Café, was an institution in Indian Rock, a haven for truck drivers, bikers, cowboys and state patrolmen. Ironically, families dined at Lucky's, probably pretending

23

that the card room behind it didn't exist.

"I'll meet you there," Cheyenne said. She'd have been safe enough with Jesse, but no way was she climbing into that truck in a straight skirt. She had *some* dignity, after all, even if she did feel like the scrawny ten-year-old who'd parked her bike in this alley and gone inside to beg her father, with a stellar lack of success, to come home for supper. Or to watch her perform in the class play. Or to take Gram to the hospital because she couldn't catch her breath . . .

"Okay," Jesse said easily. He walked her to the rental car, which looked nondescript beside his truck. Like his boots, the vehicle had seen its share of action. Like his boots, it was top-of-the-line, with dual tires and an extended cab. Definitely leather seats, custom CD player and a GPS, too.

Once she was behind the wheel of the rental, with the window rolled down, Jesse leaned easily against the door and looked in at her.

"It's good to see you again, Cheyenne," he said.

"You, too," she replied. But a lump rose in her throat. *Don't go there,* she told herself sternly. *This is business. You'll buy the land. You'll help Nigel get the construction project rolling. You'll collect your bonus and take care of Mitch and your mother. And then you'll go back to San Diego and forget Jesse McKettrick ever existed.*

"As if," she muttered aloud.

Jesse, in the process of turning away to head for his truck, turned back. "Did you say something?"

She gave him her best smile. "See you there," she said.

He waved. Hoisted himself into the truck and fired up the engine.

Cheyenne waited until he pulled out, and then followed.

If she'd been as smart as other people thought she was, she thought grimly, she'd have kept on going. Sped right out of Indian Rock, past the Roadhouse, past Jesse and all the other memories and impossible dreams he represented, and never looked back.

CHAPTER TWO

JESSE REACHED the Roadhouse first and waited in his truck for Cheyenne to catch up. Things had been dull around Indian Rock lately, with nothing much to do besides play poker and feed horses, but he had a feeling life was about to get a little more interesting.

Smiling slightly, he pulled Cheyenne's business card from his pocket and read it again. Meerland *Real Estate* Ventures, Ltd.

This time, it clicked.

The smile faded to black.

She wanted *the land.*

"Damn," he muttered, watching in the side mirror as Cheyenne's car turned into the lot and pulled up beside him.

He sighed. She'd been pretty, as a girl. Strangely

alert, too, like a deer raising its head at a watering hole at the snap of a twig, sniffing the wind for the scent of danger. Now, as a woman, Cheyenne Bridges was beautiful. Slight in adolescence, she'd rounded out real well, and if she'd let that rich dark hair down from the prim French twist and ditch the librarian gear, she'd be a showstopper.

Jesse got out of the truck, waited stiffly while Cheyenne pushed open her car door to stand teetering on those ridiculous shoes. She smiled tentatively and touched her hair.

In poker, that move would be an eloquent tell: Cheyenne was nervous.

And if his suspicions were right, she had *cause* to be nervous. He retallied the facts in his head—she worked for a real-estate company, of the "ventures" variety, and back there in the alley behind Lucky's she'd said she wanted to discuss a business proposition.

In those few moments while they both stood in the gap between silence and speech, between uncertainty and decision, he considered sparing her fruitless expectations. He wasn't about to sell the acres just beyond the eastern boundaries of the Triple M, if that was what she wanted. That land was the only thing he'd ever gotten on his own and not by virtue of being born a McKettrick.

Then again, he supposed he ought to at least hear her out. Maybe he was wrong, and she was beating the brush for investors. Being a gambler, he might be able to get behind something like that, if only because it would mean spending time with Cheyenne, unraveling some of the mysteries.

One thing was obvious. Cheyenne had come a long way since she'd left Indian Rock. The car was nothing special—probably rented—but the clothes were upscale. And while she still used her maiden name, that didn't mean she wasn't married. His older sisters, Sarah and Victoria, both had husbands, but still they went by McKettrick.

He glanced at Cheyenne's left hand, looking for a ring, but the hand was hidden by the wide strap of her purse.

"Shall we?" he asked and gestured toward the entrance of the Roadhouse.

She looked relieved. "Sure," she said. She walked a little ahead, and he opened the door for her.

Jesse had been eating at the Roadhouse all his life, but as he followed Cheyenne over the threshold, it seemed strange to him, a place he'd never been before. The sounds and smells and colors spun around him, and he felt disoriented, as though he'd just leaped off some great wheel while it was still spinning. He was a second or two getting his bearings.

He'd gone to school with the hostess, from kindergarten through his senior year at Indian Rock High, but as he and Cheyenne followed the woman to a corner booth, he couldn't have said what her name was.

What the hell was wrong with him?

Cheyenne slid into the red vinyl seat, and Jesse sat

opposite, placing his hat on the wide windowsill behind the miniature jukebox. He ordered coffee, she asked for sparkling mineral water with a twist of lime.

They studied their plastic menus, and when the waitress showed up—Jesse had gone to school with her, too, and consulted her name tag so he wouldn't be caught out—Cheyenne went with French onion soup and he chose a double-deluxe cheeseburger, with fries.

"Thanks, Roselle," he said, to anchor himself in ordinary reality.

Roselle touched his shoulder, smiled flirtatiously and sashayed away to fill the orders.

Cheyenne raised her eyebrows slightly, but said nothing.

Might as well bite the bullet, Jesse figured. "So Cheyenne, what brings you back to Indian Rock after all this time?" he asked easily.

She took a sip of fizzy water. "Business," she said.

Jesse thought of his land. Of the timber, and the wide, grassy clearings, and the creek that shone so brightly in the sun that it made a man blink. He tasted his coffee and waited.

Cheyenne sighed. She had the air of someone about to jump through an ice hole in a frozen lake. "My company is prepared to offer you a very competitive price for—"

"No," Jesse broke in flatly.

She'd made the jump, and from her expression, the water was even colder than expected. "No?"

"No," he repeated.

"You didn't let me finish," she protested, rallying. "We're talking about several *million* dollars here. No carrying back a mortgage. No balloon payments. *Cash.* We can close on the deal within two weeks of going to contract."

Jesse started to reach for his hat, sighed and withdrew his hand. He'd seen this coming. Why did he feel like a kid who'd counted on getting a BB gun for Christmas and found new underwear under the tree instead?

"There isn't going to be any contract," he said.

She paled. Settled back against the booth seat. Her hand trembled as she set down her water glass.

"The price is negotiable," she told him after a few moments of looking stricken.

He knew what she was thinking; he could read it in her face. *Money talks.* She thought he was angling for a higher price.

"You should never take up poker," he said.

The food arrived.

Roselle winked as she set the burger down in front of him.

"I hate women like that," Cheyenne told him after Roselle had swivel-hipped it back behind the counter.

Unprepared for this bend in the conversational river, Jesse paused with a French fry halfway to his mouth. "What?"

"They're a type," Cheyenne said, leaning in a little and lowering her voice. "Other women are invisible to them. If they had their way, the whole world would be a reverse harem."

Jesse chuckled. "Well, that's an interesting take on the subject," he allowed. "The soup's pretty good here."

She picked up her spoon, put it down again. "It's not as if I'm asking you to sell any part of the Triple M," she said. Another hairpin turn, but this time, Jesse was ready. "That land is just *sitting* there. Unused."

"Un*spoiled*," Jesse clarified. "I suppose you want to turn it into an industrial park. Or a factory—the world really needs more disposable plastic objects."

"Condominiums," Cheyenne said, squaring her shoulders.

Jesse winced. "Even worse," he replied.

"People need places to live."

"So do critters," Jesse said. He'd been hungry when he'd suggested supper at the Roadhouse. Now, he wasn't sure he could choke down any part of that cheeseburger. "We've got so many coyotes and bobcats coming right into town these days that the feds are about to put a bounty on them. Do you know why, Ms. Bridges?" he asked, suddenly icily formal.

"Why are coyotes and bobcats coming into town," she countered, "or why is the government about to put a bounty on them?"

Jesse set his back teeth, thought of his cousin Keegan for no reason he could have explained, and deliberately relaxed his jaws. "Wild animals are being driven farther out of their natural habitat every day," he said. "By people like you. They've got to be *somewhere,* damn it."

"Which do you care more about, *Mr.* McKettrick? People or animals?"

"Depends," Jesse said. "I've known people who could learn scruples from a rabid badger. And it's not as if building more condominiums is a service to humanity. Most of them are a blight on the land—and they all look alike, too. Stucco boxes, stacked on top of each other. What's *that* about?"

Cheyenne picked up her spoon, made a halfhearted swipe at her soup. Straightened her spine. "I'd be glad to show you the blueprints," she said. "Our project is designed to blend gracefully into the landscape, with minimal impact on the environment."

Jesse eyed his cheeseburger regretfully. All those additives and preservatives going to waste, not to mention a lot of perfectly good grease. "No deal," he said. With anybody else, he'd have played out the hand, let her believe he was interested in selling, just to see what came of it. Cheyenne Bridges was different, and that was the most disturbing element of all.

Why was she different?

"Just let me show you the plans," she persisted.

"Just let me show you the land," he retorted.

She smiled. "I'll let you show me yours," she bargained, "if you'll let me show you mine."

He laughed. "You sure are persistent," he said.

"You sure are stubborn," she answered.

Jesse reached for his cheeseburger. By that time, he'd had ample opportunity to notice that she wasn't wearing a wedding ring.

"You ever get married?" he asked.

She seemed to welcome the change of subject, though the quiet, bruised vigilance was still there in her eyes and the set of her shoulders and the way she held her head. "No," she said. "You?"

"No," he told her. He and Brandi, a rodeo groupie, had been married by an Elvis in Las Vegas, come to their senses before word had got out, and agreed to divorce an hour after they'd checked out of the hotel. They'd parted friends, and he hadn't seen her in a couple of years, though she hit him up for a few hundred dollars every now and then, and he always sent the money.

As far as he was concerned, he'd answered honestly. Brandi slipped out of his mind as quickly as she'd slipped in.

Meanwhile, he'd only taken a couple of bites of the sandwich, but the patty was thick and goopy with cheese, and protein always centered him—especially when he'd been playing cards all day, subsisting on the cold cereal he'd had for breakfast after doing the chores on the ranch. Sure enough, it was the burger that lifted his spirits.

Sure enough, said a voice in his head, *you're full of sheep dip.*

It's the woman.

"How's the soup?" he asked.

"Cold," she said. "How's the burger?"

He grinned. "It's clogging my arteries even as we speak."

Cheyenne lifted one eyebrow, but she was smiling. "And that's good?"

"Probably not," he said. "But it tastes great."

After that, the conversation was relatively easy.

They finished their meal, Jesse paid the bill, and Cheyenne left the tip.

He walked her to her car. There was virtually no crime in Indian Rock, but that kind of courtesy was bred into him, like opening doors and carrying heavy things.

"You'll really look at the plans?" she asked quietly, her eyes luminous, once she was behind the wheel.

"If you'll look at the land," Jesse reminded her. "Come up to the ranch tomorrow, around nine o'clock. I'll be through feeding the horses around then."

She nodded. A pulse fluttered at the base of her throat. "I'll bring the blueprints," she said.

"Please," he said, with mock enthusiasm, "bring the blueprints."

She laughed and moved to close the car door. "Thanks for supper, Jesse."

He went to tug at the brim of his hat, then remembered he'd left it inside the Roadhouse. "My pleasure," he said, feeling awkward for the first time in recent memory.

He watched as Cheyenne started the car, backed out and drove away. Ordinarily, he'd have gone back to Lucky's to play a few more hands of cards, but that night, he just wanted to go home.

He went back into the Roadhouse, reclaimed his hat.

Roselle invited him to a party at her place.

If her eyes had been hands, he'd have been stripped naked, right there in the Roadhouse. Clearly, the "party" she had in mind would include the two of them and nobody else.

He said some other time, adding a mental "maybe."

Back in his truck, he adjusted the rearview mirror and looked into his own eyes. *Who are you?* he asked silently. *And what have you done with Jesse McKettrick?*

"I COMPLETELY BLEW IT," Cheyenne told her mother the moment she stepped into the house that night.

Ayanna sat on the old couch, her feet resting bare on the cool linoleum floor, crocheting something from multi-strands of variegated yarn. "How so?" she asked mildly.

The sounds of cyber-battle bounced in from the next room. Mitch was playing a video game on his laptop. Mitch was *always* playing a video game on his laptop. It was as though by shooting down animated enemies he could keep his own demons at bay.

"Jesse flatly refused to sell me the land," Cheyenne said.

Ayanna smiled softly. "You expected that."

Cheyenne tossed her heavy handbag onto a chair, kicked off her shoes and sighed with relief. "Yeah," she said.

"Want something to eat?" Ayanna asked. "Mitch and I had mac-and-cheese."

"I had soup," Cheyenne said.

Her cell phone played its elevator song inside her bag.

"Ignore it," Ayanna advised.

"I can't," Cheyenne answered. She fished out the phone, flipped it open and said, "Hello, Nigel."

"Have you made any progress?" Nigel asked.

Cheyenne looked at her watch. "Gosh, Nigel. You've shown amazing restraint. It's been at least an hour and a half since the *last* time you called."

"You said you were on your way to have dinner with McKettrick," Nigel reminded her. They'd talked, live via satellite, during the drive between Lucky's and the Roadhouse. "How did it go?"

Ayanna sat serenely, crocheting away.

"He said no," Cheyenne reported.

"Just like that?"

"Just like that."

"We're doomed."

"Take a breath, Nigel. He agreed to look at the plans—on one condition."

"What condition?"

"I have to look at the land. Tomorrow morning. I'm meeting him at his place at 9:00 a.m."

"So we're still in the running?"

"Anybody's guess," Cheyenne said wearily, moving her purse to sink into the chair herself. "Jesse's direct, if nothing else, and as soon as he knew what I wanted, he dug in his heels."

"Maybe you shouldn't have sprung it on him so

soon," Nigel mused. Cheyenne could just see her boss's bushy brows knitting together in a thoughtful frown. She wondered if he'd ever considered investing in a weed eater, for purposes of personal grooming.

"You didn't give me any other choice, remember?"

"Don't make this *my* fault."

"You've been breathing down my neck since I got off the plane in Phoenix yesterday morning. If you want me to do the impossible, Nigel, you've got to give me some space."

"You *can* do this, can't you, Cheyenne?"

She felt a surge of shaky confidence. "I specialize in the impossible," she said.

"Come through for me, babe," Nigel wheedled.

"Don't call me *babe,*" Cheyenne responded. Out of the corner of her eye, she saw her mother smile. "And don't bug me, either. When I have something to tell you, I'll be in touch—"

"But—"

"Goodbye, Nigel." Cheyenne thumbed the end button.

Sounds of intense warfare burgeoned from Mitch's room.

With another sigh, Cheyenne tossed the cell phone onto a dust-free end table and rose from her chair. "You know something, Mom?" she said, brightening. "You're amazing. You've been in this house for a few hours, and already it feels like home."

Ayanna's eyes glittered with a sudden sheen of tears. "I want to do my part, Cheyenne," she said. "I know you think you're in this alone, but you're not. You have me, and you have Mitch."

Cheyenne's throat knotted up. When she spoke, her voice came out as a croak. "Speaking of Mitch—"

Ayanna set aside her crochet project and stood, pointed herself in the direction of the kitchen, which, unlike those in the condos Cheyenne and Nigel planned to build, boasted none of the modern conveniences. "I'll make you some herbal tea," Ayanna said. "Might help you sleep."

"Thanks," Cheyenne said and crossed to push open the partially closed door to her brother's room.

Mitch sat hunched over his computer, a refurbished model, bought with money Ayanna had probably saved from the checks Cheyenne sent every payday. He seemed so slight and fragile, slouched in his wheelchair, with a card table for a desk. Once, he'd been athletic. One of the most popular kids in school.

"Hey," Cheyenne said.

"Hey," Mitch responded without looking away from the laptop screen.

She considered mussing his hair, the way she'd done when he was younger, before the accident, and decided against the idea. Mitch was nineteen now, and his dignity was about all he had left.

When the deal was done, she reminded herself, she'd buy him a *real* computer, like the one she'd seen at McKettrickCo when she'd stopped in looking for Jesse earlier that day. Maybe then he'd start hoping again.

"I wish we could go back to Phoenix," he said.

She sat down on his bed. Ayanna had brought his blankets and spread from home, put them on the roll-away that had been old when Cheyenne had left for college. Oh, yes, Ayanna had tried, but the room was depressing, just the same. The wallpaper was peeling, and the curtains looked as though they'd been through at least one flood. The linoleum floor was scuffed, with the pattern worn away in several places.

"What's in Phoenix?" she asked lightly, though she knew. In the low-income housing where he and Ayanna lived, he'd had friends. He'd had cable TV, and there was a major library across from the apartment building, with computers. Here, he had an old laptop and a rollaway bed.

Mitch merely shrugged, but he shut down the game and swiveled his chair around so he could face Cheyenne.

"Things are gonna get better," she said.

"That's what Mom says, too," Mitch replied, but he didn't sound as if he believed it.

Cheyenne studied her brother. She and Mitch had different fathers; hers was dead, his was God knew where. Ten years ago, when she'd left Indian Rock, he'd been nine and she'd been seventeen. When Ayanna had followed her second husband, Pete, to Phoenix, dragging Mitch along with her, Cheyenne had been in her sophomore year at the University of Arizona, scrambling to keep up her grades and hold on to her night job. Mitch had written her a plaintive letter, begging her to come home, so the two of them could stay in this run-down shack of a house. He'd loved Indian Rock then—loved the singular freedoms of growing up in a small town.

She'd replied with a postcard, scrawled on her break at Hooters, telling him to *get real.* She wasn't about to come back, and even if she did, Ayanna would never agree to let them live alone, with Gram gone. *You'll like Phoenix,* she'd said.

"I'm sorry, Mitch," she said now, after swallowing her heart. It was true that Ayanna wouldn't have let her children stay there, if only because she'd needed the pittance she'd received for renting the place out, but there were gentler ways of refusing.

"For what?" he asked.

"Everything," she answered.

"It wasn't your fault," Mitch told her. "The accident, I mean."

I could have come back, gotten a job at the Road-house or Lucky's, waiting tables. I could have paid Ayanna some rent, and probably gotten something from the state to help with the cost of raising my little brother. If I'd even tried . . .

"It wouldn't have happened if we'd been here," she said.

"Who knows?" he asked. "Maybe it was fate—maybe I'd have rolled that four-wheeler anyhow."

Cheyenne closed her eyes against the images that were always hovering at the edge of her consciousness: Mitch, sixteen and foolish, joyriding in the desert with friends on "four-wheelers"—all-terrain vehicles designed for the hopelessly reckless. The rollover and critical spine injury. The rush to the hospital after her mother's frantic call, the long vigil in the waiting room outside Intensive Care, when nobody knew if Mitch would live or die.

The surgeries.

The slow, excruciating recovery.

Cheyenne had been just starting to make a name for herself at Meerland then. She'd driven back and forth between San Diego and Phoenix, armed with a company laptop and a cell phone. She'd held on stubbornly and worked hard, determined to prove to Nigel that she could succeed.

And she had. While spelling an exhausted Ayanna at the hospital—Pete, husband number two and Mitch's dad, had fled when he'd realized he was expected to behave like a responsible adult—she'd struck up a friendship with one of her brother's surgeons and had eventually persuaded him to invest in Meerland. When his profits were impressive, he'd brought several of his colleagues onboard.

Mitch had gradually gotten better, until he was well enough to leave the hospital, and Cheyenne had gone back to San Diego and thrown all her energies into her job.

"Do you think we could get a dog?"

Cheyenne blinked. Returned to the here-and-now with a thump. "A dog?"

Mitch smiled, and that was such a rare thing that it

made her heart skitter over a beat. "We couldn't have one at the apartment," he said.

"But you'll be going back—"

"I'm never going back," Mitch said with striking certainty.

"What makes you say that?"

"We don't have to pay rent here," he answered. "Mom's talking about painting again, and getting a job waiting tables or selling souvenirs someplace. She'll probably meet some loser and make it her life's mission to save him from himself."

For all her intelligence, Ayanna had the kind of romantic history that would provide material for a week of Dr. Phil episodes. At least she hadn't married again after Pete.

Tears burned in Cheyenne's eyes, and she was glad the room was lit only by Mitch's computer screen and the tacky covered-wagon lamp on the dresser.

"I wish—" Mitch began when Cheyenne didn't, *couldn't*, speak, but his voice fell away.

"What, Mitch?" she asked, after swallowing hard. "What do you wish?"

"I wish I could have a job, and a girlfriend. I wish I could ride a horse."

Cheyenne didn't know what to say. Jobs were few and far between in Indian Rock, especially for the disabled. Girls Mitch's age were working, going to college, dating men who could take them places. And riding horses? That was for people with two good legs and more courage than good sense.

41

"Isn't there something else?" she said, almost whispering.

Mitch smiled sadly, turned away again and brought the war game back up on his computer screen. *Blip-blip-kabang.*

Cheyenne sat helplessly on the bed for a few moments, then got to her feet, laid a hand briefly on her brother's shoulder, and left the room, closing the door behind her.

THE HEADLIGHTS OF JESSE'S truck swept across the old log schoolhouse his great-great-great grandfather, Jeb McKettrick, had built for his teacher bride, Chloe. Jesse's sisters had used the place as a playhouse when they were kids, and Jesse, being a decade younger, had made a fort of it. Now, on the rare occasions when his parents came back to the ranch, it served as an office.

He pulled up beside the barn, and the motion lights came on.

Inside, he checked on the horses, six of them altogether, though the number varied. They'd been fed and turned out for some exercise that morning, before he'd left for town, but he added flakes of dried Bermuda grass to their feeders now just the same, to make up for being gone so long.

They were forgiving, like always, and grateful for the attention he gave them.

He took the time to groom them, one by one, but eventually, there was nothing to do but face that empty house.

It was big; generations of McKettricks had added on to it—a room here, a story there. Now that his folks spent the majority of their time in Palm Beach, playing golf and socializing, and Victoria and Sarah were busy jet-setting with their wealthy husbands, Jesse was the unofficial owner.

He entered through the kitchen door, switched on the lights.

The house his cousins, Meg and Sierra, owned was reportedly haunted. Jesse often wished this one was, too, because at least then he wouldn't have been alone.

He went to the walk-in Sub-Zero, took out a beer and popped the top. What he ought to do was get a dog, but he was gone too much. It wouldn't be fair to consign some poor unsuspecting mutt to a lonely life, just so he could come home to somebody who'd always be happy to see him.

"You're losing it, McKettrick," he said aloud.

He thought about Cheyenne—*had* been thinking about her, on one level or another, ever since they'd parted in the Roadhouse parking lot.

Thought about her long legs and her expressive eyes, and the fullness of her mouth. She was good-looking, all right, and smart, too.

He wondered how far she'd go to persuade him to sell that five hundred acres she wanted.

The phone rang, nearly startling him out of his hide.

He scowled, set down his beer and picked up the receiver. "Yo," he said. "This is Jesse."

"Yo, yourself," Sierra replied. She was set to marry

Travis Reid, one of his closest friends, in a month. Jesse would be best man at the ceremony, and until tonight, when he'd run into Cheyenne, he'd wished Sierra wasn't a blood relative so he could at least fantasize about taking her away from Travis.

"What's up?" he asked and grinned. Most likely, if anything was up, it was Travis. The man had been at full mast ever since he'd first laid eyes on Sierra one day last winter.

"We're having a prewedding party," Sierra said. "Saturday night. Live music. A hayride and a barbecue. The whole works. Be there, and bring a date."

"I've got a big tournament that night," Jesse protested. "Cliffcastle Casino. No limit and plenty of tourists who think they know the game because they watch the World Poker Tour on TV."

"Come on, Jesse. You spend too much time at the tables as it is. And don't make me play the guilt card. As in, you're the best man and this is part of the gig."

"I wouldn't think of making you play the guilt card," Jesse said dryly, downing a big swig of beer. "Except that you just did."

She laughed. "It could get worse. Liam's counting on seeing you. Meg's flying in from San Antonio, and Rance and Keegan have both cleared their schedules to come. Since it would be really crass of me to point out that that involves more than missing a poker tournament, I won't."

Jesse sighed. "Okay," he said. "But I want something in return."

"Like what?"

"Send over a ghost, will you? It's way too quiet around here."

CHAPTER THREE

CHEYENNE SHOWED UP at the ranch the next morning, as agreed, at nine o'clock sharp. Jesse had just turned all but two of the horses out to graze in the pastures beyond the corral gate. He'd saddled his black-and-white paint gelding, Minotaur, first, and was finishing up with Pardner when she pulled in.

Standing just outside the barn door, Jesse yanked the cinch tighter around the horse's belly, grinned and shook his head slightly when Cheyenne stepped out of the car and he saw what she was wearing. A trim beige pantsuit, tailored at the waist, and stack-heeled shoes with tasteful brass buckles, shiny enough to signal a rider five miles away. She'd wound her hair into the same businesslike do at the back of her head—did she sleep with it up like that?—and he wondered idly how long it was, and how it would feel to let the strands slide between his fingers.

Smiling gamely, Cheyenne minced her way across the rutted barnyard toward him. Her gaze touched the horses warily and ricocheted off again, with a reverberation like the ping of a bullet, only soundless. "It's a beautiful morning," she said.

Jesse gave a partial nod, tugged at his hat brim before

45

thinking better of the idea. *Talk about tells. Why not just have a billboard put up?* Cheyenne Bridges Intrigues Me. Sincerely, Jesse McKettrick. "Always is, out here. Year 'round."

She drew an audible breath, that brave smile wobbling a little on her sensuous mouth, and huffed out an exhale. Adjusted the strap of that honking purse again. "Let's go have a look at the land," she said, jingling her keys in her right hand.

Jesse ran his gaze over her outfit, glanced toward Pardner and Minotaur, who were waiting patiently in full tack, reins dangling, tails switching. "That little car of yours," he said, watching with amused enjoyment as realization dawned in her face, "will never make it onto the ridge. Nothing up there but old logging trails."

She swallowed visibly, took in the horses again and shook her head. "You're not suggesting we—ride?" The hesitation was so brief it might have gone unnoticed, if Jesse hadn't had so much practice at picking out the very things other people tried to hide. "On horseback?"

He waited, arms folded. "That's the usual purpose of saddling up," he said. "Two people. Two horses. No special mental acuity required to figure it out."

Cheyenne shifted on the soles of her fancy shoes. They'd work in a boardroom, those shoes, but on the Triple M, they were almost laughable. "I wasn't expecting to ride a horse."

"I can see that," Jesse observed. "You do realize that those five hundred acres you're so anxious to bulldoze,

46

pave and cover with condos are pretty rugged, and not a little remote?"

"Of course I do," she said, faltering now. "I've done weeks of research. I know my business, Mr. McKettrick."

"It's Jesse," he corrected. "And what kind of 'research' did you do, exactly? Maybe you dredged up some plat maps online? Checked out the access to power and the water situation?" He waited a beat to let his meaning sink in, then gave the suit another once-over. "At least you had sense enough to wear pants," he added charitably.

"I beg your pardon?"

"Do you even *own* a pair of jeans?"

"I don't wear jeans when I'm working," she retorted. Her tone was moderate, but if she'd been a porcupine, her quills would have been bristling.

"I guess that lets boots out, too, then."

She paused before answering, and looked so flustered that Jesse began to feel a little sorry for her. "I guess it does," she said, and her shoulders slackened so that she had to grab the purse and resituate it before the strap slid down her arm.

"Come on inside," he said, indicating the house with a half turn of his head. "Mom's about your size. You can borrow some of her stuff."

Cheyenne stood so still that she might have sprouted roots. Jesse could imagine them, reaching deep into the ground, winding around slabs of bedrock and the petrified roots of trees so ancient that they'd left no trace of their existence aboveground. "I don't know—"

Jesse decided it was time to up the ante by a chip or two. "Are you scared, Ms. Bridges?"

Her mouth twitched at one corner, and Jesse waited to see if she was just irritated or trying not to smile. It was the latter; a small grin flitted onto her lips and then flew away. "Yes," she said, with a forthrightness that made Jesse wish he hadn't teased her, let alone set her up for the challenge she was facing now.

"Pardner's a rocking horse," he told her. "You could sit under his belly, blow a police whistle, grab his tail in both hands and pull it between his hind legs, and he wouldn't move a muscle."

She bit her lip. Jesse saw her eyes widen as she assessed Minotaur, then looked hopefully toward Pardner. "You're not going to let this go, are you?" she asked when her gaze swung in Jesse's direction again and locked on in a way that made the pit of his stomach give out like a trapdoor opening over a bottomless chasm. It happened so fast that he found himself scrabbling for an internal handhold, but he couldn't seem to get a grip.

"No," he said, but it wasn't because he was being stubborn. Things had gone too far, and she couldn't walk away now without leaving some of her self-respect behind. All he could do was make it as easy as possible. "Knowing the land isn't a drive-by kind of thing, Cheyenne. You gotta *be* there, if it's going to speak to you."

"Maybe you could just give the plans a glance and I

48

could come back another day—"

He put up a hand. "Whoa," he said. "I could let you off the hook here, but you wouldn't like me for it in the long run, and you'd think even less of yourself."

She paused, looked ruefully down at her clothes. Huffed out a sigh. "Just look at the blueprints, Jesse. I'm not prepared—"

Jesse dug in his heels. He sensed that this was a pivotal moment for both of them, far more important than it seemed on the surface. There was something archetypal going on here, though damned if he could have said what it was, for all those psychology classes he'd taken in college. "As *if* you'd come back out here, tomorrow or the next day, decked out to ride, and ask for the tour," he said. He narrowed his eyes. "If you think I'm going to unroll those plans of yours on the kitchen table, see the error of my ways, and ask you where to sign, you're in need of a reality check."

She chewed on that one for a while, and Jesse knew if she hadn't wanted that land half as badly as she did, she'd have told him what to do with both horses and possibly the barn, turned on one polished heel, stomped back to her car and left him standing there in the proverbial cloud of dust.

"All right," she said. The words might as well have been hitched to a winch and *hauled* out of her.

"All right, what?"

Cheyenne sighed. "*All right,* I'll borrow your mother's clothes and ride that wretched horse," she

49

told him. "But if I get my neck broken, it will be on your conscience."

Jesse indulged in a slow grin. He'd liked Cheyenne all along, but now he respected her, too, and that gave a new dimension to the whole exchange. She'd been brave enough to admit she was scared, and now she was stepping past that to stay in the game. "Nothing like that's going to happen," he assured her. "I know you're a greenhorn, and I wouldn't put you on a knot-head horse."

With that, he led the way inside. While she waited in the kitchen, he scouted up some of his mother's old jeans, a pair of well-worn boots and a flannel shirt. When he returned, she was looking out the window over the sink, apparently studying the schoolhouse.

"Is it really a one-room school?" she asked when he stepped up beside her and placed the pile of gear in her arms.

He nodded. "The blackboard's still there, and a few of the desks," he said. "It's pretty much the way it was when old Jeb built it for his bride back in the 1880s."

She looked up at him, her eyes wide and solemnly wistful. "Could I see it?"

"Sure," he answered, frowning. "Why the sad look, Cheyenne?"

She tried to smile, but the operation wasn't a success. Shrugged both shoulders and tightened her hold on the change of clothes. "Did I look sad? I'm not, really. I was just wondering what it would be like to have a history like you McKettricks do."

"Everybody has a history," he said, knowing she'd lied when she'd said she wasn't sad.

"Do they?" she asked softly. "I never knew my dad's parents. My maternal grandmother died when I was thirteen. Nobody tells stories. Nobody wrote anything down, or took a lot of pictures. We have a few, but I couldn't identify more than two or three of the people in them. It's as if we all just popped up out of nowhere."

In that moment, Jesse wanted to kiss Cheyenne Bridges in a way he'd never wanted to kiss another woman. He settled for touching the tip of one finger to her nose because she was still as skittish as the deer he'd imagined when he'd first seen her again, behind Lucky's, and he didn't want to send her springing for the tall timber.

"Ready to ride?" he asked.

"I'm never going to be any readier," she replied.

He gave her directions to the nearest bathroom, and she set out, walking straight-shouldered and stalwart, like somebody who'd been framed for a crime arriving at the prison, about to put on an orange jumpsuit with a number on the back and take her chances with the population.

THE JEANS WERE A LITTLE BAGGY, but the boots fit. Cheyenne folded her trousers, blazer and silk camisole neatly and set them on a counter. Arranged her favorite shoes neatly alongside. Looked into the mirror above the old-fashioned pedestal sink.

"You can do this," she told herself out loud. "You *have* to do this." She turned her head, looked at herself from one side, then the other. "And by the way, your hair looks ridiculous, pinned up like that."

"Nothing for it," her reflection answered.

She got lost twice, trying to find her way back to the kitchen, where Jesse was waiting, leaning back against the counter in front of the sink, arms folded, head cocked to one side. His gaze swept over her, and nerves tripped under the whole surface of her skin, dinging like one of Mitch's computer games racking up points, headed for *tilt*.

"That's more like it," Jesse drawled. He seemed so at ease that Cheyenne, suffering by contrast, yearned to make him uncomfortable.

She couldn't afford to do that, of course, so she quashed the impulse—for the moment. She'd take it out on Nigel later, over the telephone, when she reported that she'd risked life and limb for his damnable condominium development by getting on the back of a horse and trekking off into the freaking *wilderness* like a contestant on some TV survival show. Provided she didn't end up in the intensive care unit before she got the chance to call him, anyway.

What she didn't allow herself to think about was the bonus, and all it would mean to her, her mother and Mitch.

"Take it easy," Jesse said, more gently than before. She had no defense against tenderness, and consciously raised her invisible force field. With the next breath, he made the whole effort unnecessary. "I told you—Pardner's a good horse, and he's used to kids and craven cowards."

"I am *not* a coward," Cheyenne replied tersely. "'Craven' or otherwise."

Jesse grinned, thrust himself away from the counter and ambled toward the back door. There, he paused and gave her another lingering glance. "You're obviously not a kid, either. My mistake."

"You're enjoying this," she accused, following him outside into the warm spring morning. She'd been going for a lighthearted tone, but it came out sounding a little hollow and mildly confrontational.

He crossed to the horses, took the brute he called Pardner by the reins. "All aboard," he said.

Cheyenne walked steadily toward the man and the horse because she knew if she stopped, she might not get herself moving again.

"You've *never* been in the saddle before?" Jesse asked, marveling, when she got close to him and that beast. "How'd you manage that, growing up in Indian Rock just like I did?"

They'd shared a zip code and gone to the same schools, Cheyenne reflected. Beyond those similarities, they might as well have been raised on different planets. Unable to completely hide her irritation, whatever the cost of it might be, she gave Jesse a look as she put a foot in the stirrup and grabbed the saddle horn in both hands. "I guess I was so busy with debutante balls and tea at the country club," she quipped, "that I never got around to riding to the hounds or playing polo."

Jesse laughed. Then he put a hand under her backside and hoisted her unceremoniously onto the horse in one smooth but startlingly powerful motion.

She landed with a thump that echoed from her tail-bone to the top of her spine.

"You can let go of the horn," he said. "Pardner will stand there like a monument in the park until I get on Minotaur and take off."

Cheyenne released her two-handed death grip, finger by finger. "You won't make him run?"

Jesse laid a worn leather strap in her left palm, closed her hand around it, then ducked under Pardner's head to do the same on the other side. "Hold the reins loosely," he instructed, "like this. He'll stop at a light tug, so don't yank. That'll hurt him."

Cheyenne nodded nervously. The creature probably weighed as much as a Volkswagen, and if either of them got hurt, odds on, it would be her. Just the same, she didn't want to cause him any pain.

She was in good shape, but the insides of her thighs were already beginning to ache. She wondered if it would be ethical to put a gallon or two of Ben-Gay on her expense account so she could dip herself in the stuff when she got home.

"You're okay?" Jesse asked after a few beats.

She bit down hard on her lower lip and nodded once, briskly.

He smiled, laid a hand lightly to her thigh, and turned

to mount his horse with the easy grace of a movie cowboy. If Nigel had been there, armed with his seemingly endless supply of clichés, he probably would have remarked that Jesse McKettrick looked as though he'd been born on horseback, or that he and the animal might have been a single entity.

Jesse nudged his horse's sides with the heels of his boots, and it began to walk away.

"No spurs?" Cheyenne asked, drawing on celluloid references, which constituted the extent of her knowledge of cowboys. It was an inane conversation, but Pardner was moving, and she had to talk to keep herself calm.

Jesse frowned as though she'd suggested stabbing the poor critter with a pitchfork. "No spurs on the Triple M," he said. *"Ever."*

Cheyenne clutched the reins, her hands sweating, and waited for her heart to squirm back down out of her throat and resume its normal beat. The ride wasn't so bad, really—just a sort of rolling jostle.

As long as an impromptu Kentucky Derby didn't break out, she might just survive this episode. Anyway, it was a refreshing change from shuffling paperwork, juggling calls from Nigel and constantly meeting with prospective investors.

Reaching a pasture gate, Jesse leaned from the saddle of his gelding to free the latch. The fences, Cheyenne noted, now that she wasn't hyperventilating anymore, were split-rail as far as she could see. The wood was weathered, possibly as old as the historic schoolhouse

Jesse had promised to show her when they got back, and yet the poles stood straight.

Just as there were no spurs on the Triple M, she concluded, there appeared to be no barbed wire, either. Considering the size of the spread—the local joke was that the place was measured in counties rather than acres—that was no small feat.

Cheyenne rode through the gate, waited while Jesse shut it again.

"I don't see any barbwire," she said.

"You won't," Jesse answered, adjusting his hat so the brim came down low over his eyes. "There isn't any. Horses manage to tear themselves up enough as it is, without rusty spikes ripping into their hide."

In spite of all he was putting her through, before he'd even agree to look at the blueprints for Nigel's development, Jesse rose a little in Cheyenne's estimation. Spurs were cruel, and so was barbed wire. He clearly disapproved of both, and Cheyenne had to give him points for compassion.

Jesse had never been mean, she reminded herself. He'd been wild, though. Even in high school, he'd been a seasoned poker player—she'd seen him in illicit games with her dad and some of the other old-timers long before he was of age.

"Is this what you do all day?" she asked, as they rode through high, fragrant grass toward a distant ridge. White clouds scalloped the horizon like foam on an ocean tide, and the sky was the same shade of blue as Jesse's eyes.

One side of his mouth cocked up in a grin, and he adjusted his hat again. "Is *what* what I do all day? Ride the range with good-looking women, you mean?"

Cheyenne was foolishly pleased by the compliment, however indirect, though the practical part of her said she was being played and she'd better beware. She'd dated, when she had the time, and even had had one or two fairly serious relationships, but Jesse McKettrick was way out of her league. Forgetting that could only get her into trouble.

She smiled, held both reins in one hand so she could wipe a damp palm dry on the leg of Jesse's mother's jeans, and then repeated the process with the other. "You must herd cattle and things like that," she said, as if he needed prompting.

"Rance would like to run a few hundred head of beef," Jesse answered, picking up the pace just a little, so both horses accelerated into a fast walk. "The Triple M isn't really in the cattle business anymore. It's more like what the easterners call hobby farming. I train the occasional horse, ride in a rodeo once in a while, and play a hell of a lot of poker. What about you, Cheyenne? What do *you* do all day?"

"I *work*," she said, and then realized she'd sounded like a self-righteous prig, and immediately wished she wasn't too damn proud to backpedal.

He pretended to pull an arrow, or maybe a poisoned spear, out of his chest, but his grin was as saucy as ever. Nothing *she* could say was going to get under that thick McKettrick hide.

Not that she really wanted to. Much.

"How far are we going to ride?" she asked, closing the figurative barn door after the horse was long gone.

"Just onto that ridge up there," Jesse answered, pointing. His horse was trotting now, and Cheyenne's kept pace. "You can see clear across to the county road from just outside the Triple M fence line. It'll take your breath away."

Cheyenne swallowed, bouncing so hard in the saddle that she had to be careful not to bite her tongue. Her Native American grandmother, a proud member of the Apache tribe, would die of shame to see the way Cheyenne rode—if she hadn't already been dead.

Don't let me love that land too much, she prayed.

Jesse slowed his horse with no discernible pull on the reins. Reached over to take hold of Pardner's bridle strap with one hand and bring him back to a sedate walk. "Do you ever wish you could do anything else?" he asked.

The question confused Cheyenne at first because she was concentrating on two things: not falling off the horse, and not throwing away everything she'd worked for because she liked the scenery. Then she realized Jesse was asking whether or not she liked her job.

"It's a challenge," she allowed carefully. "Very rewarding at times, and very frustrating at others. Our last development was geared to the mid-income crowd, and it was nice to know younger families would be moving in, raising kids there."

Nigel had lost his shirt on that development, but Jesse

didn't need to know that. Naturally, the investors hadn't been pleased, which was why Cheyenne's boss was so desperate to secure the prime acres she was about to see in person for the first time.

She'd offered to buy one of the condos in the batch Nigel had privately called El Fiasco, for Ayanna and Mitch to live in. The price had been right—next to nothing, since they'd practically been giving the places away by the time the project had limped to a halt. Ayanna had toured the demo condo, thanked Cheyenne for the thought, and had graciously refused, saying she'd rather live in a tepee.

The refusal still stung. *This from a woman who subsists in public housing,* she thought. *A place where the Dumpsters overflow and the outside walls are covered with graffiti.*

"Where was this development?" Jesse asked.

"Outside of Phoenix," Cheyenne answered. They were riding up a steep incline now. Then, before he could ask, she added, "You wouldn't have heard of it."

"What was it called?"

She wet her lips and avoided his eyes. There was another gate up ahead, and beyond it, trees. Magnificent pines, their tips fiercely green against the soft sky. "Casa de Meerland," she said.

"Catchy name," Jesse said dryly. "I read about that in the *Republic*."

Great, Cheyenne thought. He knew about the delays, the lawsuits, the unsold units, the angry investors. "As I told you last night," she said, carefully cheerful, "we're prepared to pay cash. You needn't worry about the company's reputation—we're rock solid."

"Your company's reputation is just about the last thing I'd ever worry about," Jesse said. "Mowing down old-growth timber and covering the meadows with concrete—now, that's another matter."

Cheyenne tensed. She knew her smile looked as fixed as it felt, hanging there on her face like an old window shutter clinging to a casing by one rusted hinge. "We have a deal," she said. "I'll look at the land, and you'll give the blueprints a chance. I sincerely hope you're not about to renege on your end of it."

"I never go back on my word," Jesse told her.

Cheyenne held her tongue. If he never went back on his word, it was probably only because he so rarely gave it in the first place.

"What do you do when you're not pillaging the environment?" he asked. They were approaching a second gate, held shut by another loop of wire.

She glared at him.

He laughed.

"I don't have time for hobbies," she said. Wearing Jesse's mother's jeans and boots reminded her of the woman she'd seen only from a distance, around Indian Rock, always dressed in custom-made suits or slacks and a blazer. Evidently, there was another, earthier side to Callie McKettrick.

"I could give you riding lessons."

"Thanks, but no thanks," she answered, a little too quickly and a little too tightly.

"Suppose I completely lost my head and agreed to sell you this land. Would you be in town for a while afterward?"

The question shook Cheyenne, though she thought she did a pretty good job of hiding her reaction. Was there a glimmer of hope that he'd agree to the deal? And what did he *want* her to say? That she'd be gone before the ink was dry on the contract, or that she'd stay on indefinitely?

In the end, it didn't matter what he wanted. The truth was the truth, and while Cheyenne liked to dole it out in measured doses, she was a lousy liar. "I'd be here for six months to a year, overseeing the construction end and setting up a sales office."

They'd reached the upper gate, and again, Jesse leaned to open it. She couldn't get a clear look at his face, but she sensed something new in his manner—a sort of quiet conflict. He'd been so clear about his intention to hold on to the land. Was he relenting?

She felt a peculiar mixture of hope and disappointment.

"I guess you could rent that empty storefront next to Cora's Curl and Twirl," he said as she rode through the opening. "For a sales office, I mean."

Cheyenne's heart fluttered its wings, then settled onto its roost again, afraid to fly. "I remember the Curl and Twirl," she said. The balance was delicate, and she knew an ill-chosen word could tip things in the wrong direction. "Cora's still cutting hair and teaching little girls to twirl batons?"

Jesse grinned at her before riding slowly back to close the gate again. "Not much changes in Indian Rock," he observed. "Did you ever take lessons from Cora?"

Something spiky lodged in Cheyenne's throat. God, she'd longed for a pink tutu and a baton with sparkly fringe on each end, longed to be one of those fortunate kids, spilling out of station wagons and pickup trucks, rushing into the Curl and Twirl for a Saturday-morning session. But there had never been enough money—Cash Bridges had needed every cent the family could scrape together to drink, play cards and bail his cronies out of jail. After all, Cheyenne remembered hearing him tell Ayanna gravely, they'd do the same for him.

"No," Cheyenne said flatly. She tried for a lighter note because she didn't want to talk about her father or any other part of her past. "Did you?"

Jesse chuckled. "Nope," he answered. "But my sisters went for it in a big way."

Ah, yes, Cheyenne thought. The McKettrick sisters. They'd been grown and gone by the time she'd got out of kindergarten, Sarah and Victoria had, but their legend lingered on. Always the most beautiful, always the most popular, always the best-dressed. They'd been cheerleaders and prom queens, as well as honor students and class presidents. One had married a movie executive, the other a CEO.

Some people were born under a lucky star.

She'd been born under a dark cloud instead.

"There's the trail," Jesse told her, indicating a

narrow, stony path that seemed to go straight up. "Follow me, and lean forward in the saddle when it gets steep."

When it *gets* steep? Cheyenne swallowed hard and lifted her chin a notch or two. As for the following, the horse did that part. She concentrated on staying in the saddle and avoiding the backlash of tree branches as Jesse forged ahead.

She was sweating when they finally reached the top and Pardner stepped up beside Jesse's horse. What was its name? Something Greek and mythological.

The land spilled away from the ridge, and nothing could have prepared her for the sight of it. Trees by the thousands. Sun-kissed meadows where deer grazed. A twisting creek, gleaming like a tassel pulled from the end of one of the batons at Cora's Curl and Twirl.

Tears sprang to Cheyenne's eyes, and that drumbeat started up again, in her very blood, thrumming through her veins.

Jesse swung a leg over the gelding's neck and landed deftly on his feet. He wound the reins loosely around the saddle horn.

"I told you it would take your breath away," he said quietly.

Cheyenne was speechless.

Jesse reached up, helped her down to the ground.

The bottoms of her feet stung at the impact, and she was grateful for the pain because it broke the spell.

"It's magnificent," she said, almost whispering.

Jesse nodded, took off his hat as reverently as if he'd

just entered a cathedral. Looking up at him, she saw his face change, as though he were drinking in that land, not just with his eyes, but through the pores of his skin.

Cheyenne reminded herself that the tract wasn't part of the Triple M; if it *had* been, there wouldn't have been a hope in hell of developing so much as an inch of it. She'd been over the public records a dozen times, knew Jesse had purchased the land two years ago from the state. It must have taken a chunk out of his trust fund, even though the price he'd paid was a fraction of what Nigel was willing to pony up.

As if he'd heard her thoughts, Jesse turned slightly and looked down into her eyes. "When we were kids, Rance and Keegan and I used to camp up here. I still like to bring a bedroll and sleep under the stars once in a while. A couple of years back, about the time the governor of Arizona decided not to turn it into a state park, I won a big poker tournament, and I bought it outright."

"That must have been some tournament," Cheyenne said, as casually as she could.

"World championship," Jesse answered, with a verbal shrug. "I'm going back to Vegas in a couple of months to defend my title." He turned to survey the land again, gesturing with his hat. "That creek practically jumps with trout every spring. There are deer, as you can see, as well as wolves and bobcats and coyotes and bear—just about any kind of critter you'd expect to run across in this country." He watched her for a few moments, choosing his words, turning his hat in his hands just the way any one of his cowboy ancestors might have done. "Where do you figure they'd go, if you and your company put in a hundred stucco boxes and a putting green?"

CHAPTER FOUR

CHEYENNE LOOKED AWAY, blinked. Wished the land would disappear, and Jesse's question with it.

Remember your mother, she thought. *Remember Mitch.*

Jesse turned her gently to face him. "When Angus McKettrick came here in the mid 1800s," he said, "the whole northern part of the state must have looked pretty much like this. He cut down trees to build a house and a barn, and used windfall for firewood. He put up fences to keep his cattle in, too, but other than that he didn't change the land much. His sons built houses, too, when they married—my place, the main ranch house where Keegan now lives, and the one across the creek from it. That belongs to Rance. They've been added onto, those houses, and modernized, but that's the extent of it. No short-platting. No tennis courts. We McKettricks like to sit light on the land, Cheyenne, and I don't intend to be the one to break that tradition."

Cheyenne gazed up at him, full of frustration and admiration and that infernal drumbeat, rising from her own core to pound in her ears. The majesty of the land seemed to reply, like a great, invisible heart, thumping an elemental rhythm of its own. "You promised you'd look at the blueprints," she said. It was lame, and she could feel all her hopes slipping away, but still she couldn't let go.

Jesse put his hat on again, helped Cheyenne back up onto her horse, and mounted the gelding. Neither of them said anything during the ride to the ranch house.

"I do care what happens to the land," she told him, quietly earnest, when they'd reached the barn and dismounted again.

"Do you?" Jesse asked, but he clearly didn't expect an answer. "Get your blueprints," he urged with a nod toward her rental car. "I'll put Pardner and Minotaur away and meet you in the schoolhouse."

She ran damp palms down the thighs of Callie McKettrick's jeans and returned his nod. She watched until he disappeared into the barn, leading both horses behind him.

"What do I do now?" she asked softly, tilting her head back to look up at the sky.

She stood there for a few seconds longer, then turned and went to the rental car. Plucked the thick roll of blueprints from the backseat.

The schoolhouse was cool and shadowy, and dust particles, stirred by her entrance, bobbed like little golden flecks in the still air.

Cheyenne laid the roll on a large table with an old chair behind it, and looked around with interest. Someone had scrawled a list of stock quotes on the blackboard, and there was an old-fashioned rotary phone on the table next to a vintage globe, but beyond those things, the place probably hadn't changed much since it was built.

She ran a hand across the single row of small desks, admired the potbelly stove and returned to the globe.

The world was profoundly different now she thought sadly, giving the miniature planet a little spin. New borders. New wars. AIDS and terrorism.

Cheyenne heard Jesse come in but she didn't turn to look. For a heartbeat or two she wanted to pretend she was Chloe McKettrick, the schoolteacher bride, and Jesse was Jeb. As long as she didn't make eye contact, she could pretend.

"There were never more than a dozen pupils at any given time," Jesse said quietly. "Just Chloe and Jeb's kids, their cousins and a few strays or ranch-hands' children."

"It must have been wonderfully simple," Cheyenne said very softly.

"It was hard, too," Jesse answered. She knew he was standing next to the big table, heard him slide the rubber bands off the blueprints and unroll them. "No running water, no electricity. We didn't have lights out here until well into the 30s. Holt's place had a line in from the road from about 1917 on, but all it powered was one bulb in the kitchen."

Cheyenne forced herself to turn around and look at Jesse. Just briefly, she could almost believe he *was* Jeb, dressed the way he was with his hat sitting beside him on the tabletop. She knew which was Holt's place, which had been Rafe's and Kade's—everyone who'd ever spent any time at all in Indian Rock had heard at least the outlines of the family's illustrious history—but hearing it from Jesse somehow made it all seem new.

She shook her head, feeling as if she'd somehow wandered onto the set of an old movie, or fallen head-long into a romance novel. It was time to stop dreaming and start *selling*—if she didn't convince Jesse to part with that five hundred acres, well, the consequences would be staggering.

"It's wonderful that the ranch has been so well pre-served all this time," she said as Jesse studied the blue-prints, holding them open with his widely placed hands, his head down so she couldn't see his expres-sion. "But the land we're talking about has never been part of the Triple M, as I understand it."

Jesse looked up, but he was wearing his poker face and even with all the experience Cheyenne had gath-ered from dealing with her cardsharp father, there was no reading him. "Land," he said, "is land."

Alarms went off in Cheyenne's head but she kept her composure. She'd had a lot of practice doing that, both as a child, coping with the ups and downs of a dys-functional family, and as an adult struggling to build a career in a business based largely on speculation and the ability to persuade, wheedle, convince.

She moved to stand beside Jesse, worked up a smile and pointed to a section in the middle of the proposed development. "This is the community park," she said. "There will be plenty of grass, a fountain, benches, playground equipment for the kids. If we dam the creek, we can have a fishpond—"

Too late, Cheyenne realized she'd made a major mistake mentioning Nigel's plans to change the course of the stream bisecting the property before flowing downhill, onto and across the heart of the Triple M.

Jesse's face tightened and he withdrew his hands, letting the blueprints roll noisily back up into a loose cylinder.

"Surely that creek isn't the only water source—" Cheyenne began, but she fell silent at the look in Jesse's eyes.

"No deal," he said.

"Jesse—"

He shoved the blueprints at her. "You kept up your end of the bargain and I kept up mine. And I'll be *damned* if I'll let you and a bunch of jackasses in three-piece suits mess with that creek so the condo-dwellers can raise koi."

"Please listen—" Cheyenne was desperate and past caring whether Jesse knew it or not.

"I've heard all I need to hear," he said.

"Look, the fishpond is certainly dispensable—"

Jesse crossed the room, jerked open the door. Sunlight rimmed his lean frame and broad, rancher's shoulders. "You're damned right it is!"

He stormed toward the house and once again Cheyenne had no choice but to follow after she tossed the blueprints into the car through an open window.

He left the back door slightly ajar, and Cheyenne squeezed through sideways, not wanting to push it all the way open. She was about to make a dash for the bathroom, switch the cowgirl gear for her normal garb and speed back to town, over the railroad tracks—*home*—when she caught herself.

Jesse stood facing the sink with his hands braced against the counter in much the same way he'd held the blueprints down out in the schoolhouse. Judging by the angle of his head, he was staring out the window.

"I didn't do anything wrong," Cheyenne said, more for her benefit than his own. "That creek can't be all that important to the survival of this ranch or one of your ancestors would have grabbed it at the source a long time ago."

He turned to face her, moving slowly, folding his arms and leaning back against the edge of the sink. "If I were you, I wouldn't talk about *grabbing* land," he said.

Cheyenne squinted at him, trying to decide if he was softening a bit or if the impression was pure wishful thinking on her part. "It's enough to say no, Jesse," she said quietly. "There's no reason to be angry."

Jesse shoved a hand through his hair, then flashed her a grin so sudden and so bright that it almost set her back on her heels. "I'm sorry," he said. "I'm mad at myself, not you."

Cheyenne stared at him, disbelieving, almost suspecting a trick. In her experience, anger was a shape-shifter, disguising itself as some gentler emotion only to rise up again when she least expected, and roar in her face like a demon from the fieriest pit of hell.

"*I* should have thought about that creek," he went on as she stood frozen, like a rabbit caught out in the open by some crafty predator. "For a while there I was actually playing with the idea of making the deal. I started thinking about families, little kids on tricycles and dogs chasing Frisbees. It wasn't until you showed me where the koi pond would be that I reined myself in."

"What if we promised never to divert the creek, at any time, for any reason?"

Jesse sighed. "If you promised me that I'd probably believe it, but you can't and you know it. Once the units are sold and your company moves on, anything could happen. The homeowner's association could vote to dynamite the creek and make their own lake, and there wouldn't be much I could do about it."

Cheyenne pulled back a chair at the big kitchen table, which was not an antique as she would have expected, but an exquisite pine creation, intricately carved and inlaid with turquoise and bits of oxidized copper, and sank into it. She propped one elbow on the table top and cupped her chin in her palm. "There *would* be things you could do, though. McKettrickCo must have an army of lawyers on staff. You could get a court order and block anything like that indefinitely."

"McKettrickCo's lawyers," Jesse said, opening the refrigerator and taking out a bottle of sparkling water and a beer, "are not at my beck and call. Even if they were, they've got plenty to do as it is."

He set the water down in front of her, and she was impressed that he'd remembered her preference for it from the night before.

"This is the most beautiful table I've ever seen," she said as she gave a nod of thanks and twisted off the top of the lid to take a much-needed sip.

Jesse hauled back another chair and sat down, opened his beer. "Handcrafted in Mexico," he said. "My mother has an eye for what she calls 'functional art.'"

Not to mention a bottomless bank account, Cheyenne thought. "Maybe we should use coasters," she said practically.

Jesse laughed. "The wood is lacquered. It wouldn't qualify as functional if you could leave rings on it with a beer can or a bottle of water."

Cheyenne felt herself relaxing, which was strange given that she could almost hear everything she'd planned for and dreamed of creaking like the framework of an old roller coaster about to come crashing down around her ears. The dust wouldn't settle for years.

"Why do you want that particular tract of land so badly?" Jesse asked, catching her off guard again. "It's more than the job, isn't it?"

Maybe, Cheyenne thought, she ought to go for the sympathy vote. She sighed, took another drink of water. Jesse had already made up his mind; at this point, she had nothing to lose.

"There's a bonus in it," she said. "The money would make a lot of difference to my family."

Jesse shifted in his chair and turned his beer can around on the tabletop as he thought. "There must be a lot of other people out there, ready and even eager to sell their property. Why does it have to be my land?"

"Nigel wants it," Cheyenne answered.

He raised one eyebrow. "Nigel?"

"My boss. And this is probably going to mean my job."

"You could always get another job."

"Easy to say when you're somebody who doesn't need one."

Jesse hoisted his beer can slightly. "Touché," he said. "There might be a place for you at McKettrickCo. I could ask Keegan."

Cheyenne remembered Keegan from school. He'd been the serious, focused one. And Rance, who'd been almost as wild as Jesse. She might have gone for the sympathy vote in a last-ditch effort to pull the deal out of the soup, but accepting McKettrick charity was another thing. "I'll be all right," she said. Good thing she didn't have to say how that was going to happen, because she had no earthly idea. She smiled. "Is the Roadhouse hiring? I might be able to get on as a waitress. Or maybe I could deal cards in the back room at Lucky's—"

He reached out unexpectedly and squeezed her hand. "You're smart, Cheyenne. You always were. You have experience and a degree, unless I've missed my guess.

There are a lot of options out there."

"Not in Indian Rock, there aren't," she said. "And for right now, anyway, I'm stuck here."

Jesse circled the center of her palm with the pad of one thumb, and a delicious shiver went through Cheyenne. "I can't say I mind the idea of your hanging around for a while," he told her. "And Flag's just up the road. Probably lots of work there, for somebody with your skills."

Cheyenne bit down on her lower lip. "Sure," she said, with an attempt at humor. "There must be at least one company looking to drive wildlife out of its natural habitat and decimate the tree population. Why was I worried?"

Maybe, answered her practical side, because she'd sold her car and sublet her apartment. Once Nigel pulled the company credit cards and she'd turned in the rental, she'd either have to drive her mother's van or hope her old bike was still stashed in the garage behind the house.

"You must have done well, Cheyenne. Why are you in such a pinch?"

"What makes you think I'm in a pinch?" *How the hell do you know these things? Are you some kind of cowboy psychic?*

"I can see it in your eyes. Come on. What's the deal? Maybe I can help."

She bristled at that. "If you want to help, Jesse, sell me the land. I'm not soliciting donations here. I'm offering you the kind of money most people couldn't even dream of laying their hands on."

"Take it easy," Jesse counseled. "I didn't mean to step on your pride. We went to school together, and that makes us old friends. I just want to know what's going on."

She *would not* cry. "Medical bills," she said.

"From your brother's accident."

"Yes."

"Wasn't there insurance?"

"No. My mother worked as a waitress." *She isn't a socialite, ordering tables inlaid with turquoise.* "My stepfather was a day laborer when he worked at all, which wasn't often. He was more interested in trying to get some kind of disability check out of the government so he could play pool all day. In fact, if he'd worked half as hard at a real job as he did at getting on the dole, he might have accomplished something."

"So it all fell on you? You weren't legally responsible, Cheyenne. Why take on something like that?"

"Mitch is my brother," she said. For her, that was reason enough. The hospitals and doctors had written off a lot of the initial costs, and Mitch received a stipend from Social Security. At nineteen, he was on Medicare. But the gap between the things they wouldn't pay for and the things he needed was wide. "He can survive on his benefits. I want him to do *more* than survive—I want him to have a life."

"Enough to sacrifice your own?"

Cheyenne was silent for a long time. "I didn't think it was going to be this hard," she finally admitted, to

75

herself as well as Jesse. "I thought there would be an end to it. That Mitch would walk again. That everything would be normal."

I wish I could have a job and a girlfriend, she heard her brother telling her the night before in his room. *I wish I could ride a horse.*

"And my selling you five hundred acres of good land would change any of that? Make things 'normal' again?"

Cheyenne sighed, swallowed more water, pushed back her chair to stand. Plan A was down the swirler; best get cracking with plan B. Whatever the hell *that* was. "No," she said. "No, it wouldn't."

She returned to the bathroom then, changed clothes, brought the jeans, boots and flannel shirt back to Jesse.

"I'm sorry," he said.

She believed him—that was the crazy thing. "Thanks for the ride," she told him.

He opened the kitchen door for her, walked her to the car.

"Friends?" he asked, once she was behind the wheel.

"Friends," she said, starting the engine.

"Then maybe you'd do me a favor," Jesse pressed.

She frowned up at him, puzzled. What kind of favor could she possibly do for him?

"There's a party Saturday night, sort of a prewedding thing my cousin Sierra and her fiancé are throwing. Barbecue, a hayride, that kind of thing. I need a date."

If there was one thing Jesse McKettrick didn't lack

for, besides money, it was available women. "Why me?" she asked.

"Because I like you. Your mom and Mitch can come, too. It'll be a good way for them to get reacquainted with the locals."

On her own, Cheyenne would certainly have refused the invitation, but she knew Ayanna and Mitch were lonely in Indian Rock. They needed to be a part of the community. "Transportation's a hassle, with Mitch's chair—"

"I'll handle it, Cheyenne," Jesse said. "Saturday night. Six o'clock." He grinned. "Get yourself some jeans."

Cheyenne tried to recall the last time she'd done anything just for the fun of it, and couldn't come up with a single instance. Yes, she did a lot of upscale socializing because of her job, but that was business. "Okay," she said. "Six o'clock."

Jesse waved as she drove out, and she was actually feeling cheerful—until she reached the main road, leading into Indian Rock. Two things happened to snap her back to reality—her cell phone jangled and she remembered where she lived. When Jesse came to pick her and Mitch and her mother up that weekend, he'd see the waist-high weeds in the yard, the rusted wire, the old tires.

"Hello, Nigel," she snapped into the phone.

"You don't sound very happy, Cheyenne," Nigel said, sounding aggrieved.

"Jesse showed me the land. I showed him the blue-

77

prints. He refused to even consider selling, in no uncertain terms."

"You can change his mind," Nigel insisted.

"You've obviously never met a McKettrick," Cheyenne retorted. Suddenly, she felt sick and pulled onto the side of the road, thinking she might have to shove open the door in midconversation and throw up.

"He's an old flame, isn't he?"

"We went to the movies twice, Nigel. I was still in high school. That hardly qualifies as a flicker, let alone a flame."

"Maybe if you slept with him—"

Cheyenne went rigid. Actually considered pitching the phone out the window, into the brush alongside the road. Would have, if she hadn't known Nigel would deduct the cost of it from her last paycheck. "I can't *believe* you just said that!"

"Come on, Cheyenne. Deals are made that way all the time."

"Not by me they aren't!"

"You spent a week in Aspen with Dr. What's-His-Name, just last year, and came back with three hundred thousand dollars to invest."

Cheyenne's blood simmered in her veins. Forget the Native American drum song—this was a war dance. "His *wife* was there, too. You didn't actually think—?"

"Of course I did," Nigel said. "You've got a killer body and a fabulous face. How *else* could you have persuaded so many smart businessmen to write fat checks to Meerland Ventures?"

"Maybe because I have a brain?"

A pause ensued. Then Nigel went for a save. "Cheyenne, be reasonable. It was only natural to assume—"

"You smarmy son of a bitch!"

"Cheyenne—"

She rolled down the window, flung the phone out and, after checking her trajectory in the side mirror, ran over it before pulling onto the road again, back tires spitting gravel and probably squashed circuitry.

The drive home was an angry blur.

When she arrived, her mother stepped out onto the front porch, looking concerned.

"Nigel called," Ayanna said gravely, carefully descending the steps to approach. "I swear the phone hadn't been hooked up for five minutes when it rang—"

"Screw Nigel," Cheyenne said, staring straight through the windshield instead of looking up into her mother's face.

"I take it things didn't go well with Jesse?"

Cheyenne got out of the car, forcing Ayanna to step back quickly, and slammed the door hard behind her. "Things went *fine* with Jesse—if you don't count the fact that he'd probably rather die than sell that land to me or anybody else."

"Cheyenne." Ayanna touched her arm. "Oh, honey."

"I'm all right, Mom."

Ayanna studied her. Smiled tentatively. "I got a job today," she said. "Bagging groceries at the market. If I do well, I can move up to checker. That's *union,* Cheyenne. I'd have health insurance and vacation time."

Cheyenne wanted to cry. Her mother wasn't old by any means, but she was past the point where she should have been on her feet all day, stuffing cans and boxes into bags, schlepping them to people's cars and rounding up carts from all corners of the lot.

"Well," she said, "at least *one* of us is gainfully employed."

AFTER CHEYENNE DROVE AWAY, it was all Jesse could do to go back into that house. It was too damn big, and too damn lonely.

He brushed down the horses, made sure they had enough water and feed to get them through until morning, and headed for Indian Rock.

He intended to play a few hands of poker at Lucky's. Instead, he found himself swinging into the lot at McKettrickCo, parking his dusty truck beside Keegan's sleek, shiny black Jag.

Myrna Terp, the receptionist, greeted him with a delighted smile. "You're a day late for the big meeting," she said.

Jesse doffed his hat. "I'm here to see my cousin," he said. "And to flirt with you, of course."

Myrna laughed. Her son Virgil was a good friend of Jesse's, going back to playground days. Something of a western history buff, Myrna had three other sons— Frank, Morgan and Wyatt.

Frank, Morgan and Virgil took their family name in stride, but Wyatt called himself John these days. Jesse didn't blame him. It couldn't be easy going through life answering to a handle like Wyatt Terp.

"I'll give Keegan a buzz," Myrna said, "but I warn you, he's been a bear all day."

Jesse didn't wait for the buzz. He started down the hall and was just about to open Keegan's fancy office door when it swung inward and his cousin filled the gap.

"What?" Keegan demanded.

"Hello to you, too," Jesse replied affably, twirling his hat in his hands.

Keegan sighed, stepped back to let him pass.

"What's going on?" Jesse asked. It had been a long time since he and Keegan had confided in each other, but old habits died hard. So did old hopes.

"I've been on the phone with Shelley's lawyer for the last two hours," Keegan said. "She's getting married again, and they want to take Devon to Europe."

"She'd probably enjoy a trip like that. Devon, I mean."

"Permanently," Keegan specified.

"Ouch," Jesse said. He had an impulse to lay a hand on Keegan's shoulder, as he would have done way back when, but he stopped himself. "Shelley can't actually do that, can she? Take the kid out of the country against your wishes?"

"With the divorce settlement I paid her, she could do just about anything. It's not that hard to disappear,

Jesse—look what happened when Sierra was little."

When Eve McKettrick, Sierra's mother, had divorced her loser husband, he'd snatched the child and taken her to live in central Mexico. Although Eve had eventually found her daughter, a lot of complicated circumstances had kept her from reclaiming Sierra. They hadn't been reunited until just a few months ago, and while they were on good terms, the two women were still essentially strangers to each other.

"What are you going to do?" Jesse asked.

Keegan thrust a hand through his hair. "I don't know," he said.

"Let's just go up to Flagstaff and get Devon, right now. Bring her home to the Triple M."

Keegan gestured wearily toward a chair, and Jesse dropped into it.

"This isn't a John Wayne movie, Jesse," Keegan said as he closed the office door. "Shelley's Devon's mother. She has rights. Besides, I don't want to scare my daughter by making a big deal out of this. She's only nine years old, and this whole thing is tough enough for her already."

Jesse felt helpless, and he hated that. "It might turn into a *hell* of a big deal, all on its own, if you don't do something."

Keegan collapsed into his own chair behind that gleaming one-acre desk of his. Said nothing.

"Sorry I missed that meeting yesterday," Jesse said. He wasn't remorseful, and Keegan knew it, but maybe he'd appreciate the gesture anyhow.

Keegan grinned, but he looked tired and a little cornered. "What brings you here, Jess?" he asked.

"I thought maybe we could have a beer together."

"Try again."

"I know somebody who needs a job."

"So do I. *You.*"

"Very funny."

Keegan leaned back in his leather chair and tented his fingers under his chin. "Still practicing for the big poker tournament?"

"Just biding my time," Jesse answered.

"Wasn't one gold bracelet, fifteen minutes of fame and five million dollars enough?"

"I want to make sure it wasn't a one-shot deal."

"What if it was? Why should you care?"

Jesse shrugged. "I just do. Now, about that job—"

Keegan thrust out another sigh, gustier than the first. "I need a computer wiz. Happen to have one handy?"

"I don't know if she's good with computers or not."

"She?" Keegan put an edge on the word.

"Maybe you remember her from school. Cheyenne Bridges. She's working for some real-estate outfit now, and they're about to show her the road because I wouldn't sell them that five hundred acres I bought with my prize money."

Keegan squeezed the bridge of his nose between a thumb and forefinger. "Cash Bridges's daughter? I remember her, all right. I asked her out once or twice, but she was so hung up on you that I didn't get anywhere."

Jesse sat up a little straighter. Keegan was single again, and he was a good catch by anybody's definition. Maybe it wouldn't be such a good idea for him and Cheyenne to work together.

"Just a thought," he said and stood to leave.

"Sit down," Keegan said.

Jesse sat.

"What exactly does she do? Cheyenne, I mean. For the real-estate outfit?"

Jesse swallowed. "Builds condos," he said. "Rounds up investors, I think."

"She's good with money, then?"

"I don't know," Jesse said, wishing he'd approached somebody else about a job for Cheyenne. Maybe Mr. Mackey, over at the Cattleman's Bank. Hell, he'd rather see her hawking crystals down in Sedona than working shoulder to shoulder with Keegan. What the hell had he been thinking?

"I can find out easily enough," Keegan said. "What's her number?"

CHAPTER FIVE

CHEYENNE SURVEYED THE CONTENTS of her suitcase for the third time since she'd gotten home from Jesse's place. Tailored slacks. Suits. Silk blouses. Panty hose. Nothing suitable for a Saturday night barbecue and hayride on the Triple M.

"That Nigel dude's on the phone again," Mitch

announced from the doorway of Cheyenne's girlhood bedroom. It was a tiny place, hardly larger than the walk-in closet in her San Diego apartment, and there were still bits of tape clinging to the wallpaper where she'd affixed pictures of Jesse, all through junior and senior high. Where were those clippings and school photos now? She didn't remember throwing them away, but maybe she had, during some fit of adolescent heartbreak.

She tuned in again, just in time to hear Mitch finish with, "You'd better talk to the boss man. I don't think he's going to quit calling until you do."

Cheyenne turned to look at her brother. Here was a primary reason why she had to attend that McKettrick party. Mitch had brightened just since she'd told him about it, and so had Ayanna. They were already looking forward to the event, and God knew they had little enough to keep them going. "I'll be right there," she said, after forestalling a sigh. "Might as well get it over with."

Mitch smiled. "That's what you always told me, anyway," he said. "Whenever I had to have a spinal tap or go through another physical-therapy session."

Unknowingly, Mitch had put all Cheyenne's complaints squarely back into perspective. So *what* if she didn't have a job anymore? So what if she didn't own a car, or a pair of jeans to wear to the party? She had two good legs, and she'd never had to endure a single painful medical procedure in her life. Her employment situation, dicey as it was, probably looked pretty good to her brother.

She pointed a finger at him and pretended to shoot. "You made a direct hit, buddy," she said grinning. "Thanks."

Mitch wheeled backward to let her pass.

In the living room, she picked up the heavy receiver of the plain black rotary phone her grandmother had had installed back in the mid 1950s. The service had ebbed and flowed over the years, according to the family's financial ups and downs.

Cheyenne took a deep breath, let it out, and said, "Hello, Nigel."

"You're not fired," Nigel declared, blustering a little.

Cheyenne blinked. "I'm not? Maybe you should know I ran over my company phone, and—"

"I'm having a car delivered, and a new phone. The rental people will pick up whatever you're driving now. I want you to keep working on this deal, Cheyenne. McKettrick must have a weak point somewhere, and we're going to find it."

This kind of double-pronged approach was typical of Nigel, and while Cheyenne was certainly glad she was still among the gainfully employed, and even gladder that she would have a company car, the remark about finding and exploiting Jesse's "weak point" left her feeling disturbed and oddly protective. "Nothing underhanded, Nigel," she warned. "I won't be part of anything like that."

Nigel gave a snort—possibly disbelief, possibly even contempt, there was no telling without seeing his face—and Cheyenne wondered if she'd ever really known the man at all. She'd never suspected, for instance, that he'd believed she'd used sex to land all those deals, and just remembering the insinuation made her fume.

Ayanna was watching her from the kitchen door, though, and Mitch from his chair just inside the living room. Whatever her new reservations about her boss, and about Meerland Ventures in general, she had to stay in the game as long as she could.

"Are you hung up on this guy or something?" Nigel asked.

Cheyenne simmered. "I don't have to be 'hung up' on Jesse to play by the rules," she said. "I have standards, Nigel."

"And I don't?"

"I'm not sure," she replied. "First, you suggest that I sleep with him to get what I want. Now, you're talking about looking for a soft spot to stick the knife. I'm not about to undercut Jesse McKettrick or anybody else to push this deal through. Before you send the car and the new phone, you'd better be clear on where I'm coming from."

"I'm clear, all right," Nigel replied. "Listen, I'm sorry if I stepped on your toes. I just thought you were willing to play hardball, that's all. And furthermore, if you think people with the kind of money the McKettricks have *don't,* you are grievously naive."

Cheyenne frowned. "I'm confused, here, Nigel. Do I still have a job or not? And if I do, do I get to do it my way? Because I don't *give a rip* how anybody else conducts business. I'm only concerned with my own conscience."

Mitch and Ayanna applauded.

Cheyenne widened her eyes and mimed a gulp.

"You get the car," Nigel said. "You get the phone. And you get three weeks—twenty-one bright, shiny days—to pull this off. If you fail, no car, no phone, no job." He paused, then added solemnly, "No *company.*"

"I want one more thing," Cheyenne said. In poker terms, she thought wryly, her chips were in the center of the table and she was *all in.* Might as well call Nigel's car and phone and raise him an ultimatum. "No more phone calls. I believe I've said this before, but since it didn't get through, I'll try one more time. When I have something to say, I'll call you."

Another round of applause from the family, louder this time.

"Do you have the television set on or something?" Nigel asked with a frown in his voice.

"Yeah," Cheyenne answered, with a wink for Mitch and Ayanna. The TV, with its foil-flagged antenna, probably didn't even work. *"Wheel of Fortune."*

I'll spin, Pat.

"You'll have the car tomorrow," Nigel promised.

Cheyenne thanked him, hung up and then stood there, wondering whether to do a victory dance or burst into tears.

Ayanna and Mitch stared at her, waiting for some reaction.

"I need jeans," she said. "And let's splurge on supper at the Roadhouse. I'm buying."

She didn't want to go near Lucky's, because of old memories, and besides, the Roadhouse was more accessible for Mitch.

Their faces glowed.

"You don't own a pair of *jeans?*" Ayanna asked, sounding stunned, looking down at her own battered Levi's.

"Why does everybody make such a big deal about that?" Cheyenne retorted good-naturedly. "You'd think they were part of a national uniform or something."

"They are," Ayanna said.

Half an hour later, with everybody spit-shined and presentable, and Mitch's chair folded and loaded into the trunk of the rental car, they set out for town. Cheyenne dashed into the local Stuff-Mart, bought two pairs of jeans, two T-shirts, a denim jacket and some cheap but flashy boots. When she got back to the car, Ayanna was reading a newspaper, while Mitch, ensconced in the backseat, played a handheld video game.

"All set?" Ayanna asked, eyeing the bulging blue plastic bag Cheyenne carried.

"All set," Cheyenne replied, hoping it was true.

She had jeans.

She had three weeks to change Jesse's mind about selling his land.

And it would take a miracle.

"NO ANSWER," KEEGAN SAID, hanging up the phone and

sitting back in his chair again. His eyes twinkled as he studied Jesse, though the set of his face remained serious. "You know, cousin, you don't *look* as if you want me to bring Cheyenne in for an interview, let alone offer her a job with McKettrickCo. And I find that fascinating, given that that was allegedly the reason why you came here in the first place."

Jesse couldn't help scowling. He was losing his touch, he concluded. All of a sudden, people could read him like a book.

Maybe he ought to stay away from that big poker tournament in Vegas. Leave well enough alone.

As if he'd ever been able to do that.

"She's coming to Sierra and Travis's party with me on Saturday," Jesse said, for the sake of clarity.

"I see," Keegan said sagely, grinning with everything but his mouth. "You don't just like Cheyenne—you *like* her."

Jesse shifted in his chair. He'd drawn a line in the sand, marked his territory. So be it. "Just don't put the moves on her, okay?"

Keegan chuckled. "Now that's funny, coming from you. *I'm* not the famous heartbreaker in this family, you know."

"I mean it, Keeg. Cheyenne's vulnerable."

"*Vulnerable?* Good God, you *have* been watching talk-TV. I remember her as serious and smart. Tough, too—she had to be, to grow up with Cash Bridges for a father. But 'vulnerable'? I don't think so, Jesse."

"Think whatever you damn well please," Jesse said

tersely. "But don't mess with her."

Keegan held up both hands, palms out, in a gesture of amused concession. "I hear you," he said, but the thoughtful look in his eyes still raised Jesse's hackles.

He thrust himself out of his chair, reached for his hat. "See ya," he said.

"See ya," Keegan replied.

Jesse left the office without another word.

SUPPER AT THE ROADHOUSE was a celebration, of sorts. Ayanna was pleased about her new job at the supermarket, and Mitch flirted the whole time with a teenage waitress named Bronwyn. Cheyenne was the only one putting on an act. Behind a cheerful smile, she mentally relived that morning's encounter with Jesse, over and over again. Hadn't he *told* her, straight out, that he wasn't about to sell his precious five hundred acres? What did she hope to accomplish by staying on in Indian Rock?

Three weeks wasn't enough time to change Jesse's mind.

He was a McKettrick, genetically stubborn. Three *centuries* probably wouldn't do the trick.

All she was really doing was putting off the inevitable.

Prolonging the agony.

Maybe she ought to look into bagging groceries alongside her mother.

She was actually thinking of asking the Roadhouse

manager for a job application when some primitive sense awakened, crackling in her nerve endings, and her gaze swung, without her consciously intending to look in that direction, toward the front door.

Jesse McKettrick ambled in.

He looked straight at her.

The air sizzled.

She wondered why the smoke detectors didn't go off, and if he'd left his hat in the truck, because he wasn't wearing it.

He smiled and came directly over to their booth.

"Hello, Cheyenne," he said. He nodded to Ayanna. "Mrs. Bridges." Then he turned his easy, approving smile on Mitch. "Jesse McKettrick," he said, putting out his hand.

Mitch, parked at the end of the table in his wheelchair, shook it manfully. "Mitch Bridges," he said.

"Why don't you join us, Jesse?" Ayanna asked, beaming.

Cheyenne nudged her mother's ankle with the toe of her shoe.

"We're just about to order dessert," Ayanna added, ignoring the signal.

"Don't mind if I do," Jesse said. Cheyenne had to scoot over a little to let him sit down next to her in the booth, or he'd have landed on her lap, but she didn't give him much room.

"Do they have any horses at the ranch where we're going to for the barbecue?" Mitch asked, so hopefully that Cheyenne's throat constricted.

"Mitch," she began, "you can't—"

This time, it was Jesse who did the nudging. His right thigh whacked eloquently against her left, effectively silencing her. *And* sending a flash of heat through her entire body. "Sure there are," he said. "I'll saddle one for you if you want."

Cheyenne whacked him back. A painful flush climbed her neck and pulsed in her cheeks.

Jesse didn't spare her so much as a glance, but the pressure of his thigh increased, hard and muscular.

"That would be great!" Mitch said exuberantly.

Ayanna looked equally delighted.

Had these people lost their minds? Was she, Cheyenne, the only one with any common sense at all? Mitch was a paraplegic. He couldn't ride a horse.

Bronwyn, Mitch's new friend, strolled over to take dessert orders. She was cute, with gleaming brown hair worn in a lengthy French braid, huge green eyes and an angelic smile. Her gaze kept slanting sideways to land on Mitch, who smiled up at her as though they'd known each other from birth.

"The peach cobbler's good today," she said. Only then, apparently, did she notice the latest addition to the corner booth. "Oh. Hi, Jesse."

Cheyenne allowed a moment of smugness to distract her from her irritation over Jesse's glib promise to put Mitch on horseback. Obviously, there *were* women who were oblivious to the McKettrick charm.

"Hi," Jesse said amiably. His thigh was still pressing against Cheyenne's, and she couldn't seem to muster the coordination to move away. "I'll have the cobbler, please."

Mitch and Ayanna both followed suit.

"Ice water," Cheyenne said when Bronwyn gave her a questioning glance.

"It won't help," Jesse observed, as if the two of them were alone.

"Shut up," Cheyenne told him.

"Cheyenne!" Ayanna protested.

Cheyenne subsided. Folded her arms and slid as close to the wall as she could get. Even with several inches of distance between them though, she still felt the heat and substance of Jesse's body. They might as well have been in full contact.

Jesse turned and looked down into Cheyenne's eyes. "My cousin Keegan is trying to reach you," he said bluntly.

"Why?" Cheyenne asked.

Jesse's jaw tightened, but the move was so slight that Cheyenne almost missed it. "He wants to set up an interview at McKettrickCo."

"For what?"

"A job."

"Jesse, I *told* you—"

Cheyenne felt her mother's heel digging into her instep.

"You can always say no," Jesse reasoned. "You did tell me you were about to be out of work, didn't you?"

"Out of work?" Mitch put in proudly, probably more for Bronwyn's benefit than anyone else's. The girl lingered, though she'd already taken the order for three cobblers and Cheyenne's ice water. "She's getting a company car."

Cheyenne's cheeks heated. *Now* what was she supposed to say to Jesse?

Change of plans. I have three weeks to do the impossible.

Oh, and before I forget, my boss is probably looking for your Achilles' heel right this very moment. You don't have one—do you?

Jesse frowned. "So you still think you can change my mind?" It was clearly a rhetorical question. Why else would she be staying in Indian Rock and getting a car as a perk after telling Jesse only that morning she'd almost certainly be fired as soon as Nigel heard what his decision was?

She opened her mouth and promptly closed it again, because anything she would have said could only have gotten her in deeper.

Bronwyn left, reluctantly, and returned with desserts.

"This cobbler," Ayanna piped up hastily, "is *delicious.*"

It was an interesting observation, Cheyenne thought, since she hadn't actually *tasted* the stuff yet.

Jesse sat with his fork poised in midair, and Cheyenne didn't reach for her glass of water. Suddenly, he flashed that wicked grin, but his eyes were stone serious.

"You might want to consider working for McKettrickCo," he said. "I can't promise a company car, but

I *can* tell you this—you won't be asked to ruin a tract of land that's been pretty much the same since God spoke it into existence."

With that, he stood, tossed enough money to pay for his untouched cobbler onto the table and left the Roadhouse.

Mitch and Ayanna sat in uncomfortable silence.

After a moment's hesitation and a muttered swearword, Cheyenne got up and hurried after Jesse, nearly running over Bronwyn in the process. She caught up to him in the parking lot, just as he was about to climb into his truck.

"Jesse, wait."

He turned slowly to look at her, and it struck her that he didn't look angry. He looked hurt.

"Are we still on for Saturday night?" she asked, feeling foolish.

Jesse didn't speak.

"My mother and brother are counting on going."

"I'll be around at six," Jesse told her flatly. "Just like I said I would."

"I bought jeans and everything," she said. He'd just answered her question. Why was she prattling like this? And why couldn't she simply cut her losses and run?

He took a step toward her. "You just don't give up, do you?"

"I can't, Jesse."

"Because of the company car?"

"Because of my family."

He sighed, reached into the truck for his hat and settled it on his head. "I've got a family, too, Cheyenne. Sure, that whole creek thing got by me, but the fact is, we depend pretty heavily on that water in dry years, down on the Triple M. Even if I wanted to sell that land to a developer—and we've already established that I don't—I couldn't put the ranch in jeopardy like that."

Cheyenne clasped her hands together behind her back. "I know all that, Jesse," she said. "And believe it or not, I respect you for taking a stand. But I've got to try to change your mind, because it's my job."

Jesse surprised her with another grin. Even standing at least ten feet from him, she felt the impact of it, and had to catch her breath. The feeling roughly corresponded to being French-kissed without warning.

"I can't say I'm averse to being persuaded," he said. "As long as you understand that you don't have a chance in the furthest corner of hell." He climbed into the truck, spoke to her from behind the wheel. "Tell your brother and mother it was good to see them."

Cheyenne took a step toward him. "About saddling that horse for Mitch—"

He held up a hand to stop the flow of words. "That," he said, "is between Mitch and me." With that, he closed the truck door, started the engine and backed out, waving once as he passed.

Cheyenne stood rooted to that potholed parking lot, watching him drive away.

THE NEXT MORNING, she was breaking in one of her

new pairs of jeans and an old cotton shirt of her mother's when Jesse pulled into the front yard, with a bunch of new lumber sticking out of the bed of his truck.

Cheyenne had been clearing away debris since just after sunup, in an effort to make the place look halfway decent, but she was still waist-high in weeds. Sweat dampened her scalp and forehead, and her hair was coming down from the loose clip on top of her head.

She sighed and tried to ignore the strange jubilation she felt.

"Mornin'," Jesse said, climbing out of the pickup. He took off his hat, tossed it onto the passenger seat and approached.

"What are you doing here?" Cheyenne asked, embarrassed by both her own appearance and that of the property.

"Just a neighborly visit," he answered and rounded the truck to begin unloading the lumber. "I brought a box of doughnuts, hoping you'd contribute the coffee."

Cheyenne approached. "What—?"

"Okay, I admit it," Jesse said with another shameless grin. "I cruised by the place last night, after I left you at the Roadhouse, and noticed you needed a ramp for Mitch's wheelchair."

Cheyenne's pride kicked in. "We have—"

Jesse nodded toward the half-rotted boards stretching between the porch and the ground. "Recipe for disaster," he said.

"I appreciate your concern, but we really don't need—"

Ayanna came out onto the porch, dressed in jeans and the red cotton shirt provided by the supermarket. "Jesse," she called. "What a nice surprise!"

"You're supposed to be friendly to me, remember?" Jesse whispered, close—much *too* close—to Cheyenne's ear. "Try to get on my good side, so I'll sell you that five hundred acres?"

"But you don't have any intention of doing that," Cheyenne protested, whispering, too.

"No," Jesse said, "I don't. But 1 will enjoy your efforts at persuasion. You might start by taking the doughnuts inside, and giving up a cup of coffee. I take it black."

"This is crazy!"

"Yeah," Jesse grinned. "I don't know what's come over me."

Cheyenne gave up—at least temporarily—and went to the passenger side of the truck for the doughnuts. She and her mother bumped shoulders as they passed in the yard, Cheyenne on her way into the house, Ayanna headed straight for Jesse.

"Behave," Ayanna ordered under her breath.

Cheyenne stiffened her spine and kept walking.

When she returned a few minutes later, with Jesse's coffee and three doughnuts on a cracked plate, Ayanna was pulling out in the van, on her way to work. She must have met the rental-car people on the bend in the driveway because she'd just disappeared into the stand of cottonwoods when two guys showed up in a minibus.

Cheyenne shoved the coffee and doughnuts at Jesse and went to sign off on the car and surrender the keys. She felt oddly bereft as she watched the two vehicles speed away.

When she turned to look at Jesse, he was sipping coffee and holding a doughnut with a big bite out of one side.

"Guess you're on foot for the time being," he said.

Cheyenne lifted her wrist, then remembered she wasn't wearing a watch. "Not for long," she replied. "What are you up to, Jesse?"

"Just doing a kindness for a friend," he said.

Mitch wheeled out onto the porch, which took some maneuvering, since the door was barely wide enough to accommodate his chair. "Hey, Jesse," he said.

"Hey, dude," Jesse replied.

"What's with the boards?" Mitch asked, but the expression in his eyes said he knew, or hoped he did.

"Building a ramp," Jesse said. He finished the doughnut, set his coffee down and walked back to the truck, returning almost immediately with a toolbox swinging from one hand.

Mitch's smile broadened. "Can I help?"

Cheyenne held her breath.

"Sure," Jesse said. "You didn't expect to just sit around and watch, did you?"

CHAPTER SIX

JESSE'S SWEAT-DAMPENED HAIR curled at the nape of his neck as he bent over the ramp, arousing an unwanted and fragile tenderness in Cheyenne and, to make matters infinitely worse, he'd taken off his shirt. Between the deep tan of his skin and the play of well-defined muscles in his back and shoulders, Cheyenne was hard put to look away.

Mitch stayed right beside him, there in the tall grass, leaning forward in his wheelchair to hand Jesse nails and carrying on a rambling, one-sided conversation. Jesse hammered away, paused now and then to run a forearm across his brow, and listened in a holistic way—much as he'd taken in the view of those five hundred acres when he and Cheyenne had ridden up to the ridge the day before. Even though he wasn't looking at Mitch, he seemed to be catching every word and nuance, assimilating and integrating it, somehow making it a part of himself.

Cheyenne had never known anyone who used his senses quite the way Jesse did, and the insight both rankled and intrigued her. Wild though he was, there was an innate and wholly paradoxical stillness about him, even when he was moving, as though he revolved around some inner core rooted in the very heart of creation.

What would it be like to make love with a man like

that? A man capable of that elemental concentration? That strange singleness of heart, mind and body?

Cheyenne flushed and fanned herself with the first thing that came to hand—yesterday's newspaper—and went back to her own work, hacking at weeds with the dull hoe she'd found earlier in the shed out back. She was soaked with perspiration, blisters burned her palms, and she knew her muscles would ache like crazy by the following day, but there was something deeply satisfying about chopping away at that undergrowth.

Because of that, and because she wanted to avoid snagging her gaze on Jesse again, she focused on swinging the hoe, and wouldn't have noticed the two cars coming up the driveway if one of the drivers hadn't honked his horn.

She stopped, leaned on the hoe handle and squinted.

First came a black sedan, then a sporty blue compact.

Jesse quit hammering, and he and Mitch watched the vehicles roll to dusty stops at the edge of the yard.

Nigel got out of the dark sedan, smiling, dressed in his usual natty tailored suit and shiny shoes. His fine brown hair had that floppy look Cheyenne secretly thought of as inherently English. He pulled off his expensive sunglasses, the kind that made him look like the captain of an alien space ship, and strode toward her, nodding at Jesse and Mitch as he passed.

"Surprise!" he said. "I come bearing gifts." He gestured grandly, in an apparent attempt to draw Cheyenne's attention to the blue car. The promised company ride, no doubt.

Because she could so easily imagine Nigel putting his well-shod foot into his big mouth by making some overconfident reference to Jesse and the land deal, she made the introductions quickly. "Nigel, this is Jesse McKettrick," she said. "Jesse, my boss, Nigel Meerland. I think you know Mitch."

Nigel tried to play it cool, but he reacted visibly to Jesse's name, stiffening a little and turning to give him a second look. Then he rallied. "Of course I know Mitch," he said, approaching to put out his hand, first to Jesse, then to Mitch.

Jesse's gaze slid to Cheyenne, and she wondered if he'd known she was warning Nigel not to say anything about the condo development.

Impossible, she decided. Jesse was disturbingly perceptive, but he wasn't a mind reader.

"I've brought your car, your new telephone and a stack of files," Nigel announced, shifting the formidable force and energy of his presence back to Cheyenne. "I'd love to stay and help you with your various . . . projects . . . but I've got a plane to catch. Important meeting in L.A. tonight." He waggled his eyebrows, as if to let her know he was transmitting a secret message.

Just the thought of Nigel pounding nails or clearing weeds made Cheyenne smile. And even though the reference to the L.A. meeting troubled her a little, for reasons based more on instinct than on reason, she put it aside.

Nigel arched one eyebrow. "A word, please?"

Still smiling, Cheyenne walked him back to the sedan. Waited while he got behind the wheel and started the engine.

"That's him?" he asked, stealing a glance in Jesse's direction.

Jesse, meanwhile, had gone back to working on the ramp.

"That's him," Cheyenne confirmed.

"Looks as if you've got him right where you want him."

Cheyenne kept her feathers smooth. Where *did* she want Jesse? In her bed, for one place, she realized with a cold-water shock, followed by a surge of searing heat, though she wasn't about to let that happen—or confide the desire to Nigel. "What makes you say that?" she asked, to give herself time to recover.

"He wants you," Nigel said. "That's why he's here, doing manly man work with his shirt off. Don't tell me you don't get the message, Pocahontas. I thought your people were supposed to be intuitive."

Holy shit, Cheyenne thought. Nigel was a nincompoop, for the most part, but occasionally he hit on a solid insight.

"My people?" she echoed, indignant.

"Indians," Nigel said. He could be politically correct when it suited him, but right now, evidently, it didn't.

"Native Americans," she insisted.

"Whatever," Nigel replied. He looked at her intently as the man who'd driven the other car approached. "Say, you wouldn't happen to have a stake in a casino or something like that? Some kind of tribal rights?"

"Nigel," Cheyenne said evenly, "thank you for the car. Thank you for the new cell phone. And get out."

He grinned.

The guy from the leasing company handed Cheyenne a set of keys and got into Nigel's car on the passenger side.

Nigel honked again, a jaunty toot-toot of a goodbye, and they were off, turning around in the deep grass and barreling back down the driveway.

Cheyenne watched until they were out of sight, and so was a little startled when she realized Jesse was standing beside her.

"Nice save," he said.

She looked up at him and was relieved to see a grin on his dirty face. "I don't know what you're talking about," she lied.

"Yes, you do," Jesse countered good-naturedly. "You were afraid the boss would assume I was a handyman and give you a pep talk about sticking it to me."

Cheyenne sighed. "Nobody wants to stick anything to you, Jesse," she said, and immediately wished she hadn't phrased her answer quite that way. "It's a fair offer."

"Right," Jesse said, pleasantly skeptical.

"That development would bring a lot of business to Indian Rock. It would be good for everybody."

"Except the McKettricks, and about a dozen different species of critters," Jesse replied.

"We were getting along so well," Cheyenne said rue-fully.

Jesse's mouth quirked at the corner. "Only because we weren't talking," he replied. "By the way, you'll never get this ground cleared with that hoe. Why don't you rent a tiller?"

"Why didn't I think of that?" she asked cheerfully. She *had* thought of it, of course, but she was reluctant to stretch the budget even that far.

"Guess I'd better finish that ramp," Jesse said with an implied shrug and turned away. Mitch waited patiently, clasping a handful of nails.

Cheyenne tucked her car key into the pocket of her new jeans and went to examine her car. Boxes containing a laptop, the promised cell phone and half a dozen fat file folders sat in the backseat.

She carried the stuff inside the house in relays, piling it all on the kitchen table, and headed for the sink. There, she splashed her face and neck with cool water, then washed her hands.

After checking the pitiful store of food supplies Ayanna had brought from Phoenix, she made iced tea.

Outside, the hammering continued.

Mitch's voice was an eager drone on the hot, weighted air.

The telephone rang and, against her better judgment, Cheyenne took the receiver off the wall. This phone, like the one in the living room, dated from the fifties, so there was no caller ID.

Alas, she didn't need it.

"Hello?" she said, hoping she was wrong.

"He wants you," Nigel told her. "Use it."

JESSE EYED THE RAMP, nearly completed now, and the tumbledown porch he was about to attach it to, wondering if it would hold.

"How about letting me take a spin in that chair?" he said to Mitch.

Mitch grinned. "You want to?"

"Sure," Jesse answered with a grin.

Mitch buzzed through the grass, hoisted himself off the chair to sit on the edge of the porch and beckoned.

Jesse crossed the yard, sat down in the chair and inspected the controls. The thing was electric, but that was about all that could be said for it. Like the house and the yard, it was well past its prime.

He stood up again, dragged the ramp over to the porch and set it in place. Then he returned to the chair, whipped it into Reverse, did a 360, and tried for a wheelie.

Mitch laughed aloud.

Cheyenne appeared in the front doorway, frowning.

Jesse zipped up the boards and back down again in reverse.

Yep, he thought, the ramp would hold. For the time being, anyway. Attaching it to that porch was like putting a Band-Aid on a bullet wound, though. It was a stopgap measure at best.

He looked up at Cheyenne.

Still frowning, she turned and fled back into the house.

"What's with her?" he asked.

"She's just way too serious," Mitch replied.

Jesse remembered the shy but funny girl Cheyenne had been, before she'd left Indian Rock to start college. "I guess she's had a rough time," he said. He was fishing and he knew it, but he couldn't help it.

Mitch's face changed and he nodded. "She used to be different," he said sadly. "Before the accident."

Jesse steered the wheelchair within Mitch's reach and got out of it. "That was a hell of a thing," he said. "I'm sorry it happened."

Mitch shrugged. "Life goes on. There are a lot of things I could do, if Cheyenne and Mom weren't so scared I'd get hurt again."

Jesse perched on the edge of the porch, waiting while Mitch transferred himself back to the chair. "Like what?" he asked easily.

"I'm good with computers," Mitch said. "I could be a technician or even write programs. But they—" he nodded toward the house "—are afraid nobody would hire me. You know, because of the chair."

"You don't need legs to write programs," Jesse said.

Mitch grinned, his whole face going as bright as a harvest moon on a clear night. "You still going to saddle up a horse for me at the party tomorrow night?"

Jesse nodded. "You bet."

"Mom might be okay with that, but Cheyenne will pitch a fit."

Jesse turned his head toward the open doorway. For a moment, it was as if he could see through the sagging walls of that old house, catch sight of Cheyenne in there, wishing he'd go away.

"She'll get over it," he said.

"You don't know my sister," Mitch told him.

Jesse shook his head. No, the truth was, he *didn't* know Cheyenne, but he'd like to. Inside and out. He wanted to explore her most secrets thoughts, touch the bruised places on her soul, lay her down on a bed in some cool, shadowy room and make love to her until they both passed out from exhaustion.

"What does she do for fun?" he asked.

"Cheyenne doesn't *have* fun," Mitch answered. "All she does is work and worry, as far as I can tell."

"Maybe it's time somebody changed that," Jesse mused.

"Good luck," Mitch scoffed, but when Jesse looked at his face, he saw a hope so desperate that it twisted something deep inside him.

Jesse stood. "Guess I'd better gather up my tools and get out of here. You want to give the ramp a try before I go?"

He'd planned to spend what remained of the day playing poker in the back room at Lucky's, but now he needed a shower and a change of clothes. Instead of going all the way out to the ranch, he decided to stop by McKettrickCo—Rance and Keegan had an executive gym there, equipped with the necessary facilities, and he knew Keegan always kept extra duds on hand.

As it happened, he wanted a word with his cousin anyway.

Mitch navigated the ramp with the deftness of a

skateboarder going over a jump.

Jesse decided the thing ought to have side rails and made a mental note to stop by the lumber yard again for more boards.

"Thanks, Jesse," Mitch said from up on the porch.

"No problem," Jesse answered, wondering if he ought to go inside and say goodbye to Cheyenne. In the end, he decided against it because it might seem as though he wanted something from her, and even though he *did* want something, it wouldn't be smart to let on.

Mitch was still going up and down the new ramp as Jesse drove away, and just before he turned the bend, he saw Cheyenne in his rearview mirror, giving a half-hearted wave from the doorway.

"NICE CLOTHES," KEEGAN remarked, when Jesse came out of the workout room at McKettrickCo, freshly showered and wearing black slacks with knife-edge creases and a long-sleeved polo shirt the manufacturer would probably have described as *sea-foam green.* "The boots add an interesting touch."

Jesse grinned and looked down at his favorite pair of shit-kickers. "I don't mind duding up a little," he said, "but I draw the line at wearing oxfords."

Keegan chuckled and shook his head. "Downright noble of you to stoop to stealing from my wardrobe," he said. "And I'd pay money to see you in oxfords." He looked tired as hell, and it occurred to Jesse that his cousin might not have gone home at all the night before. He could have had his dinner brought in, worked until his eyes wouldn't focus, and stretched out on the couch in his office for a snooze. Since the divorce, he'd done that a lot, according to Myrna Terp.

"You said something yesterday about wanting to hire somebody who was good with computers," Jesse said, figuring he might as well launch right in. No sense in beating around the bush.

Keegan sighed. "What are you doing, starting an employment agency? I tried to call Cheyenne a couple of times, but evidently she doesn't have voice mail."

"I don't think she's looking for a job," Jesse replied, turning to the mirror over one of the line of sinks and getting a start for his trouble. He looked like any other corporate grunt, heading out to play eighteen holes on the golf course. The idea made him shudder. "She's still trying to persuade me to sell her the land."

Keegan, leaning one shoulder against the doorjamb, folded his arms. "You're not stringing her along, are you, Jesse? Just to see where it might lead?"

Jesse turned from the mirror, crossed the room and glared at his cousin. "I told Cheyenne flat out that I won't accept the deal on any terms. If she still wants a chance to convince me, well, I'm up for that."

"I imagine you are."

The words hurt more than Jesse would ever have let on. "My reputation must be worse than I thought," he said.

"Your reputation," Keegan replied, "is worse than you could possibly imagine. Do you actually know somebody who can handle a computer?"

"Yes," Jesse said. "Mitch Bridges. He's willing to learn, anyway. You could institute some kind of work-study program, couldn't you? On-the-job training?"

Keegan huffed out another sigh. "Cheyenne's brother? He's in a wheelchair, isn't he?"

Jesse bristled. "Yes, he's Cheyenne's brother. And so what if he's in a wheelchair? There's nothing wrong with his brain. He's young and I think he'd work hard."

"Okay," Keegan said, laying a conciliatory hand on Jesse's shoulder. "If he knows the basics, I'll send him up to Flagstaff for a crash course. And maybe some kind of local training program wouldn't be a bad idea. McKettrickCo likes to give back to the community."

"Thanks, Keeg," Jesse said.

"The kid's got to produce, Jesse," Keegan warned. "I'm not running a charity organization here."

"Maybe you ought to be."

Keegan shoved a hand through his hair.

"How come you look so worried?" Jesse asked. "More bad news on the ex-wife front?"

"It just keeps coming," Keegan admitted. "When I went to pick Devon up last night, Shelley said she was spending the night with a friend. And the board of directors is thinking of taking the company public."

By then, they were in the corridor. Keegan's office was at the end, with Rance's next to it. Rance's door was partway open—either he was back from his latest business trip, or the cleaning crew was inside.

"So you're just giving up?" Jesse asked. "This is

112

your weekend with Devon—you told me that yesterday."

"I'm leaving in a few minutes to go get her. Devon's out of school today—teacher meetings or something—and I was going to take her riding."

Rance poked his head out of his office. His dark hair looked as though he'd been ramming his fingers through it. "Well," he drawled, looking Jesse over, "if it isn't the Player. Golf your game these days?"

Jesse returned the look. "I thought you were in China making us all richer," he said. Then he remembered what Sierra had said on the telephone the other day, about Rance and Keegan clearing their schedules to come to the party on the ranch.

"Obviously," Rance retorted, stepping into the hallway, "I'm back. And it's a damn good thing. Keeg's got the bit in his teeth about letting us go public. Says it's a big mistake and he'll block it any way he can."

"Gee," Jesse said, turning to Keegan. "A shitload of money and nobody in the whole damn family has to work for the rest of their days. That *is* an awful prospect."

"Since when did you ever work?" Keegan snapped.

Since this morning, Jesse thought, but he didn't plan on mentioning the ramp-building enterprise over at the Bridges place. There was something way too personal about it, and he knew both Rance and Keegan would ask a lot of questions if they knew.

"Why work?" Jesse retorted. "I won five million dollars playing poker, and my dividend checks come in faster than I can spend them."

Keegan threw up his hands. "I tried," he told the hallway ceiling.

"How are the kids?" Jesse asked Rance. He truly wanted to know, and he also wanted to put a bend in the subject so it would head in another direction—away from Cheyenne and Mitch and his own state of chronic unemployment.

Rance smiled. He loved his daughters, but since his wife, Julie, had died a few years before, he'd left them with their grandmother a lot, while he jetted around the world making deals and soaking up smaller companies. A couple of the major news magazines had called him a pirate, and when it came to doing business, he played for keeps, no holds barred, taking no prisoners, though Jesse had never known him to do anything illegal. "Cora closed up the Curl and Twirl and took them to Disneyland for a week," Rance said. "They'll be back sometime tonight."

Jesse nodded. "You'll be bringing them to Sierra and Travis's party, then?"

"Yep," Rance confirmed.

"See you there," Jesse said on his way out.

"Make sure you bring my clothes with you," Keegan called after him.

Jesse turned, saluted and left.

CHEYENNE, FRESHLY SHOWERED and shampooed, clad in her bathrobe with her hair wrapped in a towel, set a plate of bologna sandwiches in the middle of the table, along with the iced tea she'd brewed earlier. Mitch, having already wheeled to the table, grinned up at her. "That's a seriously cool car Nigel brought you," he said. "We ought to take a spin. Maybe motor down to the supermarket and show it to Mom."

"Later," Cheyenne said. Hard as she tried to corral them, her thoughts kept straying back to Jesse. The way he looked without his shirt. The knowing glint in his eyes when he'd said, *Nice save.*

Mitch took in the boxes Nigel had left, now sitting on top of the dryer jammed up alongside the washer in the tiny kitchen. Cheyenne's jeans and T-shirt were thumping through the spin cycle. "Want me to set up the laptop and the phone for you?" he asked.

"Sure," she answered and sank into a chair to reach for half a sandwich. "I'd appreciate that. Thanks."

"I like Jesse," Mitch said solemnly, as if it were some big secret.

"Ummm," Cheyenne said.

"Do *you* like him, Cheyenne?"

She put her sandwich down on one of her grandmother's chipped plates. They'd been cheap in the first place, those dishes, but Gram had treasured them. Collected them carefully during an advertising promotion at the grocery store.

Suddenly, Cheyenne's throat tightened again, and her eyes threatened to mist over. Gram. Her mother's mother, clinging to the Apache ways, and at the same time trying to function in a predominantly white world.

"Cheyenne?" Mitch pressed, looking worried.

"I like Jesse well enough," she said.

"You have a date with him tomorrow night," Mitch prodded.

"Yes," Cheyenne replied dryly, "I remember."

"So you must like him better than 'well enough.' You like Nigel 'well enough,' but you've never gone out with him." A horrified look crossed Mitch's face. He was nineteen, and because of what he'd suffered, he was mature for his age, but at times he seemed younger, and this was one of them. *"Have you?"*

"Nooooo," Cheyenne said. "I haven't." She didn't believe in mixing business and pleasure. But, then, she'd never had to do business with Jesse McKettrick before, and the man was *built* for pleasure.

"I think Nigel's a shit," Mitch told her, going for another sandwich.

"I think you're right," Cheyenne agreed.

Mitch's forehead furrowed with confusion. "Then why do you work for him? Why don't you get another job?"

"Because it's not that easy," Cheyenne answered. "The economy isn't exactly booming."

"You could apply at McKettrickCo."

"Mitch," Cheyenne said carefully, pushing her chair back a couple of inches, "don't get carried away, here, okay? Yes, Jesse built the ramp, and that was nice of him. He invited us to the party tomorrow night, and that was nice, too. *But* the McKettricks are the McKettricks, and the Bridgeses are the Bridgeses. They live on the Triple M and we live—well, *here.* You think those railroad tracks out there are just railroad tracks? They're not, Mitch. They might as well be a stone wall, twenty feet thick and a hundred feet tall."

Mitch shook his head pityingly. "God, Chey, that's depressing."

"Maybe so," Cheyenne said. Her appetite was gone, so she put the remains of her sandwich in the fridge and cleared her side of the table. "But it's true."

"Is it?" Mitch countered, popping his chair into reverse and scooting back far enough to look her up and down. "I feel sorry for you, Chey. You've given up," he accused. "What happened to all those dreams you used to tell me about, when I was in the hospital? You were going to get married and have kids. Start your own company, so you wouldn't have to take orders from anybody. You said I could do the same thing, do whatever I wanted. Were you just shining me on? Trying to cheer up the poor cripple?"

"Mitch—"

"When did you stop believing life could be good, Cheyenne? Really *good?*"

"I didn't stop bel—"

"Yes, you did!" Mitch shouted. With that, he spun around and left the room.

"Mitch!" Cheyenne yelled after him.

She heard his bedroom door slam in the distance.

She stood very still.

Had she given up, stopped believing her dreams could come true, dreams for herself and for Mitch and her mother as well?

"No," she whispered. She'd come to Indian Rock to buy the land to build the most beautiful condominium development ever designed. If she succeeded, the bonus she received would set Ayanna and Mitch up for life, and enable her to go out on her own, once her contract with Nigel expired.

But how *could* she succeed?

Jesse wasn't about to give in. She was building a house of cards, and it was bound to fall.

What kind of game was she playing with herself, with Jesse?

Did she really think she could change his mind?

Or did she simply want an excuse to spend more time with him?

Her cheeks burned.

The washer pounded to a thunking stop.

Cheyenne crossed the kitchen, took her jeans and T-shirt out of the machine and flung them into the dryer. Fifteen minutes later, she was sitting on the back porch, towel-drying her hair, when she heard her mother's van chortle up out front.

It was too early for Ayanna to be off work. Had she been fired?

Cheyenne couldn't work up the energy to go and find out.

She stayed where she was, gazing at the backyard, which looked even worse than the front. There was the old tire swing, where her dad used to push her when she was little. When he hadn't been drinking, or playing cards, or locked up in jail, that was.

He'd made so many promises back then.

I'll take care of you, princess.

You and me and your mother, we'll get us a house of our own, in some other town, where we can start new.

Soon as I draw that royal flush, princess. Soon as I draw that royal flush.

Cheyenne wrapped her arms around her knees, laid her head down.

The screen door opened behind her.

"Everything okay?" Ayanna asked softly.

Cheyenne didn't look up. She was going to have a chenille imprint on her forehead from her bathrobe, but she didn't care. "I might ask you the same question," she replied.

"I'm on my lunch break," Ayanna said. Cheyenne felt her mother plunk down on the step beside her. Give her a shoulder-bump. "That's some company car out there, and the ramp looks great. So where's Mitch and what's with the communal glum mood?"

"Who says there's a glum mood, communal or otherwise?"

"Well, you're sitting on the back step in your bathrobe, in the middle of the day. You won't look at me. Your brother must be shut up in his room, and he isn't playing a video game unless he switched the sound off on his laptop. The atmosphere around here is thick as yesterday's gravy. I don't have to call the psychic hotline to know there's something going on." She began to rub Cheyenne's back in slow, comforting circles. "Come on, kiddo. What's up?"

Cheyenne turned her head on her knees, looked into her mother's kind, tired face. "You've been through so much, Mom," she began. "Dad. Mitch's accident. Pete taking off when you needed him most. How can you keep the faith the way you do? How do you stay so optimistic?"

"I have my down times," Ayanna said quietly. "But there are plenty of things to be thankful for. Mitch could have been killed when that four-wheeler rolled over, but he wasn't. You've made me so proud, working your way through college, landing such a good job."

"I'm a complete fraud," Cheyenne moaned and pressed her face into her knees again.

Ayanna laughed softly and continued the back rub. "How so, sweetheart?"

"You saw that car out front. Nigel brought it, after you left for work, along with another phone and a new computer. He still believes I can get that land. I know I can't. I've accepted all that stuff on false pretenses— along with a continuing paycheck."

"Business is speculative, Cheyenne. Yours more than most. Methinks something—or some*one*—else is bothering you."

Cheyenne didn't reply.

Ayanna got up, without another word, went into the house and came back a few minutes later, nudging Cheyenne until she sat up straight.

"What's that?" Cheyenne asked. Her mother was holding a battered shoe box in both hands.

"See for yourself," Ayanna said, placing the box in Cheyenne's lap.

Cheyenne lifted the lid, and inside were the pictures of Jesse she'd collected in high school, and the clippings, with yellowed edges now and smidgens of tape still clinging to their corners.

Cheyenne's throat went dry.

"*That's* why you came back to Indian Rock," Ayanna said, and then she left Cheyenne alone again, with her box of memories.

CHAPTER SEVEN

BRANDI BISHOP SHIFTED uncomfortably in her chair and checked her watch for the third time since she'd arrived at the little street-corner café near her Santa Monica beach condo. She drew the usual number of sidelong looks from the men at the surrounding tables, to the usual irritation of the women they were with. She'd finished work for the day, but she still had three hours of class ahead, and her poor dog, Shimmy, was at home, waiting to take his walk.

A waiter wafted over. "May I bring you something, madame?"

Madame? She was twenty-seven, not *fifty*-seven. "Cappuccino," she said, deliberately leaving off her customary *please.* "Non-fat, extra espresso."

The waiter, immune to her charms, tightened his mouth and executed a terse little bow.

Gay for sure, she decided wearily. Not that it mattered.

She uncrossed her legs, then crossed them again. Looked at her watch. Ten minutes to six. Sighing, Brandi took out her cell phone and called her neighbor and best friend, Geoffrey. Maybe she should introduce him to the waiter, she thought. They'd probably hit it off right away—except that Geoffrey was nice and the waiter was snooty.

"Hey, girlfriend," Geoffrey said with his usual warmth.

"Shimmy needs a walk," Brandi answered, as a tall, elegantly dressed man appeared, stopped to speak to the hostess and immediately turned to sweep the gathering with his gaze, which immediately stopped on her. "And I'm not going to make it home before class starts—again. Can you help me out? Please?"

"As if the world needed another lawyer," Geoffrey teased as Brandi watched the stranger approach, weaving his way confidently between tables, his lithe frame dappled in the shadows of palm leaves. "Sure, sugarplum. I'll take care of Shimmy. You just concentrate on torts and depositions or whatever it is you're learning."

"Thanks, Geoff," Brandi replied. "Bye for now."

"Use me and throw me away," Geoffrey said.

Brandi laughed and hung up.

"Mr. Meerland?" she asked. He was looming over her table now, smelling of expensive cologne and money.

The man nodded. Smiled. His teeth were capped, and the tan was probably fake. "Ms. Bishop, I presume? May I join you?"

Brandi suppressed another sigh. Until she'd met Dan Simmons a few months ago, she'd measured every man she encountered against Jesse McKettrick. Handsome and smooth as he was, Nigel Meerland fell short either way. "I don't have much time, Mr. Meerland," she said.

He dragged back a chair, sat down and turned to the waiter, who was just mincing over with Brandi's cappuccino. "I won't keep you long," Meerland promised her after putting in an order for a scotch, neat.

All Brandi knew about Nigel Meerland was that he ran a real-estate development company based in San Diego. He'd looked her up on the Internet, he'd explained when he'd called her at work, promising it would be "worth your while" to meet with him. She'd been about to refuse when he'd mentioned Jesse's name, and something inside her had gone on red alert. Instinct told her this was something she needed to deal with. Beyond that, she was mystified.

"I have a class in forty-five minutes," she said. "And traffic will be bad, since rush hour's on."

Meerland smiled easily. *I've got all the time in the world,* his manner said. "You sell shoes in the daytime and attend law school at night," he commented. "Impressive. You're obviously ambitious, and I like that in a person."

Brandi's internal warning system spiked to *shrill.*

She scooted back in her chair, her spine stiffening. "What do you want, Mr. Meerland?" she asked.

"I understand you were briefly married to a man named Jesse McKettrick."

Brandi frowned. She hadn't touched her cappuccino, even though she *really* needed the caffeine. It was more than disquieting to realize just how much of her personal information and history was available to anybody with access to a computer.

"You're a beautiful woman," Meerland went on, when Brandi didn't speak. "McKettrick was a fool to let you go."

"The parting was mutual," Brandi said. The guy was really beginning to creep her out. What if he was a serial killer or some kind of stalker?

The waiter brought Meerland's scotch, presented it solicitously, and gave Brandi an irritated glance.

Meerland took a sip, his eyes smiling at Brandi over the rim of the glass. "Relax," he said after swallowing. "I'm here to present you with a significant financial opportunity."

Brandi pushed her chair back, tossed down a bill to cover the cost of her cappuccino. "You're selling something, all right," she said. "But I'm not buying."

"Please hear me out," Meerland wheedled.

Brandi remained seated, though she couldn't have said why. "Make it quick," she told him.

"You're aware that your husband won some five million dollars in a poker championship last year and bought a significant tract of land with the proceeds?"

"Ex-husband," Brandi clarified. "I saw the tournament on TV. What Jesse did with the money is his own business."

Meerland rubbed his chin thoughtfully. "Search though I might, I can't seem to find a record of the divorce," he said.

Brandi sat up straighter. She and Jesse *were* divorced. She'd signed the papers, and so had he. She had a copy at home, in her file cabinet. "What are you getting at?"

"My company desperately needs that land I just referred to. We're offering almost double what Mr. McKettrick paid for it. He refuses to even consider the deal. If you take this to court—whether you're divorced or not—you can probably claim as much as half his winnings. *Or* you can force him to sell the property he purchased, and collect your share of the proceeds."

Brandi swallowed. She made good money, selling shoes on commission in an upscale department store, and whenever she was in a pinch, all she had to do was call Jesse and he'd transfer funds straight into her bank account. She'd kept a tally, intending to pay him back when she got out of law school.

Now, as the possibilities of what Meerland was suggesting crashed over her like a tsunami, she felt herself go pale.

"We're talking about approximately four and a half million dollars here," Meerland said, pressing his advantage. "That would be your share. *If* McKettrick sells us the land."

"No," she said. "*No*. I couldn't do that to Jesse. Anyway, we *are* divorced, and I can prove it." Not that she *intended* to prove anything to Nigel Meerland. She didn't have to.

"Your marital status may not matter, if you get the right lawyer and the right judge." Meerland turned his glass round and round with one hand, idly, frowning into the amber swirl of liquid. "I understand your dad got hurt at work," he said. "He'll be out of commission for a while. Bills are bound to accumulate. And you're up to your eyeballs in student loans, aren't you? So is your fiancé, the soon-to-be doctor. It takes a lot of money just to start a practice, what with the cost of malpractice insurance, for example—"

Brandi stood up, shaking. "I've heard enough," she said. "I'm not for sale, and I'm not selling Jesse out to make a few bucks. Goodbye, Mr. Meerland, and thanks for nothing."

Her dad drove an armored car for a security company, over in Phoenix, and six weeks ago he'd been shot in an attempted robbery. He'd need several surgeries to repair the shattered bones in his right leg. Brandi knew his disability payments would barely allow him to keep body and soul together—and he had a second wife, a mortgage and four kids. It *would* be nice to help him out.

Meerland fell into step beside her as she left the café by the outside gate.

"I hope I didn't offend you," he said mildly.

Brandi's eyes burned and her stomach pitched. She'd

never loved Jesse McKettrick, and he hadn't loved her. She'd forgotten whose crazy idea it was to get married—though neither one of them normally drank to excess, they'd met in a club one night in Vegas and had gone on a bender together. Brandi had just been through a bad breakup, and Jesse had been having some kind of hassle with his family. They should have skipped the wedding entirely and gone straight to the sex, which had turned out to be nuclear. After a week locked away in a hotel suite on the Strip, practically swinging from the chandeliers, they'd discovered how little they shared in terms of common interests and long-term goals and had filed for a quickie divorce and gone their separate ways.

"Four and a half million dollars," Meerland reiterated.

"No," Brandi said. Her wheels were parked at the curb, an old wreck of a pickup truck, painfully out of place in Santa Monica, and she wished Meerland hadn't seen it. Hoped it would start when she cranked up the engine so she could peel out.

"It would be so easy," Meerland persisted. "Solve so many problems. Think of the start you and Dr. Dan could make with that much money. No debts. Maybe even private practice for both of you, right out of the chute. Smooth sailing."

Everybody had a price, and for all her high regard for Jesse, who had been both generous and fair, for all her protests that she wasn't for sale, Brandi was dangerously tempted.

She couldn't help imagining what it would be like to make things easier for her dad, untangle her own financial snarl, and help Dan get established on top of that. She wouldn't mind going straight into private practice herself, skipping all the hoops she'd have to jump through working her way up in someone else's firm.

She climbed into the truck, slammed the door and fired up the engine.

Thank God, the motor roared to life.

Thank God, no parts fell off.

Brandi sped away. Half a mile from the restaurant, she pulled into a parking lot, fumbled for her telephone and called Dan.

FIRST THING SATURDAY MORNING, Cheyenne called the local equipment-rental place and ordered a tiller. Ayanna had already gone to work, and Cheyenne and Mitch were sharing an awkward breakfast—they'd barely spoken since yesterday's argument—when the wonder machine was delivered.

Wearing a pair of her mother's jeans and an old T-shirt she'd found in a bureau drawer, Cheyenne went outside to watch as the small tractor was unloaded from a flatbed truck. She'd cleared away the twisted coils of barbed wire and the old tires the day before, so she was good to go.

"Big job," the deliveryman said, assessing the half acre of weeds surrounding them. "For a C-note, you can leave the driving to me."

"Just show me how to run this thing," Cheyenne

answered, after considering the proposition for a few moments. A hundred dollars was a hundred dollars, and since Nigel might pull the plug on her paycheck at any time, considering how precarious his financial situation was, she wasn't inclined to be extravagant.

The fellow shrugged. "Okay," he said doubtfully.

The screen door slammed, and Cheyenne looked back to see Mitch coming down the ramp in his wheelchair.

"Just turn this key," the deliveryman told Cheyenne. He pointed out the brake pedal, with exaggerated care, glanced at Mitch and shoved a clipboard into Cheyenne's hands. "Sign here," he told her. "I'll come back for the tractor sometime this afternoon. If you're not going to be around, leave the key under the seat."

Cheyenne nodded, signed, and waited until the man got back into his truck and left before turning to Mitch.

He'd wheeled himself up on the other side of the tractor.

"Does this thing have a hand brake?" he asked. Cheyenne knew by his distracted tone that he was thinking aloud, rather than expecting an answer from her.

She answered anyway. "I don't know." She could start the machine and shut it off. The tilling blade was already attached, and there was a slide lever on the dash that probably raised and lowered it.

"It does!" Mitch cried, exultant, and before Cheyenne could react to that, her brother had hoisted himself out of the wheelchair and onto the seat of the small tractor. Granted, it was fairly low, but she'd never imagined he had that much upper-body strength.

The pit of her stomach quivered. "Mitch—"

He glared her into silence. Turned the key and fired up the engine. "I can *do* this," he told her, and just like that, he was moving.

Cheyenne looked on, shading her eyes from the sun with one hand, as her brother began mowing under more than a decade's worth of weeds. Like a farmer who had been tilling fields for years, he started at the outside of the yard and worked his way inward in ever-narrowing circles.

The smell of freshly turned earth awakened an old, half-forgotten joy in Cheyenne. She remembered working in the vegetable garden out behind the house, with Gram and Ayanna, planting tomatoes and corn that grew so tall, from a small child's perspective, anyway, that it blocked out the sky.

It would be nice to have a garden, she reflected, with uncharacteristic whimsy. To sit on the back porch and listen to the whoosh-whoosh-whoosh of a sprinkler, flinging droplets of shimmering water over green and growing things.

At a gesture from Mitch, she moved the wheelchair out of his way. A smile broke over her face as she watched him pass.

And then two things happened simultaneously.

Jesse McKettrick drove in, and the tractor over-turned, pitching Mitch onto the ground.

Cheyenne raced toward her brother.

Jesse got there first and shut off the tractor.

"You okay, buddy?" he asked with another of his easy grins, crouching at Mitch's side, opposite Cheyenne, who'd dropped to her knees.

Mitch nodded uncertainly. "There must have been a hole, hidden in the grass," he said, sounding dazed. "I didn't see it."

"It could happen to anybody," Jesse told him, but he was looking straight into Cheyenne's eyes. Silently warning her not to panic.

She put a hand to her chest, trying not to hyperventilate. "You're sure you're not hurt?"

Mitch grinned. Now that the initial shock was past, he seemed almost proud of the spill he'd taken. "No," he said. "I *think* I'm okay, but I can't feel the lower half of my body. For all I know, I've broken both legs."

"Better get you checked out," Jesse said calmly. "Okay to move you, or do you want an ambulance?"

"No ambulance," Mitch said.

At that, Jesse slipped both arms under Mitch, lifted him and carried him to his truck.

Cheyenne, still stricken, got to her feet and hurried after them. Opened the door on the passenger side, so Jesse could set Mitch on the seat.

"I'll get my purse," she said.

Mitch snapped his seat belt into place and tilted his head back, closed his eyes. Was he in pain? Pretending, perhaps for her sake, that he wasn't?

"Take a breath," Jesse told her. "There's no emergency here."

How did *he* know that? Cheyenne, feeling both exasperated and grateful that he was there to help, dashed into the house, got her bag and ran out again.

Jesse's truck had an extended cab, and he was holding one of the back doors open for her when she returned.

"I hope this doesn't mean I can't ride that horse," Mitch said as she buckled herself in.

"Forget the damn horse," she said. "And I shouldn't have let you *near* that tractor!"

Jesse, about to climb behind the wheel, paused with one foot on the running board and gave her another quelling look.

She swallowed, defiant and chagrined at the same time, and felt heat surge into her face.

"I'm probably all right," Mitch said, and turned in the front seat to look back at her. "Anyhow, if one of us had to take a header off a tractor, I'd rather it was me than you."

Jesse got into the truck, started the engine and drove out of the yard as calmly as if they were going for a drive, instead of heading for the hospital.

Did Indian Rock even *have* a hospital? Cheyenne knew there hadn't been when she'd lived there before, but maybe one had been added.

"Want me to call your mom?" Jesse asked quietly. Clearly, he was addressing Mitch, not Cheyenne.

She opened her mouth to answer, just the same, then closed it again.

"No," Mitch said. "She just started her new job, and I don't want to get her upset for no reason."

"No reason?" Cheyenne echoed. "You *fell off a tractor—*"

"Chill," Mitch told her.

Five minutes later, they pulled up in front of the local clinic.

Jesse looked back at Cheyenne. "Wait here," he said and got out of the truck to sprint across the ambulance bay.

A gray-haired doctor came outside almost immediately, followed by two nurses pushing a gurney. Jesse brought up the rear.

With a gentle smile, the physician opened Mitch's door, assessed him with wise, gentle eyes, the color of old blue jeans. His face was rugged, etched deep with character lines.

"I'm Dr. Krischan," he said to Mitch, before sparing Cheyenne a brief, kindly glance. "I hear you got bucked off a tractor."

"I don't think I'm hurt," Mitch said.

Cheyenne's heart pinched. Mitch had been through so much. *What* had possessed her to let him get on that monstrous piece of equipment? She should have known something like this would happen. . . .

"Let's just make sure," Dr. Krischan said.

He and the nurses helped Mitch out of the car and placed him carefully on the stretcher. By then, Cheyenne was standing beside Jesse, and when he reached out and took her hand, she didn't pull away, even though that was her first inclination.

Inside, Mitch was whisked off to an examination

room while Cheyenne filled out the necessary forms. She'd been through the medical maze so many times, she knew the information by heart.

When that was done, though, she was at a loss.

There was nothing to do now but wait.

"Maybe I should call Mom after all," she told Jesse.

He shook his head, led her to a chair, sat her down and brought her a bottle of water from a nearby vending machine. Took a seat next to her. "Mitch doesn't want her to worry, remember?"

"She's his *mother,*" Cheyenne fretted.

"And he's a grown man."

"He's only nineteen."

"A grown man," Jesse repeated.

Cheyenne heaved a frustrated sigh. "Thank you, Jesse. For being there. For helping."

He grinned at her. "Why, shucks, ma'am," he drawled, eyes twinkling. "It's nothing."

"Does anything ruffle you?"

"Not much," Jesse replied.

"Things always work out for you, don't they?"

"McKettrick luck," Jesse said. "It's never failed me yet."

Cheyenne felt a sort of fascinated envy. "Must be nice," she said, and then wished she'd kept her mouth shut.

"Luck isn't something you're born with," Jesse told her. "It's a choice."

She couldn't keep the skepticism out of her voice. "A *choice?*"

"Yes," he answered. And she couldn't figure out whether the look in his eyes was a caress or an expression of sympathy.

"You're crazy."

The corner of his mouth jutted upward. "Maybe so," he conceded. "But I figure I'm lucky because I expect to be. And since I could just as well expect to be the *unluckiest* SOB on earth, that makes it a choice."

"I could choose all I wanted to, and I'd still be Cash Bridges's daughter," Cheyenne heard herself say. She took a great swallow of water, but it was too late to wash the words back down her throat.

"Who you are has nothing to do with your dad," Jesse reasoned, "and everything to do with you. If you've decided it's a bad thing to be 'Cash Bridges's daughter,' though, then that's the way it will be."

"What are you, some kind of philosopher?"

"No," Jesse grinned. "I just think a lot."

Cheyenne got out of her chair to pace. And to get a little farther from Jesse, because he had a way of pulling her into his orbit, like some central star system with whole galaxies revolving around it.

When she'd expended enough nervous energy, she stopped, looked down at Jesse. "Why did you come by our place this morning?" It had just occurred to her to ask.

"I have a knack for being in the right place at the right time," Jesse said. "Just part of my charm."

Cheyenne took another swig from the water bottle. Swallowed. "You must have had a reason."

"I decided Mitch's ramp needed side rails. So I bought some lumber, loaded it in the back of my truck, and headed for your house."

"Why?"

"I just told you why."

"I mean, why are you so determined to help?"

"It's what we do, out here in the country. Or have you forgotten that, living in the big city?"

"Don't try to come off as a country boy, okay?" Cheyenne said, but she was relaxing. It was a strange paradox, his having that effect on her, when nobody had ever rattled her more than Jesse McKettrick did. He made her stomach jump and her palms sweat. "You've led a sophisticated life—traveled all over the world."

"So I have," Jesse allowed. "But Indian Rock is home. Always has been."

Cheyenne began to pace again.

After an eternity, Dr. Krischan returned. "Nothing broken," he said, watching Cheyenne. "Mitch can go home."

Jesse got to his feet. "See you at the shindig tonight, Doc?"

The other man chuckled. "I'll be there."

"Good to know," Jesse said, with a nod toward the back, where Mitch was, "since the kid is hell-bent on taking up bronc busting."

Cheyenne stiffened.

"I'm *kidding*," Jesse told her.

She sighed.

A nurse wheeled Mitch out of the examining area in a clinic chair, and once they reached the truck, Jesse took over. As much as he unsettled her, Cheyenne was touched by the way he lifted Mitch onto the passenger seat without making it seem like a big deal. From his manner, anybody would have thought he dealt with paraplegics every day.

Humiliation was a virtual way of life for Mitch, but with Jesse, things were different. Jesse treated Mitch with quiet respect and utter normality.

Once they were home, and Mitch was back in his chair, Jesse righted the rented tractor, got on it and finished spading up the weeds. Ayanna came home for lunch, and while Mitch was inside regaling her with an account of what had happened, Cheyenne sat on the porch step and watched Jesse in action.

"How do you do it?" she asked when he finally parked the tractor and came over to sit beside her.

"Do what? Drive a tractor?"

"You know that isn't what I mean," Cheyenne said. "You make Mitch feel—well—*normal*. How do you do that?"

"It's easy, Cheyenne," Jesse answered gently. "He *is* normal."

"He—" Cheyenne stopped herself. She'd been about to point out that Mitch was confined to a wheelchair, and list all the things he couldn't do. But Jesse was right. Her brother wasn't a medical case. He wasn't a label. He wasn't a number on a chart somewhere.

He was a person. Somewhere along the line, with all

the crises and all the worry, she'd forgotten that.

"Guess I'd better unload the wood for those rails," Jesse said, standing up. "I'll have to put them up another time, though. I promised Travis I'd help him unload a bunch of rented chairs after lunch, and he's probably watching the road for me. See you at six."

"See you at six," Cheyenne echoed. The words sounded hoarse, and she cleared her throat.

Jesse pulled the boards out of the back of the truck, stacked them neatly, got behind the wheel and drove away.

Cheyenne rose off the porch step and went inside the house.

She found Ayanna alone in the kitchen, looking unusually tired and a little glum.

"Mitch is going through his suitcases," she told Cheyenne, "looking for something to wear to the party tonight."

Cheyenne smiled, crossed to her mother and put an arm around her shoulders. "You doing okay?" she asked. "I know it was probably a shock, but Mitch really is all right—"

Ayanna bit her lip. The shadows under her eyes seemed to deepen. "I know he is," she said. "It's not that. It's—I'm not sure I can do this job, Cheyenne."

Cheyenne's heart ached. "Then quit," she replied gently. "There must be something else you could do."

Tears brimmed along Ayanna's lower lashes, and she gave a brave little nod that made Cheyenne feel even worse. "Mama begged me to go to secretarial school," she said. "I wish I'd listened. But, oh, no—I was young and in love with Cash Bridges, of all people, and I knew everything—"

Cheyenne gave her a hug. "You could attend junior college in Flagstaff," she said. "It's never too late."

"Of course it's too late," Ayanna responded, with a combination sniffle and laugh. "Or is it?"

"Only if you decide it is," Cheyenne said and heard the echo of Jesse's voice in her own words.

"You're right," Ayanna said, perking up. "I'll stop by the library after work and pick up a catalog."

Cheyenne nodded. Suddenly, she wanted that five hundred acres Jesse wouldn't sell with a new ferocity. Okay, so she *didn't* like the idea of cutting down ancient trees to put up condos, or of damming the creek. She'd make sure the McKettricks retained water rights, in perpetuity. And she'd find a way to make up for the condominiums. Gather some investors, once she went out on her own, and build a beautiful assisted-living center for senior citizens, perhaps, or try to bring some sort of light industry to Indian Rock.

Of course there was still the problem of Jesse—he'd made up his mind not to sell, and it would take drastic measures to change that.

"I'd better get back to the store," Ayanna said. Grabbing up the keys to that ratty old van with a resignation that made Cheyenne even more determined, she left.

Cheyenne was still standing in the middle of the kitchen floor when the telephone rang.

"Hello?" she answered, prepared to summon Mitch

or explain that her mother wasn't home. No one besides Nigel ever called her, and he probably would have used her cell number.

"Cheyenne?" a man's voice asked. It was familiar—like Jesse's, but *not* Jesse's. In the next moment, she understood why. "This is Keegan McKettrick."

"Keegan," Cheyenne said, smiling. "Are you looking for Jesse? He was here earlier, but he left a little while ago. Said something about helping unload chairs for the party—"

"Actually," Keegan said, "I wanted to talk to you."

Cheyenne waited, confused.

"Jesse says you might be interested in coming to work for McKettrickCo."

At first, Cheyenne's temper flared. She'd *told* Jesse, quite clearly, after their ride to the top of the ridge the other day, that she wasn't looking for charity. Now, in light of her renewed determination to buy the land and collect the promised bonus from Nigel so her mother wouldn't have to box groceries like some teenager and Mitch could live with some dignity, the glimmer of an idea sparked.

"What kind of job did you have in mind?" she asked.

"Human resources," Keegan answered. "Jesse said something else the other day—made me think. I'd like to set up some kind of work-study program, maybe in conjunction with the high school. Train some local people to run computers and the like. I need someone to head it up."

Cheyenne sank into a chair, slightly dizzy. "Why do

you think I'd be qualified?"

There was a smile in Keegan's voice when he replied. "I checked you out on the Internet," he said. "You've got a degree, and your current job requires a lot of initiative and creative thinking. That's what I'm looking for. Maybe we could talk about it tonight? At the party?"

Cheyenne's palm grew moist, where she gripped the old-fashioned receiver. "I'll be looking forward to it, Mr. McKettrick," she said.

"Keegan," he corrected. "See you tonight."

CHAPTER EIGHT

GOLD HOOPS GLISTENED on Cheyenne's earlobes, and her hair, glistening ebony in the light from the bulb over the front door, fell in loose waves around her shoulders. She wore new jeans and a close-fitting white top, and Jesse's breath caught at the sight of her, the way it did when he drew a royal flush in a high-stakes game.

His knees felt a little unsteady as he got out of the truck and walked toward her. Damn. Why hadn't he stopped off at the florist's and picked up a bouquet?

She smiled. "Mom and Mitch are still getting ready," she said.

"No hurry," Jesse replied, still feeling shaken. "You look great."

She took in his getup—best boots, fairly new jeans, a

white shirt open at the throat—and favored him with another smile. It settled over him, that beneficent smile, felt like an undeserved gift. "Thanks," she said. "You look pretty spiffy yourself."

The sounds of activity came from inside the house. Voices, murmuring, cheerfully rushed. The gathering of things. Mitch and Ayanna were just on the other side of the screen door, but they might as well have been in the next universe, as far as Jesse was concerned. Only Cheyenne seemed real; the house—the first faint shadows of twilight in the cottonwoods—the ground under his feet—all of that might have been an illusion.

"Thanks," Jesse remembered to say, and the word came out hoarse.

"Would you like to come in?" Cheyenne asked.

Jesse didn't want to move. Didn't want anything to change. The moment was golden, and he wanted to stay in it for good.

He shook his head.

Cheyenne turned to open the screen door, so Mitch could roll through in his chair, followed by Ayanna. Both of them looked so eager that Jesse would have invented a party if there hadn't been one waiting out on the ranch.

"Hey, Jesse," Mitch called, heading down the ramp.

Jesse held his breath. He'd played it cool that morning, when he'd seen Mitch go flying off the tractor, but inside, he'd been as panicked as Cheyenne. He wished he'd put the rails on the ramp before setting it up and fastening it to the porch.

"Hey, buddy," he responded, a beat or two late.

Ayanna, resplendent in turquoise and silver conchas, beamed at him. "Thanks for helping Mitch today," she said. "I appreciate it."

Jesse nodded, feeling shy. Since he'd never felt shy in his life, he was confounded by the emotion, couldn't have called it by its name until he'd reflected on it for a while. "Not a problem," he said.

It was a project, getting Mitch installed in the back-seat with Ayanna and loading the wheelchair in the truck bed. By the time Jesse finished all that, Cheyenne had already climbed in on the passenger side.

He'd been close to her before, but for some reason, her proximity made every nerve in Jesse's body jump. Her scent found a place inside him, nestled in to stay. What was it? Perfume—shampoo? Or did she just naturally smell that way, sort of soft and flowery and clean?

The drive to the ranch seemed shorter than usual. Jesse concentrated on the road, even though he knew it so well he could have driven it in his sleep. He figured if he looked at Cheyenne, his eyes would get stuck and he'd run them all into a ditch.

The Chinese lanterns that he and Travis had spent the afternoon hanging from tree limbs glimmered up ahead, in festive shades of red and green and yellow and blue. Cars and pickups, along with a limo or two, lined both sides of the long driveway leading up to the main house, and the music was loud enough to set

Jesse's inner ears vibrating.

"What a sight," Ayanna marveled from the backseat. No one else spoke.

Jesse drove up in front, put the truck in park, and got out to open doors for Cheyenne and Ayanna, then unload the wheelchair. Once he'd gotten Mitch situated, he'd head back down, find a place to leave the truck and walk back.

It wasn't dark yet, and wouldn't be for a couple of hours. Still, the lights of the party shimmered in Cheyenne's eyes as she took it all in. Jesse had the odd notion that she was stashing the spectacle away somewhere, inside herself, like a keepsake.

Mitch headed for the center of the party as soon as he'd landed in his chair, and Ayanna followed.

Cheyenne lingered beside Jesse, watching them go with a slight, sad smile. "They're so happy," she mused.

"I'll park the truck," Jesse found the words to say. "You go ahead."

Cheyenne turned, assessed the line of cars zigzagging like a chain of staples almost to the main road. Shook her head. "I'll go with you," she said and climbed back into the truck before Jesse had a chance to talk her out of it.

Jesse got behind the wheel again, and fought a powerful urge to drive and keep on driving, until there was no one else around except him and Cheyenne.

"Are we just going to sit here?" Cheyenne prompted wryly when they didn't move.

He shifted the rig and gave it some gas. His neck felt

hot, and he still wasn't sure that, now that he had the truck in motion, he wouldn't just keep going. There was so much he wanted to say to Cheyenne, so much he wanted to ask. And damned if he could corral any of it into words.

Cheyenne laughed softly. "Is something wrong?"

Jesse shook his head, but he didn't risk looking her way.

They parked at least half a mile from the house, in the field, and got out to walk back. Cheyenne fell in step beside Jesse, and it only seemed natural to take her hand. He was inordinately glad when she didn't pull away.

The music seemed to roll out to meet them, thrumming. Cheyenne tilted her head back to look at the darkening sky.

"I'd forgotten how bright the stars are out here," she said.

Jesse chanced a sidelong glance at her. He'd spent whole nights lying on a bedroll up on the ridge overlooking those five hundred acres, with his horse grazing nearby, watching the constellations shift like slow-moving pinwheels, but he didn't want to talk about that. First, because it was a private thing, one he didn't readily share, and second, because it would mean bringing up the land, and that was a subject best avoided, at least for that night.

"Do you like living in the city?" he asked because it seemed like a safe question, and it was something he really wanted to know.

"It has its perks," she said. "Restaurants. Book stores. Live theater. I just never seem to have time to enjoy them."

The obvious response was that she worked too much, if that was the case, but he didn't want to head in that direction, either. "I have a place in New York," he said. "I go there when I need an urban fix."

He felt her surprise, even before she stopped, and because they were holding hands, he had to stop, too.

"New York City?" she said, in the same tone as the voice-over in those salsa commercials.

Jesse chuckled. "They do allow cowboys, you know," he said.

She pulled on his hand until he had to look at her, and then he felt as though he was about to tumble right into her eyes. "What do you do there? In New York, I mean?" she asked.

"Hang out with friends, mostly," he said, baffled by her interest, and a little nettled by her continued surprise. "I like to take in a show, hit some of my favorite restaurants, and check out the bookstores." He paused, smiled. "Yeah," he said. "I do read. Without even moving my lips."

For the first time that evening, she looked flustered. "I didn't mean—"

"It's okay, Cheyenne," Jesse told her, pulling her into motion again. Earlier, he'd considered hijacking her, taking her somewhere for coffee, just to talk. Now he had the presence of mind to realize that Keegan and Rance and probably Travis would notice the disappearance and either razz him until three weeks after the end of time or just corner him someplace and ask him too many questions. "Do you get to New York often?"

She sighed. "For the occasional meeting," she said. "Most of them last all day, then there's the obligatory business dinner. By the time that's over, I usually go back to the hotel and crash."

"Maybe you ought to go just for fun sometime," Jesse suggested.

She looked puzzled, as though the concept of doing anything just for enjoyment had never crossed her mind. "Just for no reason?"

He laughed. "Fun *is* a reason, Cheyenne."

She blinked. "I guess you're right," she said.

They'd reached the edge of the lawn by then, and thus the fringes of the party. Liam, Sierra's seven-year-old son, came dashing toward them, the colored lights of the lanterns flashing on the lenses of his glasses.

"Yo, Jesse!" he whooped.

Jesse ruffled the little boy's hair. "Yo, Liam," he said. "Seen any ghosts lately?"

Liam looked from Jesse's face to Cheyenne's and back again. "Tobias," he said, with patient goodwill, "is *not* a ghost. He's a real boy."

"This is my friend, Cheyenne," Jesse said. "Cheyenne, Liam McKettrick. He sees dead people."

"I do not," Liam protested, but he looked pleased by the accusation just the same. He reached out, snatched Cheyenne's free hand. "Come on," he said. "My mom says she wants a look at the woman who could get under Jesse McKettrick's skin."

Cheyenne's gaze shifted briefly to Jesse's face, then back to Liam. "Your mom," she said lightly, "must have me mixed up with somebody else. Nevertheless, I'd really like to meet her."

Jesse watched as Liam pulled Cheyenne into the crowd, and followed at a pace designed to let a fresh rush of blood recede from his neck. He'd rather have been invisible, so naturally Travis waylaid him, handed him a beer.

Jesse took it gratefully.

Travis's gaze followed Cheyenne as she and Liam zeroed in on Sierra, who was greeting guests at the edge of the yard. "Is she the one?"

Jesse bristled. "The one what?"

Travis chuckled. "Take it easy," he said. "I *mean,* is she the one who wants to buy your land?"

"Yeah," Jesse answered, letting out his breath. Shoving a hand through his hair. He hadn't worn a hat, but now he wished he had because then he could have pulled the brim down low on his forehead, hiding his eyes. "That's her."

Travis slapped him on the back. "I'll be damned," he said.

"What?" Jesse snapped.

"There's more going on here than a real-estate deal, that's what," Travis replied.

Jesse recalled Liam's remark about Sierra wanting to meet the woman who'd *gotten under his skin.* "Not a damn thing more," Jesse protested. "The rumor mill

148

must be in high gear, if you think that."

Travis's smile was easy. "I don't have to depend on rumors for my information," he said smugly. "All I had to do to figure this one out was watch the two of you walking up the driveway."

"All right, so I like her," Jesse said, lowering his voice in case anybody in the crowd was eavesdropping. "I like a lot of women. It's nothing more than that."

Travis looked unconvinced. He slapped Jesse's shoulder again. "You'd better go and say howdy to Sierra," he said. "She'll track you down and demand an accounting if you don't."

Jesse scanned the gathering again and, sure enough, Sierra was approaching, with Cheyenne at her side. There was no sign of Liam.

Reaching them, Sierra stood on her toes to plant a sisterly kiss on Jesse's cheek. Her dark blue eyes gleamed with amusement as she looked up at him, and her short brown hair shone. "I hear Liam put his foot in his mouth," she said, twinkling.

Jesse's gaze slid to Cheyenne. She shook her head, smiling a little.

He shifted his attention back to Sierra.

She laughed. "Cheyenne didn't say a thing," she said. "Liam told me."

Jesse grinned at her. Yeah, he was a little rattled, but he'd had a soft spot for his long-lost cousin, and for Liam, ever since he'd met them one day last January when they'd pulled up in an old car, a pair of wayfaring strangers just finding their way home. "Nice party," he said. "Is there anything to eat?"

"Chuck wagon's over there," Sierra responded, with another smile, linking her arm through Travis's, but looking at Cheyenne again. "Let's talk some more, after you've eaten," she said. "I want to tell you about the poker tournament."

Cheyenne seemed taken aback, but before she could ask any questions, Sierra and Travis were moving on, breaking into a laughing circle of friends.

"What tournament?" Cheyenne asked, sounding worried.

"No idea," Jesse said. "Let's go get some supper."

The caterers were serving everything from corn bread and beans to filet mignon out of a rig designed to look like a chuck wagon. People came and went from a dozen or so picnic tables, imported for the occasion, and Jesse was glad to see that Ayanna and Mitch were already eating. Ayanna was talking to Cora Tellington, Rance's mother-in-law, while Mitch sat at a little distance. Bronwyn, the kid from the Roadhouse, sat cross-legged in the grass next to him, talking a blue streak.

Liam, Keegan's daughter, Devon, and Rianna and Maeve, Rance's girls, chased each other between the tables, shrieking with laughter.

Jesse felt unusually self-conscious as he and Cheyenne got into the chow line. He knew everybody was curious; he'd caught several of them looking his way.

Cheyenne filled a plate, and Jesse followed suit.

They found a spot under a maple tree and sat on the ground to eat.

The band kicked it up a notch, and people started dancing under a canopy of trees in the side yard.

"This is quite a house," Cheyenne said, and Jesse was grateful for the opening because for once in his life, he didn't have the first idea what to say.

"It's old," he said. "When Holt—Sierra's great-great-great-etcetera grandfather—bought the place, it was part of another ranch. Later, when he reconciled with old Angus, our common ancestor, it became part of the Triple M."

Cheyenne was quiet for a few moments. "What did you mean when you asked Liam about ghosts?" she asked. "He mentioned someone—Tobias, was it?"

Jesse grinned. "He claims he sees another kid around the place sometimes. One of his and Sierra's ancestors. Sierra's done a lot of research on the family connection, and says she's had some strange experiences herself."

Holding a chicken drumstick in one hand, Cheyenne assessed the long, hulking log place. All the houses on the ranch were made to last, constructed in the same way, with thick, sturdy walls and big windows, hardwood floors and massive stone fireplaces. "That McKettrick history again," she said.

Jesse nodded. "Tobias is right there in the family tree, so he existed all right. He died a couple of years ago, a very old man, in Santa Fe, New Mexico."

"In Santa Fe?" Cheyenne sounded a little disappointed. "Why not on the Triple M, or at least in Arizona?"

"Lots of the McKettricks leave the land," Jesse said. It was a fact of life, and something he still didn't understand. "I guess if they'd all stayed, the place would be jammed to the outside fence lines. There's a pretty big bunch in Texas, around San Antonio, but most of them are scattered all over the world."

Cheyenne nodded. "That's where the home offices of McKettrickCo are," she said. "In San Antonio, I mean." Then she paused, as though she wanted to say something more, but wasn't sure about it. She met Jesse's gaze again. "You don't seem very interested. In the company, I mean."

"Rance and Keegan are interested enough for all three of us," Jesse said.

Cheyenne bit her lower lip. "Did something happen? Some kind of rift?"

Jesse shook his head. "I was never a businessman," he told her.

"So all you want to do, for the rest of your life, is ride horses and play poker?"

"I'd like to have a wife and family sometime," he said, watching as the kids snaked by again, in a long, noisy chain, holding hands. "Nobody has everything."

Cheyenne nodded. Mitch was in the middle of the dancing, with Bronwyn, and her gaze went straight to him. "Maybe he'll forget about riding the horse," she said, and then looked as though she wished she hadn't spoken.

"Not likely," Jesse said.

They'd finished their food. He took Cheyenne's plate, stacked it on top of his own, got to his feet, and helped her up with his free hand. He disposed of the plates, dropping them into one of several barrels provided for the purpose. Again, Cheyenne cast a look around the party, and he wondered what—or who— she was on the lookout for.

His question was answered almost immediately when Keegan came strolling over, looking a lot less buttoned-down than usual in jeans, a blue shirt and polished boots.

Cheyenne smiled warmly.

Jesse's stomach clenched.

"Hello, Cheyenne," Keegan said. It wasn't an idle greeting; from the look of him, and the tone of his voice, he'd clearly been anticipating this encounter, maybe for a long time.

Jesse moved a little closer to Cheyenne.

"Hello, Keegan," Cheyenne responded. Did she just bat her eyelashes, Jesse wondered, or was it a trick of the rapidly fading light?

Jesse cleared his throat.

Keegan ignored him. "Is this a good time to talk?" he asked Cheyenne.

She nodded.

At last, Keegan acknowledged Jesse. Up till then, he'd have thought he'd gotten his wish to be invisible. "Would you excuse us for a few minutes, Jesse?"

Like he had a choice. Cheyenne was already moving

to Keegan's side. They were about to walk away—together—whether he "excused" them or not.

Jesse gave a terse nod.

Keegan and Cheyenne had gone a few steps when Keegan returned. "I'll give her back," he said in an undertone. A grin flickered in his eyes, never touching his mouth.

Jesse didn't respond, not verbally, anyway. He just glowered. Watched as the two of them moved off, approached a table on the far side of the yard, sat down facing each other. Keegan was careful to pull back Cheyenne's chair, Jesse noted.

"Jesse?" It was Mitch. "How about saddling that horse for me?"

Jesse sighed inwardly. Rubbed his chin. Had trouble looking away from Keegan and Cheyenne. He knew the confab was probably about a job at McKettrickCo, and he had nobody to blame for that but himself. He'd been the one to come up with *that* brilliant idea.

Just the same, if he could have gone over there, grabbed Cheyenne by the hand and taken her away without making a scene, he would have done just that.

"Sure you're up to it?" he asked Mitch. "After the tractor incident, I mean?"

Mitch nodded. "Yes," he said. "I'm sure. If the guy from the rental place hadn't already taken that thing back, I'd ride it again, just to prove I could."

"Who says you have to prove anything to anybody?"

"I've got a lot to prove to myself," Mitch said quietly.

"Okay," Jesse answered. After one last glance in Cheyenne's direction, he set off for the barn, with Mitch trundling and bumping along beside him in the chair. Travis had been teaching Sierra and Liam to ride, and he kept a couple of rocking horses on the place. Either of them would be safe for Mitch to mount.

The doors stood open, and the interior lights were on.

Jesse flipped the switch for the floodlight in the smaller corral, the one Travis used to train horses, grabbed some gear out of the tack room, and tossed it all down outside Pony-boy's stall door. "How about a little exercise?" he said to the gelding.

Pony-boy nickered and bobbed his head. He was a buckskin, more than twenty years old; Travis had picked him up at an auction for a song, mainly because nobody else wanted him, and the next stop would have been the slaughterhouse. The horse had proved gentle enough for Liam and Sierra, both of them greenhorns, and if Travis trusted the animal, so did Jesse.

While Mitch watched from the breezeway, Jesse went into the stall, leaving the door open so the rest of the tack would be in easy reach, and tossed a saddle blanket onto Pony-boy's slightly swayed back. Stroked the animal's neck and spoke quietly to him.

During the saddling process, Jesse chanced to glance toward Mitch, and the combination of determination, fear and pride he saw in the younger man's face gave him pause.

"Maybe we ought to wait for Cheyenne," Jesse said,

offering Mitch an out if he wanted one.

Mitch shook his head. "This isn't about Cheyenne," he retorted. "It's about me."

Jesse nodded to show he understood. Offered a spare grin. "Maybe it's a little about Bronwyn, too," he ventured. "She already likes you, Mitch. She's all but hired a skywriter to let you know. You don't have to impress her by riding a horse."

"Don't I?" Mitch countered, as Jesse led Pony-boy out of the stall, ready to ride. "Have you *looked* at her? She could have any guy she wanted. She probably just feels sorry for me, because I'm in a wheelchair."

Jesse stopped, turned, looked straight in Mitch's face. "Whoa back a second," he said quietly. "I've known Bronwyn and her family for a long time. They're a real decent bunch. She's shown an interest in you. It's not an act, and it's not pity. She really wants to be your friend, Mitch, and I'd be willing to bet the chair isn't a factor."

Mitch bit his lower lip, the way Jesse had seen Cheyenne do.

"I need some help getting on that horse," Mitch said after a few moments of silence. "After that, I can handle it."

"Let's go out to the corral, then," Jesse said. The picture of that tractor overturning in the Bridgeses' yard, and Mitch tumbling helplessly onto the ground, was still fresh in his mind.

Don't let this be a mistake, he thought.

The smaller of the two corrals was well lit. Jesse

156

opened the gate, led Pony-boy through and waited while Mitch made his way over uneven ground.

By the time Jesse had gotten Mitch into the saddle, a few small groups of spectators had gathered along the fence rails outside the corral, and more were wandering that way.

"Stay clear of the chair until I can move it," Jesse told Mitch. "Pony-boy's a good fella, but the machinery might spook him."

Mitch nodded.

Jesse set his feet in the stirrups.

"How do I make him go?" Mitch asked.

"You don't," Jesse answered, "until I've moved that chair."

"Oh, yeah," Mitch said with a nervous chuckle. "Right."

Jesse spotted Ayanna Bridges standing on the lowest rung of the fence, but there was no trace of Cheyenne. Ayanna waved, and Jesse waved back.

He pushed the chair back out of the corral, returned to Pony-boy's side.

"You got any grip at all in your legs?" Jesse asked, looking up at Mitch.

Mitch shook his head. He was sweating a little.

"Then hold on with your mind," Jesse said. "Just as if your legs worked. The horse will feel it, and he'll respond."

"Okay," Mitch agreed.

Jesse gave Pony-boy a light swat on one flank, and the animal ambled across the corral. Mitch gripped the saddle horn with both hands, but his face was brighter than the motion light fixed to the side of the barn.

"Use the reins," Jesse coached, standing in the middle of the corral while Mitch circled. "Lightly, though. Just enough to let him know which way you want to go."

"Is it all right to yell?" Mitch called.

Jesse took a step toward the horse and rider. "Why? Are you scared?"

"No," Mitch said. "I'm *happy*."

Jesse grinned broadly. "Then go for it."

Mitch Bridges cut loose with a *Yippee!* that would have done an old-time cowpuncher proud.

SOMEBODY YELLED, BUT IT WAS a peripheral sound, one Cheyenne barely noticed.

The job Keegan described to her, at their table under the trees, sounded better than good. There was only one problem, as he saw it—the distinct possibility that McKettrickCo would go public within the next six months to a year, and if that happened, Keegan said forthrightly, he couldn't guarantee that her position wouldn't be eliminated after the changeover. In the meantime, though, she'd have benefits and a competitive salary, and work she could feel good about doing.

Her contract with Nigel had another few months to run, and he wasn't likely to let her out of it. Unless, of course, his company folded in the meantime.

"Take some time to think about it," Keegan said. "I don't need an answer tonight."

Cheyenne nodded. Looked around. They were practically alone, except for the caterers. Even the band had stopped playing and wandered off, leaving their instruments unattended.

Keegan looked momentarily puzzled—until he turned toward the barn. A bright light burned, setting the corral aglow, and there was Mitch, riding a horse.

Riding a horse.

Cheyenne went from a standstill to a sprint, her heart pounding in her throat, and wriggled through the milling guests to the fence, climbing up onto the first rung next to her mother.

"Shhh," Ayanna whispered. "He's doing fine."

Cheyenne, who had been about to scramble over the top rail and put a stop to the whole dangerous experiment, swallowed and forced herself to look at Mitch.

His poor, useless legs dangled on either side of the horse, but his spine was straight, and his head high, and he was beaming. Somehow, he urged the animal into a trot.

"Easy," Jesse warned, but he was grinning as he stood in the middle of the corral, watching.

"I'm going to kill him," Cheyenne whispered. Jesse McKettrick had boundless confidence in his *own* physical prowess, probably with good reason, but what he *didn't* have was the right to take reckless chances with Mitch's safety.

"He knows what he's doing," Ayanna assured her.

"I'm talking about Jesse, not Mitch," Cheyenne bit out.

"So am I," Ayanna said. "Look at him. He's calm, but

if anything went wrong, he'd have control of that horse in a millisecond."

A millisecond, Cheyenne thought bitterly, was all it had taken to snap Mitch's spine. He'd been lucky that day with the tractor, but an accident that might leave a healthy person with nothing more than bruises could *kill* Mitch.

"Has everybody around here gone crazy?"

Ayanna smiled at her daughter's anxious words. Her gaze tracked Mitch proudly as he reined in close alongside Jesse.

"I guess I'm done now," Mitch said. Then, looking absolutely translucent with joy, he pretended to sweep off a hat and wave it at the crowd, like some cowboy movie star taking center stage at a rodeo.

The crowd laughed and applauded.

Jesse pushed the wheelchair as far as the corral gate, helped Mitch down off the horse and got him settled, and led the animal away, into the barn.

While Mitch soaked up the admiration, Cheyenne leaped backward off the fence and made for the barn doors, standing open to the warm night, spilling light and the earthy scents of hay and horse.

Jesse tugged the saddle off the animal's back, pulled the bridle over its head, careful to remove the bit with one hand, presumably so it wouldn't bang against the animal's teeth.

"That was a *stupid,* arrogant thing to do!" Cheyenne blurted, standing a dozen feet from Jesse with her hands on her hips.

"Maybe," Jesse conceded, pausing to look at her, then leading the horse into its stall.

"You *saw* Mitch get thrown from that tractor today!"

Taking his time, Jesse closed the stall door, fastened the latch, stroked the horse's long face appreciatively. "That's right," he answered. "And if Mitch hadn't gotten on old Pony-boy here, he might have been scared for the rest of his life."

Ever since she'd come back to Indian Rock, Cheyenne had kept her emotions in check. Now, suddenly, she started to cry, and not delicately, either. She gave a strangled sob, and the floodgates opened.

"It was *just like* the first accident," she wailed. "He was on a four-wheeler and—"

Jesse paused a moment, then came to her, took her in his arms, held her against his chest. "I know," he said. "I know."

Against her better judgment, Cheyenne didn't pull away.

CHAPTER NINE

"THERE'S BEEN A LOT TO BE afraid of," Jesse said gently, there in the middle of the breezeway, his breath warm in Cheyenne's hair. "I understand that. But this is a safe place. This is home."

Cheyenne didn't know whether he meant his arms were a safe place, or the Triple M, or Indian Rock. She sniffled and tilted her head back to look up into Jesse's face. "What's happening?" she asked, not addressing Jesse, but thinking aloud. She felt confused, disoriented, even a little light-headed.

"I don't know." Jesse grinned, his voice throaty and low. "But I like it. I like it a lot."

She finally found the strength to step back out of his embrace, but it took all her determination. She'd never leaned on anybody before, at least not since she'd been an adult, and she didn't dare start now. Not with Jesse McKettrick, at least.

"Thanks for bringing us to the party," she said, dashing at her cheeks with the back of one hand. Ashamed of her emotional display. "But I think we should go home now."

"I'll take you if you want to go," Jesse allowed. "But I don't believe Mitch is ready to leave. He's having too good a time out there, grandstanding."

In spite of everything, Cheyenne laughed. It was a moist, spare sound, made against her will. "You'd think he was Roy Rogers," she said.

Jesse reached out, ran the backs of his fingers lightly along her cheek. It was over so briefly that if his touch hadn't left a trail of fire along her nerve endings, she wouldn't have counted it as real. "Just for a few minutes," he told her, "Mitch wasn't the kid in the wheelchair. He was a cowboy. He had legs again. That counts for something, Cheyenne. Don't take that away from him by trying to rush him out of here."

He had legs again.

Cheyenne knew that phrase would stay with her,

long after she'd left Indian Rock for good. Long after memories of Jesse had faded, she would remember that.

"Why did this have to happen to him?" she cried. She wasn't asking Jesse. She was asking the universe.

"Why does anything happen to anybody?" Jesse countered quietly. "We've all got a part to play, when we come into this world. Nobody gets to approve the script."

Cheyenne thought of the Triple M, of the big McKettrick family and its colorful history. "What if you lost it all tomorrow, Jesse?" she asked. It wasn't a challenge. It was an honest question. "Would you still have that same easygoing attitude?"

"I guess I'd be real sad for a while," he said. "Then I'd make the best of things. Find myself a horse to ride—just like Mitch did tonight—and ante up for a game of poker."

Before Cheyenne could respond, Mitch whirred in from the corral, his face dusty and his grin broad.

"Did you see, Cheyenne?" he asked eagerly. "Did you see me ride that horse?"

Something softened inside Cheyenne. "I saw," she said very quietly.

Mitch turned the chair, so he could look up at Jesse. "Can I do it again sometime? Maybe you and I could ride together?"

Jesse's gaze touched Cheyenne's face, like the faintest whisper of a breeze, and went immediately to Mitch. "Sure," he said. "Sure."

The horse nickered, and Mitch went over to the stall. Remarkably, the animal lowered its head so its erst-while rider could stroke its neck. "Thanks, Pony-boy," Mitch said.

Cheyenne's eyes stung, and she swallowed. When she looked Jesse's way, she caught him watching her.

"You'd be hard put," he said, ostensibly addressing Mitch, "to find a better friend than a horse."

Bronwyn rushed in next, her pretty face alight with excitement.

"You were *great!*" the girl told Mitch.

He blushed. "Thanks," he said, sounding shy.

"The band's playing again," Bronwyn enthused, taking Mitch's hand. "Let's go dance some more!"

Dance? Cheyenne thought, befuddled.

The pair of them disappeared.

"I think that's a great idea," Jesse said.

"What?" Cheyenne asked, distracted.

"Dancing," Jesse answered.

She barely stopped herself from moving back into his arms. Best to keep some perspective here, she thought.

Jesse stepped forward, took her hand.

So much for perspective.

Then, with only the horses to see, he pulled her close, bent his head and kissed her.

Cheyenne had kept her passions under wraps for a long time—she'd had to because she needed almost all her wit and energy to do her job, and what was left over went to her mother and brother.

Now, with Jesse's mouth touching hers, gently, but hungrily, too, her soul stirred. A pleasant buzz of electricity zipped through her, a spreading warmth. She slipped her arms around Jesse's neck and kissed him right back.

When they broke apart, Cheyenne was breathless, and a little bedazzled. A simple kiss wasn't supposed to feel like that, was it?

Was there a rule book somewhere, a part of her mind chided, with a code of kissing?

Jesse smiled at her expression, squeezed her hand.

"We'd better get out there and dance," he told her. "Indian Rock is a typical small town. We stay in here too long, they'll be wondering what we're doing."

Cheyenne laughed, gave away too much by touching the tips of her fingers to her mouth, where Jesse's kiss still tingled against her skin.

His eyes lingered there, for a moment, and she thought he might kiss her again. The mere possibility was cause for a curious tangle of anticipation and sweet terror.

"We can't have that," she said, and then a blush pulsed in her cheeks. "People wondering, I mean. Not—"

"Let's go," he said, "before they use up all the music."

For the rest of that night, it was as though a golden space had opened between Jesse and Cheyenne, and then surrounded them, a magical, non-place where they could step out of their very separate worlds, however briefly, and meet in the middle.

Cheyenne knew it wouldn't last, and Jesse probably did, too.

As it got later, sleeping children were carried inside the house, probably to lie among piles of coats, dreaming dreams charged by adrenaline and sugar. The adults spoke in softer voices, the band toned it down, and all the dances were slow ones.

At midnight, Travis stopped the music and pulled Sierra up onto the porch with him.

The guests all stopped to listen and watch.

Cheyenne felt that peculiar tightening in her throat again, the one she'd left behind years before, and had found again when she'd returned to Indian Rock.

Travis drew Sierra against his side, and she nestled there, smiling, embarrassed and happy. He kissed the top of her head. "I guess you all know we're in love," he said to the onlookers, "and we're getting married in three weeks—you have your invitations, and if you don't, show up anyway."

A patter of laughter drifted through the crowd, and some light applause.

"Some of you have noticed that Sierra isn't wearing an engagement ring," Travis went on. "That's because not just any ring would do."

A drumroll sounded.

More laughter.

Sierra looked up at Travis, her eyes shining.

Rance McKettrick stepped up, handed something to Travis.

Travis turned to Sierra. "I love you," he said.

Sierra put her hand to her throat. Her reply was inaudible, but Cheyenne and everyone else at the party knew she'd responded in kind.

A diamond glinted in the light of the porch, like a captured star.

Travis took Sierra's hand, slid a ring onto the appropriate finger.

Sierra looked down at the ring, then flung both arms around Travis's neck.

The party guests cheered.

The band struck up a celebratory little ditty.

And Cheyenne's eyes smarted.

After Travis and Sierra had exchanged an exuberant kiss, it was Sierra's turn to address the crowd. "Mom and Meg were sorry they couldn't be here tonight, but they'll be at the wedding, and I hope each and every one of you will be, too."

More applause followed, and Sierra and Travis danced, alone, to the poignant strains of an old Patsy Cline song.

After that, the party wound down.

Jesse went to get the truck, while Cheyenne searched for Ayanna and Mitch. When she'd found them, she sought out Sierra.

"Thank you," she told the hostess. "It was a wonderful party."

Sierra smiled wearily. "Yes," she said. "It was. I meant to ask you about the ladies' poker tournament—"

"I don't really play—" Cheyenne began.

Sierra cut her off, taking both Cheyenne's hands in her own. "It's just for fun," she said. "Nobody expects you to be any good."

Nervous as she was, Cheyenne laughed. She'd watched a million hands of poker in her time, waiting for her father, and had even played, when they'd needed someone to round out a game. "I see," she said.

"We're playing for a seat at the big tournament in Las Vegas," Sierra went on. "We have a pact—if one of us wins, the pot goes to the clinic, for their building fund. They need to add an in-patient wing, and they've almost got enough money to break ground."

Cheyenne had no desire to play poker, but she'd be staying in Indian Rock for a while, whether working for Nigel or for McKettrickCo. She wanted to make friends in the community, and expanding the clinic was certainly a good cause.

Of course, Sierra and her friends didn't have a prayer of getting all the way to Vegas—they'd be coming up against serious players from all over the United States. Players like Jesse.

"I'm not sure I'd be an asset," Cheyenne said.

"Please join us," Sierra coaxed, smiling and still holding on to Cheyenne's hands. "We're having a practice session tomorrow afternoon, in the poker room behind Lucky's. Lunch at eleven-thirty, then a card game. Say you'll come."

Cheyenne relented. It wasn't as if any of them would get past the first few rounds of the local tournaments. And while Lucky's held a lot of sad memories for her, she wasn't that little girl waiting hopelessly for her daddy anymore. She was a grown woman.

"Only if you promise to tell me more about the ghosts."

"It's a deal," Sierra said, pleased.

By then, Jesse had returned, and Mitch and Ayanna were both inside the truck. Cheyenne watched a little longer than she'd intended as Jesse deftly folded Mitch's chair and lifted it into the back of his pickup. When she turned back to say goodbye to Sierra, she saw a knowing look in the other woman's eyes.

"See you tomorrow," Sierra said.

Cheyenne nodded.

Jesse stood with the truck door open on the passenger side. Cheyenne thanked Sierra again and went to him.

BACK AT THE BRIDGES PLACE, Jesse helped Mitch out of the truck and back into his chair, and he and Ayanna chorused their thanks and hightailed it into the house.

Jesse and Cheyenne stood alone, at the base of the porch steps, in the light of a three-quarter moon, with crickets chirping in the brush and the smell of newly turned dirt ripe in the warm air.

"I had a good time," Cheyenne said.

"Me, too," Jesse answered. He hesitated, then laid his hands on Cheyenne's shoulders. "I'm about to kiss you again," he told her, wondering if she'd allow it or just turn and walk away.

She sighed, whether from impatience or anticipation

he didn't know, closed her eyes and tilted her head back.

Jesse chuckled and brushed her lips with his.

She put her arms around his neck, the way she had in the barn earlier, when he'd kissed her the first time. Jesse felt a charge go through him, felt the echo of it pass into her.

When she stepped back, she blinked, like somebody waking up from a deep sleep. "I'd better go in," she said, but she didn't move.

"I'll call you tomorrow," he told her.

"I'm busy tomorrow," she said.

Jesse waited. If Keegan had used their discussion about the job at McKettrickCo to move in—

"Poker game," she explained. He wondered if he'd heard her right, and his confusion must have shown in his face because she laughed. "It seems some of the women of Indian Rock are plotting to win a seat at the big tournament in Vegas. You've got some competition."

Jesse laughed, too, but it was more relief than amusement. Now he wouldn't have to go by Keegan's place and call him out. "Is that right?" he asked.

Cheyenne raised an eyebrow. "I take it you don't feel particularly threatened," she said lightly.

Hell, no, he didn't feel threatened, though he wasn't about to say as much. There were dozens, if not hundreds, of these mini-tournaments springing up all over the country, in local casinos and even online. The pros bought in, for a hefty fee, and, as last year's winner,

170

Jesse was comped by the organizers, expected to defend his title.

"And you're going to play?" he asked as a frisson of excitement shivered down his spine.

"Why not?" she said. "It's just a friendly game." Was she trying to convince him of that, or herself? It felt like something more to Jesse, though the truth of it was he didn't think any of the townswomen had an ice cube's chance in hell of getting beyond the local casino just up the road.

He kissed her again, but briefly this time. He didn't want to push his luck with Cheyenne; she was as skittish as a field-born filly, and there was still the issue of those five hundred acres standing between them. He was a good judge of character, but Cheyenne was a puzzle. She might really like him—or she might be angling to get that land.

"I could make coffee," she said uncertainly.

Jesse wanted to go inside with her—wanted any excuse to stick around for a while. But he sensed that it was time to step back, take a breath. "Another time," he told her.

He waited until she went into the house, then got back in the truck and started for home.

AYANNA WAS IN THE KITCHEN, where she'd set out two cups and put a kettle on the stove to boil. Mitch had apparently gone straight to bed.

"You were eavesdropping on Jesse and me from the living room," Cheyenne accused, smiling.

Ayanna blushed guiltily.

My God, Cheyenne thought. *She's still young. She's still pretty. She had a wonderful time at the party.*

"I was *not* eavesdropping," Ayanna insisted, but her color was still high, and her eyes sparkled with cautious mischief.

Cheyenne pointed to the cups. "I doubt you'd offer Jesse tea," she said. "You knew he wasn't coming inside, and furthermore, you're gearing up for serious girl talk."

Ayanna looked both pleased and embarrassed. "All right, so I might have walked past the screen door at an opportune moment and *accidentally* overheard a tiny part of the conversation—"

Cheyenne crossed the kitchen floor, with its buckling linoleum, and hugged Ayanna. " 'Accidentally'?" she asked, grinning. "Did you have fun tonight?"

"Yes," Ayanna said, "and so did Mitch. So did *you,* from the looks of things. You and Jesse made such a nice-looking couple, dancing like that."

"Don't make too much out of this, Mom," Cheyenne warned gently. "I'm not in the McKettricks' league, and I suspect Jesse's just trying to see how far I'll go to get him to sell me those five hundred acres."

"Did it ever occur to you that he might actually *like* you?" Ayanna asked, huffily. "You're not an adolescent anymore, adoring him from a distance and pinning his picture up on your wall. You're a beautiful, accomplished woman, and he'd be lucky to have you."

"Mom," Cheyenne said.

"Well, it's true," Ayanna insisted.

"You might be a little prejudiced." *I don't want you to get your hopes up,* she added silently. *Happy endings are for storybooks. This is real life.*

"And *you* might be a little jaded." The kettle boiled, and Ayanna snatched it from the burner, and filled Gram's cracked but beloved old cups with hot water. "What's this about you playing in a poker tournament?"

"You only 'overheard' part of the conversation?" Cheyenne teased, carrying the cups to the table. The water was turning a lovely dark pink, and the scent of raspberries rose with the steam.

The two women sat down across the table from each other. Cheyenne flashed on a memory of playing five-card stud there, when she was barely big enough to see over the edge. She and her dad had used matchsticks and pennies in place of chips.

"I thought you hated poker," Ayanna said, blowing on her tea and dodging Cheyenne's gaze.

"Sierra invited me to join her and some of her friends for a friendly game, that's all."

Ayanna shifted uncomfortably on her chair. "Cheyenne, you know I never tell you what to do, but I shouldn't have to remind you that your father—"

Cheyenne sat up a little straighter. "I'm not my father," she said. Then, aware that those years when Cash Bridges had spent his days and nights playing cards had surely been even worse for Ayanna than they had for her, she softened. Reached across the table to squeeze her mother's hand. "I'm not going to turn into a compulsive gambler, Mom," she promised.

Ayanna leaned forward. "I want you to make friends here, of course," she said, quietly earnest. "But a poker tournament?"

Cheyenne sighed. "If a miracle happens, and one of us gets all the way to the big game in Vegas, and *wins* on top of that, the money will go to build a wing onto the clinic in Indian Rock."

Ayanna seemed relieved. "Talk about a long shot," she said.

Cheyenne laughed. "They don't get much longer," she answered.

Unless, of course, added a little voice in her mind, *you happen to be Jesse McKettrick, born under a lucky star.*

"Keegan as much as offered me a job tonight," Cheyenne confided, after a few moments of reflective silence. "At McKettrickCo."

Ayanna's face lit up. How she could stay so optimistic, so hopeful, after all they'd been through as a family, was a mystery to Cheyenne. "Really? Doing what?"

"I'd be setting up a human resources department," Cheyenne answered slowly, wishing she hadn't mentioned the opportunity until she'd had more time to think about it.

"Which means?" Ayanna prompted.

Cheyenne smiled, but her misgivings made her lips wobble slightly. "Keegan wants to start a work-study program. Train some of the local people to join McKettrickCo—especially kids."

"That's wonderful!" Ayanna paused, studying Cheyenne's expression. "Isn't it?"

"Maybe," Cheyenne said. "According to Keegan, some of the family wants the company to go public. That could mean a leadership change, and the whole project might be scrapped."

"Oh," Ayanna whispered, looking downcast. But then she brightened again, with a resilience Cheyenne both admired and envied. "Mitch could apply," she said.

Cheyenne reached across the table to touch the back of her mother's hand. Felt it tremble beneath her fingertips. *She's afraid,* Cheyenne thought. *Because I'm always the naysayer. I'm always the devil's advocate.* "Mom," she said carefully, "it's early. My contract with Nigel still has a while to run, and he probably won't let me out of it."

Something seemed to cave in, inside Ayanna. Her shoulders drooped, and the light in her eyes dimmed a little. "Couldn't you try?" It was a forlorn question.

"I can try," Cheyenne conceded.

"Call him," Ayanna urged, immediately jumping up to fetch Cheyenne's bag from the top of the clothes dryer, where she'd set it down. "Get your cell phone out and call Nigel right this minute!"

"Now? Tonight? It's late—"

Ayanna cut her off. "No excuses," she said. "You won't know what he's going to say until you ask."

Suppressing a sigh, Cheyenne opened her bag, excavated for the phone and punched in Nigel's number.

"Good news, I hope?" he said, picking up on the first ring.

"I've been offered a job at McKettrickCo," Cheyenne said, figuring she might as well just get it out there, on the table.

"Wonderful!" Nigel enthused.

Cheyenne blinked. "What?"

"We can attack them from within," Nigel said. "Find their weak spot and—"

"Wait," Cheyenne said. "I'm not suggesting a spy mission. It would mean resigning from Meerland, Nigel. Giving back the cell phone and the computer and the company car."

"Well, we'd certainly want it to *look* that way," Nigel gushed.

"Nigel," Cheyenne said patiently, "you aren't listening to me—as usual. I wouldn't be working for you anymore. In any capacity."

A stunned silence followed.

"Nigel?"

"In that case," Nigel mused. "I would have to enforce your contract."

Cheyenne sagged against the back of her chair, rolled her eyes for her mother's benefit. Ayanna, ready to skip down the Yellow Brick Road a moment before, looked deflated again.

"Unless, of course," Nigel went on, once he'd given the threat time to sink in, "you were actually still in my employ. Then it would be a case of corporate intrigue."

"It would be *spying*," Cheyenne insisted. "And, besides, the land you want to develop belongs to Jesse, not McKettrickCo."

"Maybe on paper," Nigel said, "but I know how these families work. It's all about the money, and the common good. If you were on the inside, you could learn things that would be invaluable to me." He paused, and the distance between them seemed to shiver with some disturbing energy. "I know this all seems pretty bottom-of-the-bag to you, Cheyenne, but believe me, all is not lost."

Suspicion flashed through Cheyenne. There it was again. That intimation that he knew something, that he'd found some way into the McKettrick stronghold. He'd said a similar thing earlier, after dropping off the company car.

"What—?" she began.

But he headed her off again. "You wouldn't be thinking of going over to their side, would you?"

"Their side?"

"You know what I mean. Jesse is attractive. He's rich. It's not hard to connect the dots. You hook him, move onto the ranch, and live in style from then on. Is that your plan, Cheyenne? Well, just remember that we have a binding contract, and I *will* seek redress if you don't honor it."

"I'm not trying to 'hook' anybody—that's your style, not mine—and contract or no contract, you can't force me to spy!"

Ayanna went pale.

"I'm not asking you to spy," Nigel lied blithely. "I just want you to keep your ear to the ground, that's all. I'll just check my PDA, here—yes—you're committed to Meerland until the first of September. It's what— June 15? That gives you two and a half months. Not such a bad deal, really. You'll have to give back the car, but you'll still be collecting double paychecks." His voice changed to a smarmy purr. "Tell me, Cheyenne, what's so terrible about that?"

"It's sneaky and dishonest, that's what!" She might just as well have said nothing at all.

"You're not really accomplishing much as things stand, are you?" Nigel pressed. "It's time for definitive action. If you don't do this, Cheyenne, I'll not only sue you for breach of contract, I'll be forced to resort to more drastic measures."

"*What* drastic measures?" Cheyenne demanded.

"You'll know soon enough," Nigel said cheerfully.

"*Damn* it, Nigel—"

"When I hired you, I didn't want to demand a contract. But my grandmother pointed out the fallacy of that. There were big accounts at stake. You could have pulled them out from under me at any time, without that written agreement, gone out on your own, and left me high and dry. Suffice it to say, Cheyenne, I'm glad I made you sign on the dotted line."

Cheyenne closed her eyes. The contract in question was in a storage unit in San Diego, along with just about everything else she owned, locked away in a file cabinet, but she didn't need to read it to know Nigel had her. The thing was ironclad; if she undermined Nigel's business in any way, he could take her to court.

No judge would back him up, at least not when it came to corporate espionage, but in the meantime, she'd not only go broke paying lawyers, she'd be in debt for the rest of her life.

"I hate you, Nigel," she said.

"Right now, I'm not too crazy about you, either," Nigel replied. "Crunch time, sweetheart. Show me what you're made of."

With that, he hung up in her ear.

CHAPTER TEN

JESSE CHECKED ON THE HORSES, found them all settled in for the night, and headed for the house. Inside, he flipped on the kitchen lights, rummaged through the fridge for a beer, and listened to the silence. The place seemed to pulse around him.

"Shit," he said, just to hear a voice. Tough luck that it was his own.

His glance slid automatically to the phone on the wall next to the coffeepot, where it had been ever since he'd been too short to reach it. He'd told Cheyenne he'd call her the next day, but damned if he didn't want to do it now.

Maybe she was asleep.

In bed.

In a thin nightgown, or even naked.

Don't go there, he thought.

And what the hell would he say if he *did* call her?

Sorry to bother you?

Hope I didn't wake you up?

Are you naked?

Whatever he said, she'd know he couldn't get her out of his head. Couldn't even wait until morning, like a normal human being.

Talk about tipping his hand.

Nope, he had to play this one close to his chest.

He snatched up the phone receiver, thumbed through the missed-calls list. Maybe she'd called him after he'd dropped her off at home.

The numbers were familiar. His mother. One of his poker buddies trying to get up a game.

Brandi.

He sighed. Much as he'd yearned for some conversation, he didn't want to talk to any of those people. His folks were getting old, though—in their midsixties—and one of them might have broken a hip or something.

He listened to his mother's message.

She wanted to know how he was. He hadn't called in a while. She and his dad were fine. What did he think about taking the company public?

All quiet on that front. He hit the delete key and made a note to call his parents back in the morning.

He'd been right about the second call. Utah Slim Jackson was passing through town with some friends and looking for a game. If Jesse wanted in, he'd better get himself down to Lucky's, pronto.

Jesse grinned and the mechanical operator said, "To return this call, please dial eighty-eight." He dialed.

"Big money changing hands in this here smoky room," Utah Slim said. Away from the poker tables, Utah was an insurance salesman named Milton. "Save you a seat?"

"Save me a seat," Jesse confirmed.

There was still Brandi's message to get through.

She'd want to rhapsodize about her poor but honest lover, the future doctor. She probably needed money, and he could send that tomorrow, via the Internet. With only a twinge of guilt, Jesse hung up without hearing what she had to say.

He climbed the stairs to his room, exchanged his party duds for old jeans, a T-shirt and a baseball cap. Swapped out the fancy boots for shit-kickers, and he was good to go.

He stopped off at the barn, filled all the feeders for morning and made sure the automatic waterers were working. The horses were all down for the night, and a few of them nickered at him, but most paid him no mind at all.

He got back into the truck, started the engine and headed for town.

THE SLEEPLESS NIGHT WOULD HAVE made more sense, Cheyenne thought, studying her haggard face in the bathroom mirror, if she'd been worrying about Nigel suing her up one side and down the other, but the embarrassing truth was that she hadn't. She'd been reliving Jesse's red-hot kisses, over and over, and waiting for her fever to break.

It hadn't.

At dawn, she'd finally given up, crawled out of bed and dragged herself to the shower. After that, she'd put on her bathrobe and made breakfast for Ayanna, who wanted to get to work early, and for Mitch. Her brother went on and on about last night's party, and wondered aloud if he ought to call Bronwyn and see what she was "up to."

Cheyenne was too distracted to comment.

"Don't you dare call that girl before nine o'clock," Ayanna told her son, stopping to plant a kiss on the top of his head as she whizzed by his wheelchair. She paused in the kitchen doorway, gave Cheyenne a worried glance and rushed out.

"You'd better get dressed before Jesse stops by to build those rails or something," Mitch told her sagely, after giving the bathrobe a disapproving once-over.

"Thanks for nothing," Cheyenne retorted. She had an appointment with Keegan at nine-thirty, and that meant full regalia—power suit, panty hose, makeup and high heels. She had to force herself to stay in the kitchen, finish clearing the table and wash the dishes. Jesse *did* have a way of dropping in unannounced, and even though they definitely weren't dating, the thought of him seeing her in that ratty old robe gave her the horrors.

The dress-for-success getup would be worse, though. She was dashing for her room when the phone rang. Nigel?

She hesitated, then snatched up the receiver. "Hello?"

"Cheyenne? This is Sierra. I was just calling to remind you about poker practice. Lucky's. Lunch at eleven-thirty, then a few practice games."

"Right," Cheyenne said. She'd have to stop somewhere between McKettrickCo and Lucky's, and change into jeans and a top. No way she'd show up looking like a contestant on *The Apprentice.* "It was a great party, Sierra. Thanks again for inviting us."

"Our pleasure," Sierra told her warmly. "See you at Lucky's."

"See you," Cheyenne echoed.

At nine twenty-five she pulled into the lot at McKettrickCo. She sat there, in Nigel's company car, her palms damp on the wheel, her stomach churning.

Maybe she'd just tell Keegan straight out that she was still legally bound to Nigel, and he wanted her to spy for him.

Excellent idea.

Keegan would send her packing.

Jesse wasn't about to sell the land.

Nigel's deal was toast, whatever trick he *thought* he had up his sleeve, and that meant his company would implode like an outdated Vegas casino standing on prime real estate. She not only wouldn't have the bonus, she wouldn't have a job, either.

Hello, Square One.

She sighed. Okay, so she was stuck. She'd wait Nigel out, tell him absolutely nothing about the inner workings of the McKettrick family, in the unlikely event that she stumbled across any such information in the first place, and send his paychecks back when her contract was up. In the meantime, she'd accept the job if Keegan offered it, set up the work-study program and earn every penny she was paid. If the corporation went public, she might survive the transition—or be given her walking papers by a new board of directors.

It was a crapshoot. Six of one, half a dozen of the other, as her dad used to say. Nothing to do but play the cards she'd been dealt and bluff like crazy.

Cheyenne drew a deep breath, let it out slowly, plastered an I'm-ready-to-conquer-the-world smile on her face, and headed for the door.

Her reflection in the polished glass gave her pause— she'd pinned her hair into a tight bun at the back of her head before leaving the house, as usual. She'd always thought the style made her look businesslike and efficient, but today the effect seemed severe instead.

Despite her careful makeup, there were shadows under her eyes, and her smile looked desperately perky.

She swallowed, lowered her head to concentrate on getting her face under control, and nearly collided with a tall, dark-haired man as she opened the door.

"Whoa," he said and grabbed her by the upper arms before she could fall over backward. "Sorry—I was looking over my shoulder and I didn't see you there—"

Cheyenne straightened her short black-and-white tailored jacket. The suit was a knockoff, bought at a trunk sale, but it looked good and she'd skipped meals for three weeks to buy it. "Rance?" she asked, squinting up into a smiling, square-jawed face.

He nodded, pushed the door open and squired her inside. "Hello, Cheyenne," he said. Then he flashed her one of those patented McKettrick grins. "Keegan told me you weren't coming in until around two this afternoon. Sneaky sidewinder."

Cheyenne blushed. "Maybe I misunderstood," she said. "I thought Keegan and I were supposed to meet at nine-thirty."

"You were," Rance said. "He was just trying to get rid of me. How are you, Cheyenne? Caught a glimpse of you at the party last night, but I didn't get a chance to say hello."

"I'm fine," she replied, suddenly shy.

He chuckled. "Oh, you surely are that, all right," he said.

"I thought you were going out for doughnuts," Keegan remarked from a nearby doorway, obviously addressing his cousin.

"I'll just bet you did," Rance replied.

"We always send out," put in the receptionist, standing behind her counter.

"You do that, Myrna," Rance said, keeping one massive hand cupped under Cheyenne's elbow as he steered her toward Keegan and, presumably, the inner office where they would discuss her employment.

Myrna winked at Cheyenne. "Double-glazed?" she asked. "Chocolate-frosted? Bavarian cream?"

"I beg your pardon?"

The older woman laughed. "Doughnuts. What kind would you like?"

"Oh," Cheyenne said, blushing again. What was it about Indian Rock that made her face heat up all the time? "Nothing for me, thanks."

"No wonder you're skinny," Myrna said with a sigh, picking up the phone.

"Coffee, too," Rance added.

"Get your own coffee," Myrna told him. "Do I look like a maid?"

Grinning a little, Keegan turned and led the way to a conference room at the end of the hall. Seated at a large table, Cheyenne looked at Keegan and then at Rance and, again, considered telling them the truth.

The meeting lasted forty-five minutes.

Myrna delivered the doughnuts and, with a concessionary air, three cups of coffee.

Keegan outlined his ideas for the work-study program and asked Cheyenne some penetrating questions. He seemed impressed with her responses, and so did Rance, and she felt guiltier with every passing minute.

"The job is yours if you want it," Keegan told her.

Rance nodded agreement. "When can you start?"

Don't do this, Cheyenne's conscience protested.

"Tomorrow?" she said.

Keegan smiled. "Great," he said. "You'll need a

company car, of course. We'll have one sent down from Flag today."

Cheyenne had been expecting to share the patchwork van with her mother, so the offer of a car came as a happy surprise. Conversely, it also made her feel worse. "Thank you," she said.

Keegan and Rance rose from their chairs.

She shook hands with both of them.

"I'll show you your work space on the way out," Rance said.

Keegan glared at him.

Rance took her elbow again, grinning.

Even with the high salary and the car, Cheyenne had been expecting a cubicle at best. Instead, she had a corner office with a desk almost as big as her front yard. She resisted an urge to sit down in the pricy leather chair and take a couple of spins.

"It's great," she said.

Rance escorted her all the way to her car.

"I'd ask you to lunch," he told her, with charming bluntness, "if I hadn't seen you dancing with Jesse last night. Welcome aboard, Cheyenne."

She nodded, shy again. "Thanks."

She zoomed to the supermarket, where Ayanna worked, grabbed her change of clothes out of the backseat and rushed inside, headed for the restroom.

She was in a stall, shinnying out of her panty hose, when the outside door opened and she heard her mother's voice.

"Cheyenne, are you sick?"

"No," Cheyenne answered. "I'm taking off my panty hose."

Ayanna laughed, but she sounded a little nervous. "How did the meeting go? Did you tell Keegan that Nigel asked you to spy on them?"

Cheyenne squatted, checking the other stalls for feet. All clear, unless somebody was standing on a toilet seat. "Gee, Mom," she said through the door, stepping out of the panty hose and pulling on her jeans. "Why don't you just go to Customer Service and ask if you can use the microphone? That way, you could announce it to half of Indian Rock."

"Sorry," Ayanna said, in an after-the-fact whisper. "Did you tell them, Cheyenne?"

"No," Cheyenne told her.

Ayanna gasped. Cheyenne didn't need X-ray vision to know her mother had slapped one hand over her mouth in shame and horror.

She zipped and buttoned her jeans, pulled a T-shirt on over her head, pushed open the stall door and came out, carrying her neatly folded suit over one arm. Kicking off her heels, she tugged on the shoes she'd dropped on the floor on the way in.

Ayanna looked swoony. "You're not actually going to—?"

"Spy?" Cheyenne snapped, pulling the pins out of her hair and letting it fall around her shoulders. "Of course not, Mother."

"You only call me *Mother* when you're irritated."

"I'm not irritated." She did the feet test again, just to

be sure. "I'm also not a spy!"

"Cheyenne," Ayanna reasoned, still whispering, "you are on *very* dangerous ground. When the McKettricks find out that you're still working for Nigel Meerland—"

Cheyenne juggled her suit and heels to finger-fluff her hair. "I've got this under control, *Mom,*" she said. "You're going to have to trust me. And—please—don't put this out over the PA system, okay? Don't breathe a word to anyone—not even Mitch."

Ayanna's eyes were huge with worry. "This is a mistake," she said.

"This is *damage control,*" Cheyenne replied.

The door opened and a middle-aged shopper entered, looked Ayanna up and down, and said, "No wonder you can't get any service around here. The employees hide out in the restroom."

Ayanna rolled her eyes.

Cheyenne laughed, kissed her on the cheek as she passed. "Remember, Mom," she said. "Mum's the word."

Five minutes later, she pulled into the lot at Lucky's. Her hand shook noticeably as she rummaged for her cell phone and speed-dialed Nigel.

"Send someone for the car," she said. "I took the job."

"Excellent," Nigel answered. "Just for show, I'll take back the laptop, too. You can keep the phone."

"Nigel—"

"Good work, Pocahontas," he said and hung up

before she could tell him what he could do with the car, the laptop *and* the cell phone.

A rap on the car window startled her out of her dark musings, and she jumped, dropping the phone in the process.

Sierra McKettrick smiled through the glass.

Cheyenne rolled down the window. "Oh, hi," she said, feeling as though a transcript of her conversation with Nigel had been written on her face.

"I didn't mean to scare you," Sierra said. She scanned the front parking lot. "Looks like the others are here. Let's go inside and grab some lunch. Fortify ourselves for the poker game."

The others were Janice White, a petite blonde who lived on a ranch neighboring the Triple M, and Elaine Perkins, co-owner of Perkins Real Estate.

After the introductions had been made, everyone settled in a booth to examine menus.

"That game's been going on since midnight," the weary waitress announced, cocking a thumb toward the back room. "It meant a double shift for me, and I'm dead on my feet, but, hey, the tips are good."

"What game?" Sierra asked idly, focused on the menu.

"Five-card stud," the waitress answered. "And I'm tellin' you, it's cutthroat, too."

"Great," Janice said. "We get to share the room with a bunch of sweaty poker fiends. I'll take the fish and chips. Extra tartar sauce."

"Chef's salad," Elaine chimed in. "Thousand Island on the side."

"Gotya," said the waitress. Her tired eyes came to rest on Cheyenne. "What'll it be, honey? I gotta put this order in and sit down before I *fall* down. Trust me, these dogs are barkin'."

"That's way more information than we need, Delores," Janice remarked.

"Club sandwich on wheat," Cheyenne said. "Easy on the mayo."

Delores scribbled dutifully and turned to Sierra, who immediately asked, "Can we play poker out here, in the restaurant?"

"Against state law," Delores said, tapping her order pad with the tip of her pencil. "What's your poison?"

Sierra smiled. "I've got a wedding dress to fit into. Make mine tomato soup, and hold the crackers."

Delores gave a wistful sigh, and her eyes looked dreamy. Maybe, Cheyenne reflected, it was the mention of a wedding dress, accompanied by a fantasy of some cowboy-prince coming into Lucky's for a burger and fries, falling madly in love and taking her away from it all.

"Travis Reid," Delores said. "He's a looker."

"He sure is," Sierra agreed.

Delores limped away to hand in the orders.

"I'll *bet* she's been taking her shoes off in the back room and rubbing her feet on breaks," Janice whispered, making a face. "I just hope she washed her hands."

"Again," Elaine said dryly, "more information than I really find necessary."

"I don't think I'm hungry anymore," Cheyenne said.

"Delores is the worst housekeeper in Indian Rock," Janice confided.

Elaine elbowed her. "Shut up, or I'm going home, and taking my poker expertise with me."

"What expertise would that be, pray tell?" Janice asked archly.

"I'll have you know," Elaine said, "that I play Texas Hold 'Em on my computer at least twice a week."

"Oh, well, then," Janice replied, "the world championship will be a cinch." She gazed at Sierra. "Tell me again why we're doing this? We'd have a better chance of winning a triathlon."

"To get out of our comfort zones," Sierra answered. "Expand our horizons. Test our limits."

"You McKettricks," Janice sighed. "You just can't stand to be ordinary. We could start a bowling league or something, you know. Trust me, wearing rented shoes is going to take *this* gal way beyond her comfort zone!"

Sierra laughed, looked down at the doorknob diamond shining on her left-hand ring finger.

Cheyenne felt a little pang of envy.

Elaine turned to Janice, who was sitting beside her, opposite Cheyenne and Sierra. "You can't ask the poor woman to *bowl* with that boulder weighing down her hand," she teased. "It probably weighs more than the ball."

Delores shuffled over with the food. Glanced poignantly at the big clock behind the counter, and went away.

Sierra watched her go. "Poor thing," she said. "Waitressing is hard work. Believe me, I know."

Cheyenne glanced at her, surprised. "You do?" She didn't have to voice the rest of the thought—it hung in the air as if it had been spoken aloud.

But you're a McKettrick.

"I'm sorry," Cheyenne said, miserably embarrassed. She just wasn't good at this girlfriend thing; she hadn't had enough practice. Her feet didn't hurt, and she wasn't a half-bad housekeeper, but other than those things, she probably had more in common with Delores than with Elaine, Janice and Sierra.

"It's okay," Sierra replied, smiling. "I was the family's lost sheep," she explained. "My mother and sister and I reconnected last winter. I'm still getting used to being a McKettrick."

"But she's not changing her name when she gets married," Janice said. "The McKettrick women don't, you know. They don't even hyphenate. And if they have girl children, *they're* McKettricks, too."

"How does Travis feel about that?" Elaine asked.

Cheyenne realized she was hungry and began wolfing down her sandwich. The process served a dual purpose—filling her stomach *and* making it impossible to stick her foot in her mouth.

"He's fine with it," Sierra said, "as long as the boys are all Reids."

"I guess that's fair," Janice allowed.

They finished their meals, pooled their money to pay the tab and left Delores a generous tip.

Cheyenne was the last to step into the poker room, and when she did, she froze on the threshold.

There was Jesse, in the thick of the all-night game Delores had mentioned, unshaven, with a baseball cap pulled down low over his forehead and enough chips in front of him to fill a five-gallon bucket.

As if sensing her presence, he looked up. One corner of his mouth tilted slightly upward. His gaze lingered.

Something caught fire inside Cheyenne, and she felt like a complete fool for being so stunned. Indian Rock was Jesse's hometown, after all, and Lucky's was one of his regular haunts. Why was she so taken aback to find him here?

Delores's words echoed in her head. *That game's been going on since midnight.*

Sierra, already halfway across the room to the table where Elaine and Janice were pulling back chairs, came back, whispered in Cheyenne's ear, "He doesn't bite," she teased.

Everything about Jesse said he *did* bite—in the kinds of places that made a woman catch her breath and arch her back.

Heat surged through Cheyenne's body. She gathered her composure, by force of will, smiled a wooden smile and ordered herself to act normally.

It wasn't seeing Jesse that had thrown her, she realized, as she took her chair at the poker table with Sierra and the others. At least, not initially. It was seeing Jesse *here,* where she used to come looking for her dad, with his clothes rumpled and his beard growing in. It was knowing he'd been there since midnight.

"Are you all right?" Sierra asked her quietly.

"I'm fine," Cheyenne said. She sat with her back to Jesse, but she could feel it when his gaze rested on her back, like a caress, and on the nape of her neck, too. Like a kiss.

It was bad enough, being reminded that neither she nor her mother had ever meant as much to Cash Bridges as this seedy poker room. Her visceral responses to Jesse's presence only made things that much more complicated.

"You girls need a dealer?" It was Nurleen Gentry. She'd aged some, of course, since Cheyenne's last visit when she was twelve, but she still smelled of stale cigarette smoke, cheap perfume and musty, half-forgotten dreams.

"Might as well make it as real as we can," Elaine said.

Nurleen pulled back a chair, sat down next to Cheyenne and nudged her with a plump arm while reaching with the other hand for the new deck of cards in the middle of the table. "How you doin', kid?" she asked. "It's been a long time."

Cheyenne's throat ached. She swallowed, summoned up a smile. Met Nurleen's knowing eyes. "I'm doing okay," she answered. "How about you?"

"It's a living," Nurleen said, opening the package of cards, setting aside the jokers and beginning to shuffle. "Your daddy was a good man. We miss him around here."

Sierra, Elaine and Janice all pretended not to be listening, fiddling with purses, shutting off cell phones, fluffing their hair.

Busy, busy, busy.

And not missing a word or the slightest nuance.

Suddenly, Cheyenne was twelve again. She wondered if she could speak without bursting into tears.

"Everybody ante up," Elaine said brightly.

"You sound as though you know what you're talking about," Janice marveled.

"I told you, I play Hold 'Em on my computer all the time."

"Then you ought to know," Janice told her, "that there's no ante in this game. There are blinds."

Blinds, Cheyenne recalled, were the gradually increasing amounts players had to contribute, in turn, after every new hand was dealt. As the game progressed, the blinds got progressively steeper. It gave her a curious kind of comfort having something to think about besides Jesse, and what her dad's penchant for poker had done to the family.

Nurleen produced a tray of multicolored chips from beneath the table and began dividing them.

"We'll worry about blinds later," Sierra said, biting her lower lip. "Like, when we figure out what they are."

Masculine laughter rumbled, low, around the other table.

Cheyenne squirmed on her chair.

"I'll teach you all you need to know," Nurleen said. She turned to look toward the other table. "You guys keep it down over there. We're trying to play some serious poker here."

More laughter.

Nurleen faced the novices again. Sighed. Dealt two cards, facedown, to each player.

Sierra, Elaine and Janice all peeked at their cards.

Cheyenne didn't touch hers.

Elaine raised an eyebrow.

"I'll wait for the flop," Cheyenne explained.

Nurleen gave a barely perceptible smile, set one card aside and laid three more faceup in the middle of the table.

King of clubs. Ace of diamonds. Ace of spades.

"Bets?" Nurleen asked when nobody moved or spoke.

Cheyenne separated three red chips from a stack and pushed them forward.

"You're betting without even looking at your cards?" Janice asked dubiously.

"She wants to see the turn," Nurleen said.

"Fourth card," Elaine clarified.

"I'm not betting, then," Janice said.

"That's called folding," said Sierra. She glanced in Cheyenne's direction, then tossed in three chips of her own.

Elaine took another look at her cards. "Fold."

That left Sierra and Cheyenne still in play. Cheyenne met Sierra's bet and raised.

Sierra shook her head, mystified. Then she matched and raised.

The fourth card came down. Ace of clubs.

Cheyenne felt a slight movement behind her and knew, without looking, that Jesse had left the other table to watch the women's game. Pretending he wasn't there, she turned back the corners of her cards.

Sierra stayed in the game.

So did Cheyenne.

The fifth card, the river, was the king of diamonds.

More bets were made.

Jesse exuded heat.

Sierra, flushed with excitement, went all in, pushing all her chips to the center of the table.

Cheyenne called.

"Three of a kind!" Sierra crowed, laying down the king of spades, to go with the pair of kings on the table and a six of hearts.

Jesse whispered a mild expletive.

Cheyenne turned over an ace of hearts and the fourth king. "Full house," she said.

"Does that beat what I have?" Sierra asked.

Jesse groaned, dragged up a chair between Sierra and Cheyenne.

"Ladies," he said, "you need help."

CHAPTER ELEVEN

LADIES, YOU NEED HELP. Having spoken in haste, Jesse now realized he would be repenting at leisure.

Three pairs of female eyes narrowed on him, glittering with indignation.

Definitely not the smartest thing you've ever said, McKettrick.

On top of keeping his mouth shut, he should have kept his distance, too.

Cheyenne's hair was down, tumbling to the middle of her back in fresh-scented splendor. She wore a tight little pink T-shirt and jeans that clung snugly to her sleek figure, and just being in close proximity made Jesse want her with a kind of primitive ferocity he'd never experienced before.

He rubbed his beard-stubbled chin with one hand. What he ought to have done was go home at a decent hour, sleep like a dead man, then get up and lather his face, scrape off a layer of ugly with a razor. *After* a long, hot shower, with the sprayer set on Sandblast.

Then, remembering that Sierra and her friends had a poker game planned for today, right here at Lucky's, he could have shown up as if by accident. Ambled in and acted surprised.

Too late for all that now.

The truth was, he'd forgotten about Sierra's game, not to mention her lame-ass plan—for one of the group to get all the way to the final table in Vegas, *and* carry off the big pot—until the moment she'd walked through the doorway with Elaine and Janice, with Cheyenne bringing up the rear. She'd paused on the threshold when her gaze had met and locked with his, with an almost audible impact.

Now, he was sinking fast. It was Sierra who threw him a lifeline.

"Well, Jesse," she drawled, with a little smile, "fancy meeting *you* here."

Cheyenne wasn't looking at him, but she shifted in her chair, as though to move it an inch or two away. But she *didn't* move, and Jesse was more relieved than he liked to admit.

"Of all people," Elaine added wryly. Her eyes moved from him to Cheyenne and back again, adding up the numbers. He'd gone to school with both Elaine and Janice; knew them better than his own sisters, since they were closer to his own age. Unfortunately, they knew him just as well. The mild indignation they'd greeted him with at first had given way to speculative amusement.

"Just imagine," Janice said, heaping it on. "Jesse McKettrick in an all-night poker game. Will wonders never cease?"

At last, Cheyenne spared him a glance.

We don't need your help, it said.

Jesse supposed that was preferable to *Get lost, you loser.* Nothing to do but brazen it out. Make the best of an awkward situation.

"On second thought," he said with an ease he didn't feel, "Cheyenne can probably show you everything you need to know."

She frowned.

"About poker," he clarified.

Still room for the other boot, he thought. *Just open your mouth a little wider, hotshot. You can jam it right in there, alongside the first one.*

"Looks as if you've been winning," Sierra remarked, glancing toward the pile of chips he'd left on the other table. Without looking that way himself, he knew Utah Slim and the others were glaring at him. He was holding up the game; they wanted a chance to win their money back.

"*I* always *win,*" he might have answered, if he hadn't caught himself in time. Still one boot on the floor, anyway. The other one was halfway down his throat and fixing to choke him to death.

Jesse pushed back his chair, stood. "I guess I'd better finish what I started," he said.

"Guess so," Sierra agreed.

He looked down at Cheyenne, risked laying one hand on her shoulder for a moment, then turned and walked away.

Utah Slim's hound-dog eyes were smoke-reddened and bleary. "For a minute there, McKettrick," he said, low and gruff, "I thought you were about to duck out on us. Play another game. And I'm not talking about poker."

Jesse's temper surged, but he kept it under wraps.

Mostly. "You a sore loser, Utah?" he asked easily. He'd almost said *Milton* instead of *Utah,* but the old man probably would have overturned the table in a rage if he had. Then there'd have been a fight, and he didn't want Cheyenne and Sierra and the others in the middle of a knock-down, drag-out brawl.

Utah checked his watch—a thin Rolex at odds with his baggy trousers, stained polo shirt and ancient Diamondbacks jacket—and winced visibly. "I gotta get out of here, soon. Who's dealing?" He threw an irritated glance in Nurleen's direction. She was still busy at the estrogen table, but she caught the look and threw it right back. Overhand.

"I'll do it," sighed Fred Gibbons, the only other local in the game besides Jesse himself. Five men remained, counting Jesse and Utah. The other two were Utah's buddies; Jesse was acquainted with them, since they played on the same circuit, but he didn't figure them for insurance salesmen like Milton "Utah Slim" Jackson. They were hard-bitten, experienced players with cold, watchful eyes. The kind of men who never offered their names.

Jesse stacked his chips, waiting out the deal. He didn't look at his cards until the flop was down and, as usual, the poker gods were with him.

"Fold," he said, when it was his turn to bet.

"You gonna stonewall us?" Utah asked.

"I wanna see them cards," added one of his friends.

"I don't have to show them," Jesse said, "and you know it."

An uncomfortable silence settled over the table, heavy and charged.

Jesse waited.

"He's right, Utah," Fred, the dealer, put in, but only after a swallow that made his Adam's apple travel up and down his neck a couple of times, like an elevator with a button stuck.

Utah stared at Jesse.

Jesse stared back.

Happy chatter wreathed the women's table.

"Next time," Utah said with resignation, tossing in his cards.

Reluctantly, his friends did the same. They didn't look resigned, though; they looked pissed off.

Nurleen, who had a finely honed sense of when things might go south in a hurry, left the ladies to trundle over.

"You want to cash in those chips, Jesse, or shall I put them in the safe?" she asked.

"Put them in the safe," Jesse answered, as he always did.

Utah and the buddies pushed back their chairs, got up. Jesse figured the bulge under the one man's denim jacket for a piece, but guns weren't uncommon in Arizona, especially in card rooms like Lucky's. Half the people in the state were packing.

If Cheyenne and Sierra and the other women hadn't been around, he wouldn't have been worried. As it was, he calculated how long his reach would have to be to get hold of the snub-nosed .45 Nurleen kept in an old holster nailed sideways to the underside of the tabletop.

Nurleen shunted Fred aside and sat down in her regular chair. No doubt, she was picking up the same vibes as Jesse. "Any trouble starts here," she said, addressing Utah and his posse, "and I'll be the one to finish it."

"We'll go," Utah said quickly, all bluster. He probably had insurance up the yingy, and didn't want his wife collecting. "Don't want to wear out our welcome."

"See that you don't," Nurleen said.

Jesse slid a glance toward the women's table. Wished they'd all get up and leave. Utah might be concerned about wearing out his welcome, and there was his alter ego, Insurance Man, who had a lot of good customers in Indian Rock, to consider, but the buddies clearly didn't give a rat's ass if they made a bad impression. There were other games, in other towns. They knew Jesse'd thrown the last hand, quit while he was ahead, and they weren't happy about it.

"We been losin' all night," complained the one with the bulge, while Utah and the friend gathered chips.

"That's why they call it gambling," Jesse observed. Once again, he looked toward Cheyenne, and this time, their gazes connected.

Cheyenne's eyes widened, and he saw a knowing there that could only have come from sitting through a thousand games, waiting for her dad to lose the rent money.

Jesse gave a nearly imperceptible nod.

Cheyenne was quick; he'd give her that. She sprang to her feet, hesitated a fraction of a second and then blurted out, "I think I'm going to be sick!"

With that, she slapped a hand over her mouth and dashed from the room.

Sierra, Elaine and Janice, being women, rushed after her.

Jesse gave a silent sigh that seemed to rise from the soles of his feet.

The man with the gun slipped a hand inside his jacket.

But he wasn't fast enough on the draw. Nurleen had the snub-nose out before the outsider could clear denim.

"You get out of here," she said, cocking the pistol with an ease that would have given Doc Holliday pause, "and don't *ever* come back."

"Put that thing away, Nurleen," Utah grumbled. "We're leaving. We can cash in our chips some other time."

Without looking away from the buddy, Nurleen answered, "You ought to run with a better crowd of people, Milton. These yahoos are going to get you into serious trouble one day."

The buddy flushed a muddy-red at the insult, but there wasn't much he could do, unless he wanted to get himself shot, and nothing he could say. He flung a bowie knife of a glare at Jesse, turned on his heel and headed for the back door, slamming it behind him.

Utah and buddy number two followed.

Nurleen lowered the .45 and let out a long breath when they were gone. "I'm getting too old for this shit," she said.

Jesse got out of his chair, leaned down to plant a kiss on top of her graying head. "Thanks, Dead-eye."

"You'd better not go out the back way," Nurleen said. "Milton's probably past the city limits by now, but I'll bet that pair of snakes he brought in here with him will be watching the door, just waiting to jump you."

Jesse took the gun out of Nurleen's hand, crouched and slid the weapon back into place under the table. Looking up into her face, he grinned. "I'll be all right," he told her.

"All you McKettricks think you're invincible," Nurleen said huffily. "Whole damn outfit's cocky, if you ask me." She smiled, but tears gleamed in her eyes. She took his hand and squeezed it, hard. "You be *careful,* Jesse."

"I will," he said, straightening.

"You're a damn liar," Nurleen retorted.

"Don't spread it around."

Nurleen got up from her chair, looking a little shaky, and crossed the room to lock the back door.

"Quick thinking on Cheyenne's part," she said, throwing the bolt. "There's a lot of Cash Bridges in her. You see the way she played that first hand?"

"I saw," Jesse confirmed thoughtfully, and headed for the inner door.

The restaurant was stone empty—even the fry cook was gone.

Through the front windows, Jesse could see Cheyenne and Sierra and the other members of the ladies' poker club huddled in the parking lot. Delores was out there, too, along with a straggle of customers. They were all staring at the place as though they expected flames to shoot through the roof.

To complete the scene, Deputy Terp's cruiser zipped in, lights whirling.

With a grin, Jesse made for the front door.

"Wyatt," he said, with a nod, as Myrna's eldest son got out of the car and took a few steps toward him.

Wyatt's plain-featured face tightened. "You know you're supposed to call me John," he said, frowning.

Jesse tugged at the brim of his baseball cap. "Yes, sir, Wyatt," he replied. "I know that."

Wyatt's jaw tightened. "What's going on here, anyway? Why's everybody out here in the parking lot?"

Jesse hooked eyeballs with Cheyenne again before answering. "Just a little disagreement in the card room," he said, addressing the whole assembly, as well as Wyatt Terp. "It's safe to go back inside."

Just then, an old red pickup shot out of the alley that ran behind Lucky's, bald tires flinging up gravel.

Nurleen had been right, then. Utah was long gone, but the buddies had hung around, out by Jesse's truck, hoping to take a few strips out of his hide.

"Damnation," Wyatt sputtered, dashing for the

cruiser to give chase. "This ain't the Indianapolis Speedway!"

Jesse went after him. Caught up to him just as he slid behind the wheel. "One of them's packing, Wyatt," he warned.

Wyatt nodded, reached for his radio, asked for backup, slammed the door and shot out of the lot with his siren blaring. Jesse would have followed, to even the odds a little, but Terp was an experienced cop. There would be more deputies converging up the road—and, anyway, it was unlikely the buddies would be stupid enough to draw on an officer of the law just to avoid a speeding ticket.

Cheyenne broke away from Sierra and her friends to approach Jesse. "Are you all right?" she asked.

Jesse wanted to kiss her till her toes curled. Instead, he resettled his hat and countered, "Are you? I know the food isn't the best at Lucky's, but I've never known it to give anybody an instantaneous case of food poisoning."

She flushed, threw a pretend punch at his chest and then laughed. It was a self-conscious sound, though, and she wouldn't quite meet his eyes.

He curled a finger under her chin, not giving a damn who was watching or what conclusions they might draw. "You've got good instincts, Cheyenne," he said quietly. "You picked up on something in there that a lot of people would have missed."

"I've seen a lot of games go bad," she said. Wyatt's siren gave a couple of distant whoops, far up the road, and then went silent. She looked that way, then back to Jesse's face. "You'd better watch your back," she told him. "The big guy's nobody to worry about, but those other two—"

Jesse was moved by her concern in a way he hadn't been by Nurleen's, and it didn't take a shrink to say why. "Be careful," he said. "You might give me the impression that you give a damn about me, and not just those five-hundred acres you want to buy."

She looked away. Folks were meandering back into Lucky's, flowing past them in a divided stream.

Jesse let his hand fall to his side.

"I took a job with McKettrickCo," Cheyenne said. "I start tomorrow."

Jesse felt a peculiar mixture of relief and dread. If she was going to work for Keegan and Rance, then she must have resigned from the real-estate outfit, which meant the land wouldn't be an issue between them anymore. On the other hand, his cousins were both single, and not above charming an attractive woman whenever the opportunity afforded itself.

Cheyenne was one hell of an opportunity.

"That's good, I guess," he said.

A brief silence buckled in the air between them, like a live wire getting too much charge.

"Jesse, I—" Cheyenne began. But then she stopped. Bit her lower lip.

"What?" he prompted.

She seemed fascinated by the gravel at their feet, but she finally looked up at him again. Smiled thinly. "If you change your mind about selling that land, I can still facilitate the deal."

Disappointment hollowed his middle. "Guess I'd better get on home," he said. "See to the horses. Maybe grab a little sleep." He'd noticed her car, parked next to Sierra's SUV. If it hadn't been for that, he'd have offered to drop her off on the way back to the ranch.

She caught at his arm as he turned to walk away. "Jesse?"

He stopped. Waited.

Another struggle played out in her face. "I—we need to talk. Do you think you could come by our place for supper tonight? Mom and Mitch will be there, but—"

Something quickened inside Jesse, an uneasy exhilaration. He'd felt the same way the first time he'd ridden a bronc in a rodeo. "Sounds serious," he said when she left the sentence hanging in midair. "Tell you what. I'll grill a couple of steaks at the ranch. Seven o'clock?"

If he hadn't been holding his breath for her answer, he might have smiled at her obvious consternation. She knew as well as he did that, one of these times, the circumstances were going to be just right and the two of them would end up in a sweaty tangle between the sheets.

Maybe even tonight.

The prospect electrified Jesse. Woke up everything inside him, tired as he was.

"Okay," she said uncertainly and after a long internal deliberation.

Jesse wanted to give a jubilant yell and toss his hat in the air, but he didn't. He'd spook Cheyenne if he did, and he wasn't about to take the chance.

Sierra, Elaine and Janice came out of the restaurant, in a chattering gaggle, and Sierra was schlepping an extra purse.

"Guess the practice game is over," Cheyenne said with a faint smile.

"Guess so," Jesse agreed.

"Should we walk you to your truck?" Sierra asked him, looking worried as she forked over Cheyenne's handbag. All four of them must have left their gear behind when Cheyenne had caught Jesse's signal and had bolted from the poker room. "Those guys might have doubled back, or they could have friends—"

Jesse chuckled. "This isn't Tombstone, Sierra," he said. "I'll be fine."

Sierra clearly wasn't convinced. "I could call Travis—he's in town, meeting with the contractor about our new house. I'd feel better if he followed you out to the ranch, just in case—"

"Sierra," Jesse interrupted. "Chill."

"I'm calling him," Sierra decided aloud, reaching into her purse to pull out her phone.

"Sierra."

"Oh, okay," Sierra said. "But I don't like it."

Jesse kissed her cheek, tipped his hat and left.

"I THINK IT WOULD BE SAFER," Elaine said as Cheyenne watched Jesse disappear around the side of Lucky's

211

Bar and Grill, "to hold the next practice game at some-body's house."

"Good idea," Sierra replied thoughtfully. Out of the corner of her eye, Cheyenne saw that her friend had watched Jesse out of sight, too. "We have lots of food left over from the party. How about tomorrow night on the Triple M?"

Elaine and Janice nodded.

A moment passed, then Cheyenne nodded, too.

They all agreed to meet at Sierra's the next evening, at seven, and went their separate ways.

Cheyenne sat stone still in her car, her heart pounding, her stomach churning.

Now that she'd let her guard down, she had to deal with the near-miss that had just taken place in Lucky's card room. Sierra and the others probably didn't sus-pect *how* near a miss it had been, even with all the drama of exiting the building at Cheyenne's insistence, the arrival of the deputy sheriff, and the red truck roaring out of the alley at top speed.

Cheyenne knew only too well what might have hap-pened.

She'd seen men pull knives over a hand of cards.

She'd hidden behind bars during fistfights, with glass from broken bottles and shattered mirrors raining down on her head.

She'd been driven home in the backseat of squad cars because Cash, bloody from some brawl, had been arrested for disorderly conduct. More than once, angry players had come pounding at the door of the house out

212

beyond the railroad tracks in the middle of the night, shouting threats. Another time, she and her mom and dad had been out for a drive, on one of Cash's rare poker-free Sunday afternoons, when a car full of sore losers had run them off the road.

Her dad had greeted them with a shotgun, pulled out from under the car seat, and Cheyenne had been so scared, she'd almost wet herself.

"Get down!" Ayanna had ordered, breathless with fear, but Cheyenne hadn't obeyed. She'd seen the whole thing.

Oh, yes. There was an energy to that kind of trouble, and she'd felt it again, back there in that room behind the restaurant. It made the tiny hairs on her forearms stand up, and the bottom fall out of her stomach.

Clutching the steering wheel, she closed her eyes.

Swallowed the bile that rose, stinging, into the back of her throat.

She hadn't had to fake the throwing-up part.

Sierra and Elaine and Janice had all scrambled into the restroom to find her heaving up her lunch. She'd taken the time to rinse her mouth and splash her face with cold water before herding them all outside, along with everyone in the restaurant.

Then she'd dialed 911 on her cell phone.

Feeling dizzy now, she leaned her head back against the top of the seat and tried to breathe slowly and deeply.

Surely Jesse wasn't so naive as to think those men were gone for good.

They obviously believed he'd cheated them.

They had a score to settle, and one small-town sheriff's deputy wouldn't scare them off.

Cheyenne fought the need to hyperventilate.

Jesse shouldn't have refused Sierra's offer to call Travis.

Damn his stupid pride, anyhow.

Damn his stupid McKettrick pride.

Still shaking, Cheyenne turned the key in the ignition, shifted into Drive and drove out of Lucky's parking lot. She cruised down Main Street, keeping to the speed limit, but at the edge of town, she gunned the engine.

She raced past the turnoff that would have taken her home.

After ten minutes or so, she spotted Jesse's truck up ahead. Slowed down a little. Silly to hope he wouldn't see her, recognize her car.

Crazy, what she was doing.

She wouldn't be any use at all in a fight.

Jesse rounded a bend, disappeared.

Cheyenne sped up.

Rounded the same bend.

Jesse was parked alongside the road, leaning against the side of his truck, with his arms folded. He'd taken off the baseball cap, and his rumpled hair gleamed in the sunlight.

Cheyenne considered sailing right on by, pretending she hadn't been following him at all but just traveling the same road, purely by chance, but she knew the tactic wouldn't work. So she pulled in behind the truck, shut off the car and got out.

"What are you doing?" Jesse asked reasonably, as she approached.

"Making sure you get home all right," she answered, lifting her chin.

He chuckled. Shook his head. "You're protecting me?"

She came a step closer. His beard was golden, like his hair. His eyes were the same color as the high-country sky arched over their heads.

She couldn't tell by his expression whether he was insulted or flattered. "Those guys are bad news, Jesse," she said quietly. She was already in over her head, so she might as well start treading water. "The kind who don't take kindly to losing."

"Nobody does," Jesse said, watching her. "They'll cool off, Cheyenne. Move on to the next game."

"Maybe," she replied, remembering her dad facing down those flushed and cursing men on the side of the road, with a shotgun in his hands. She'd screamed when he'd fired it into the air, could still smell the gunpowder and see the flames shooting from the double barrels.

"Suppose they turned up right now," Jesse speculated, his tone gentle. "What would you do?"

"I don't know," Cheyenne said, wanting to cry. "Something."

Suddenly Jesse reached out and hooked an arm loosely around her shoulders, pulled her against him.

Propped his chin on the top of her head. "You know, don't you," he said, "what'll happen if you follow me out to the ranch?"

She buried her face in his T-shirt. Even after playing poker all night, in a smoky room, he smelled dangerously good. After a long, long time, she nodded.

He held her a little more tightly. "Want to ride in the truck with me?"

She pulled back, just far enough to look up at him. "I can't leave the car here," she said. After all, the vehicle didn't belong to her. She was supposed to give it back. She didn't follow the chain of thought any further than that because it would lead to Nigel.

Right now, she was pretending her boss didn't exist.

Jesse nodded, walked her back to the driver's side door, which was still standing open, and waited until she was inside.

"Now's your chance, Cheyenne," he told her gravely. "You can turn around and head back to Indian Rock, and I'll understand. There'll be no hard feelings."

He was offering her a way out, and she ought to take it. She knew that. She also knew she *wouldn't* go back to Indian Rock, not before she'd spent the afternoon, and maybe the night, too, in Jesse McKettrick's bed.

It wasn't too much to ask, after all the doing without, all the fear, all the hopeless waiting in card rooms, all the pain of watching Mitch struggle to recover from the accident and not being able to do anything about it.

She didn't answer Jesse. Just waited until he walked away, got back into his truck, started it up.

She followed him along the winding road, leading ever upward, toward the house where McKettricks had lived and loved for almost a century and a half.

She had no illusions.

There would be no fairy-tale endings.

She'd hate herself in the morning. Maybe even before then.

But for one brief interlude in eternity, she was not going to be Cash Bridges's daughter.

She was not going to be Nigel Meerland's hired gun.

She was not going to be Ayanna's support system.

She was not going to be Mitch's protector.

She was going to be one thing, and one thing only.

A woman.

A flesh-and-blood *woman,* freely giving herself up to a flesh-and-blood man. And damn the consequences.

CHAPTER TWELVE

JESSE WAS AS AWARE OF Cheyenne, as he traveled that familiar road, as he would have been if she were sitting next to him on the truck seat. He'd invited her to supper, and he sure as hell hoped she'd come, but the time lapse would have given her time to think things through.

Now, there would be no interval, no space to change her mind.

For his own sake, he was glad about that. For *her*

sake—well, it might have been better if she'd taken the afternoon to chill out. Get some perspective.

Despite the brief fiasco with Brandi after he'd won the big tournament, he wasn't the marrying kind. Sure, he hated rattling around alone in the ranch house most of the time—that was the main reason he was always looking around for a game to jump into.

But he wasn't husband material, like Rance and Keegan were.

He didn't even have a damn job.

Furthermore, he didn't *want* one.

He was fixated on Cheyenne, there was no denying that, but he knew himself. He was a one-trick pony, and that trick was winning at poker, not loving Cheyenne the way she deserved to be loved.

The sex would be hot, a nuclear fusion, but even fusions cooled, in time.

Ultimately, he'd get bored. Cheyenne's bone-deep belief that no man could be trusted would be reinforced, and the whole thing would fade to a sad memory that haunted him whenever he slowed down enough to think.

He glanced at the rearview mirror, half hoping that she wouldn't be there.

But she was.

"Hell," he muttered. Then he laughed and shoved a hand through his hair and swore again, exultant.

CHEYENNE WAS ABOUT TO jump out of her skin. Desperate for a distraction, she switched on the radio, set to an oldies station.

A girl-band version of Rick Springfield's "Jessie's Girl" filled the car.

She switched it off instantly, blushing.

The hot flashes were back. Cheyenne rolled down the window.

The wind blew her hair across her face in strands that stung like little whips, and she nearly went off the road before she got the window closed again.

The whole universe seemed to throb around her, like one big, cosmic heart.

Jesse turned in at the gate to his place. The house Jeb McKettrick had built for his bride, Chloe, loomed against the sky, looking like something out of an old western on TV.

All wrong, Cheyenne thought, gnawing on her lower lip.

There should have been stormy darkness, not sunshine. Lightning, not the sparkling leaves of cottonwood trees rippling in the breeze. There should have been bats flying around, and ragged curtains blowing past broken shutters. There should have been gargoyles, instead of sturdy, peeled log pillars supporting the roof of a long porch.

Jesse parked close to the barn, and Cheyenne pulled in beside him, sat there shaking while he got out of the truck and came toward her.

He rapped on the glass, grinning at her, when she didn't move to roll down the window.

Belatedly, she pushed the button.

Now there was no barrier between them.

"I'm going to check on the horses," Jesse said practically. His voice was low and throaty, though, and his eyes searched her face. "You can head on inside, if you want to. Make yourself comfortable."

Make yourself comfortable.

Yeah. Right.

"Do you need any help?" Cheyenne heard herself ask, as though it were an ordinary day. As though she weren't about to make the most spectacular mistake of her very unspectacular life. "With the horses, I mean?"

He shook his head. "I won't be long."

Cheyenne nodded, watched until he'd disappeared into the barn.

The car was running. The gas tank was full.

She could still turn around, drive back to town and forget she'd ever been stupid enough to let things go this far.

Instead, she shut off the engine, dropped the keys into her bag and got out of the car.

The back door was unlocked, and the kitchen was even bigger than she remembered. Bigger, in fact, than the house she and Mitch and Ayanna lived in.

She'd never been any farther inside than the bathroom, down the corridor, where she'd changed clothes to ride up to the ridge with Jesse only a couple of days before.

Now she was going to see more of the place.

She swallowed.

Like, for instance, Jesse's bedroom.

What would it be like?

He nearly knocked her over with the door when he came in behind her.

"Look around if you want to," he said, apparently amused to find her rooted to a spot just beyond the threshold. "I'm hitting the shower."

It all sounded so ordinary.

Look around if you want to.

I'm hitting the shower.

What should she do?

Bolt for town?

She obviously didn't intend to do that.

Find his bedroom, then? Strip off her clothes, lie down and wait to be taken?

She shook her head, mortified by the image. She'd been ambushed by her own senses. Ambushed and hog-tied.

Jesse bent his head to look at her curiously.

"I'll be fine," she said.

Liar.

Jesse grinned. Brushed her cheek lightly with the backs of his fingers. "You could always join me in the shower," he ventured.

Curiously, the remark broke the tension. She laughed. "I think I'll explore instead."

He spread his hands. *"Mi casa es su casa,"* he said. *My house is your house.* And then he left her standing there, disappearing through an archway on the far side of the room.

Cheyenne stayed where she was for a few more moments, then worked up the nerve to take the tour.

Following the route Jesse had taken, she found herself in a massive, rustic dining room, with floor-to-ceiling windows on one end, overlooking the grassy pasture, a stand of cottonwoods, the winding creek and the distant tree-lined ridge she and Jesse had ridden to.

The table was plain and heavy, made of some dark wood, and at least twelve feet long by Cheyenne's best guess. There was a matching china cabinet, crammed with antique dishes, and a stone fireplace took up the entire wall opposite the windows.

Above the mantel hung a huge, framed oil portrait of a handsome, fair-haired man in his mid-thirties, looking ingenuously miserable in the garb of a nineteenth-century gentleman. Beside him stood a knockout redhead, in a blue gown trimmed with froths of lace at the high neckline and the sleeves. Mischief danced in her eyes.

Jeb and Chloe McKettrick, the original owners of this house.

Looking up at them, Cheyenne was suddenly thunderstruck by the resemblance between Jeb and Jesse. Dress Jesse up like a Victorian dandy, in a tight collar and a waistcoat, and he could pose for a duplicate portrait, with no one the wiser.

Chloe, Cheyenne reflected, with a strange, seismic sadness, looked nothing like her. The first Mrs. McKettrick—at least the first to be mistress of this castle of timber and stone—had fair skin, wide, intelligent eyes and fiery hair, indicating a Celtic heritage. Cheyenne was part Apache, and it showed.

Pocahontas, Nigel called her.

Not a good time to think about Nigel, she decided, turning away from the portrait to continue the expedition. Next, she stepped into a living room the size of most high-school gymnasiums, but it wasn't the dimensions that made her breath catch on a gasp.

It was the view. Another entire wall of windows, three times the length of the one in the dining room, looked out over miles of ranch land. At night, the lights of Indian Rock would be clearly visible, a shimmering sparkle tucked into a valley on the far horizon.

Cheyenne stood spellbound for a long time. The big house was so quiet that she could almost hear her own heartbeat.

Presently, she turned from the windows, took in the rest of the room. Another fireplace, with a modern portrait hung over the mantel, this one done by a photographer rather than a painter.

Cheyenne recognized Jesse's parents, his stunningly beautiful sisters. She saved Jesse for last—a small, mischievous boy, eight or nine years old, captured forever at one moment in his charmed life. His hair was lighter, tumbling over one eye, and the familiar, born-to-make-trouble grin was already evident.

"I was always a good-lookin' devil," the real, grown-up Jesse drawled, making Cheyenne pull in a startled breath and whirl to find him standing only a few feet behind her.

He'd shaved. His hair was damp, and he'd pulled on clean jeans and a white T-shirt. His feet were bare.

223

"Can I get you something? Some of that fizzy water you like?"

Cheyenne found her voice. "Uh—no—thanks. This is a beautiful house."

"It's big," Jesse allowed.

"Do you ever get lonely here, all by yourself?" Now *what* had made her ask a dumb question like that? Most likely, he had a parade of women streaming in and out. His family probably came and went, too.

"Yeah," Jesse said, surprising her. "Sometimes."

Cheyenne began to panic.

What was she supposed to do now?

What was she supposed to say?

Jesse approached, took her hand, raised it to his mouth. Brushed the knuckles with a light pass of his lips.

Cheyenne shivered, but not because she was cold.

"I'd like to brush my teeth," she said, and then wished the hardwood floor would part so she could fall through and vanish forever.

"This way," Jesse said, smiling at her burning face. Still holding her hand, he led her through yet another archway and down a short, wide corridor with museum-quality Western art framed on either side.

Russells. Remingtons.

Originals.

Beyond was a huge master suite. The bed was round, and encircled by more towering windows. The ceiling must have been eighteen feet high, and it was painted, Sistine Chapel–style, with scenes of cattle stampeding

224

beneath a dark sky sundered by lightning. Cowboys rode among the panicked beasts, on horseback, waving their hats. "Bathroom's over there," Jesse said, pointing. "You'll find the necessary supplies in the top left-hand drawer."

"Uh-huh," Cheyenne said, wandering in that direction, still checking out the stampede. "You could sell tickets to this place."

Jesse laughed.

The bath, of course, looked like something out of a sultan's palace—if that sultan happened to be part cowboy. Like the bed, the room was round, with a hotel-size hot tub taking center stage. The brass faucets gleamed, and the dome-shaped roof was made of glass.

Cheyenne found the stash of packaged toothbrushes, helped herself to a new tube of paste, and scrubbed her teeth. She'd thrown up back at Lucky's, but that wasn't something she wanted to share with Jesse—especially when the man was about to make love to her.

She rinsed the brush, set it aside on the marble counter. The sink came equipped with a little sprayer, so she gave it a spritz.

When she returned to the bedroom, Jesse was sitting cross-legged in the middle of the round bed. A gas fire leaped on the hearth, and the curtains had been drawn. Shadows danced over the stampeding cattle in the modern fresco overhead.

Cheyenne stopped, drawn to Jesse, but intimidated, too.

"This is your parents' room," she said, voicing only one of several misgivings.

"Used to be," Jesse answered. He patted the bed beside him. "Come and sit down, Cheyenne. I'm not going to jump your bones. Nothing will happen unless and until you're ready."

She was both unnerved and reassured, looking up at the painted ceiling again and simultaneously indulging her earlier yearning to take off her shoes. The chill of the stone floor was deliciously sensual. "Doesn't it make you dizzy?" she asked. "Looking up at those cattle running around and around in circles, I mean?"

Jesse chuckled, stretched out on the bed with his hands cupped behind his head. "I guess I never thought of it that way," he said lazily.

Slowly, she approached the bed, crawled onto it, stretched out next to Jesse to look up at the ghost-riders in the sky. It felt strangely natural to lie down beside him. Not scary at all.

In fact, she thought she might drift off to sleep.

Jesse rolled onto his side, facing her. She waited for him to rest a hand on her cheek or her hip, maybe even her breast, but he didn't touch her.

"Where do your parents sleep when they're here?" she asked.

Jesse laughed. "They have a suite upstairs. What's the matter, Cheyenne? Are you afraid they're going to walk in on us?"

Cheyenne blushed. "Of course not," she said, and

wondered if she'd told the truth. "They're probably miles away."

"Palm Springs," Jesse said, twisting one of her dark brown locks loosely around his finger. "I like your hair down," he told her.

She turned onto her side, so they were facing each other. "Are we crazy?" she asked.

He smiled, slid his hand down along her upper arm, brought it to rest on the curve of her hip. "Probably." He was close now, breathing the word against her mouth. As she opened to him, he hooked a thumb under the button of her jeans.

She gave a slight whimper, then slid both arms around his neck.

He kissed her, very lightly at first, then with deepening passion. He unfastened the button, then slipped his hand beneath the hem of her clingy T-shirt, splaying his fingers wide on her belly.

Cheyenne groaned, twisting onto her back.

Jesse didn't break the kiss, but found the front-catch on her bra and snapped it open, setting her breasts free. Cupping one, chafing the nipple with the tips of his fingers until it hardened, straining toward him.

Cheyenne gasped when he finally let her take a breath. Gasped again when he shoved her shirt up, bent his head and took her nipple full into his mouth.

She cried out, arching her back, and plunged her fingers into his shower-damp hair. Overhead, the stampede blurred, came into sharp focus, and blurred again.

Jesse tongued her other breast, then suckled, at the

same time unzipping her jeans.

She lifted her hips, peeled the fabric away with frantic motions of her hands. Jesse paused long enough to pull the jeans down and away, and her panties went with them.

While Cheyenne lay dazed and needing, naked except for her displaced bra and the T-shirt pushed up to her shoulders, Jesse knelt beside her. With one hand, he unbuttoned his jeans. With the other, he stroked the thatch of curls between Cheyenne's thighs, never going quite deep enough.

She moaned softly, lifting her hips a little, craving his touch.

He hauled off his T-shirt, tossed it aside. Played with Cheyenne in a way that made her give a little whim-pery yelp of need.

When he thrust a finger inside her, she made a sob-bing sound, threw back her head and closed her eyes. The lower half of her body moved in delicious rhythm with the slow, steady movement of Jesse's hand.

He must have shed his jeans then; Cheyenne was aware of nothing but the sensations of his thumb, making wet circles around her clitoris, while his finger set fire to the little nest of nerves inside her. Sure enough, he'd found her G-spot. Until that moment, she hadn't known she *had* one.

No doubt about it. G-spot up and running.

"Jesse," she whispered, pleading.

"Not yet," he said, between her legs now.

"But I'm going to—oh, *God*—"

He continued to tease her, leaned over her to capture her mouth for another kiss.

She couldn't lie still, even for his kiss. Tossing her head from side to side, she moaned again, fevered. "*Jesse,* I'm—"

"I know," he said. Then he nibbled his way back down her body, draped her legs over his shoulders, slipped his hands under her buttocks and raised her to his mouth.

The moment his tongue flicked against her, she erupted in a shattering orgasm, and a low, keening sound came from her throat. The spasms seemed to go on and on, and just when she thought she couldn't bear the shrill pleasure of it for another moment, Jesse began to suck on her.

The climax intensified. And then intensified again.

And still it went on.

Cheyenne clawed at the bedding with both hands.

Jesse drew on her harder, and then harder still.

Cheyenne's body went slick with perspiration.

She screamed Jesse's name, and then the apocalypse came. She splintered, flew apart like an expanding universe in microcosm, and then dissolved into tiny particles, conscious only of desperate, consuming release.

When the flaming pieces drifted back together, and she became aware of herself as a solid being, she was on her knees, straddling Jesse, and he was gliding inside her. The friction ignited her all over again, and she tried to move faster, hungry for more, but, grasping her hips, he kept slowing her down.

Stroke by long, slow stroke, he drove her into a frenzy of satisfaction, caressing her breasts and urging her on as she rode him.

They came simultaneously, their bodies locked together, seemingly suspended in midair, in the final, catastrophic collision.

When it was over, Cheyenne collapsed onto Jesse's chest.

He caressed her back, her buttocks, the flesh of her thighs.

She felt his heart, beating against her own. Felt his breath, warm and raspy in her hair.

He was still deep inside her, warming her flesh, making her expand to accommodate him.

She moved to roll off, blissfully exhausted, but he didn't allow that.

Remarkably, he was getting hard again.

"Oh, Jesse," she murmured. "We can't—"

He cupped her face in his hands, drew her head down for his kiss. "Sure we can," he said, after he'd taken her breath away again. And he began to move beneath her, inside her.

The friction—the friction. She was catching fire again.

Clasping her hips now, he guided her, up and down, up and down, with excruciating leisure, along the length of him. She rode, trembling with need and anticipation, while he told her, in low, gruff words, all the delicious things he meant to do to her.

Over the course of the next few hours, he did them all.

Every one.

Finally, they slept, exhausted, as one flesh.

A few hours later Cheyenne awakened alone, to the sound of running water.

She sat up, momentarily alarmed. "Jesse?"

"In here," he called.

She crawled off the bed, tested her legs, and stumbled toward the bathroom. The hot tub brimmed with steaming, bubbling water, and candles flickered on the painted tile rim surrounding it on three sides.

Jesse was already in the bath. Two glasses of red wine glistened in the dancing glow of the candles flames.

He beckoned.

Cheyenne joined him.

The water, exquisitely warm, surged against her spent muscles.

Jesse handed her a glass of wine. She sipped, set it aside.

Jesse drew her astraddle of him again, his hands strong on her waist.

"Jesse," she sighed, wriggling just a little, "I can't stand one more orgasm."

He chuckled. "I'd love to test that theory," he said.

She splashed him.

He laughed and dipped a finger into her wineglass, dabbled the burgundy drops onto her nipple and licked them away.

She moaned.

He repeated the process with her other nipple. Beneath the surface of the water, he found her clitoris again, plucked at it gently, until she writhed with wanting.

She was lost.

That easily, she was lost.

He turned off the jets. Flipped the lever that opened the drain.

The water began to recede.

Jesse knelt, parting Cheyenne with his fingers. Teasing her back to madness with the tip of his tongue.

THE SUN WAS FRINGING the eastern hills with pinkish-gold light when Cheyenne drove into the yard at home. Ayanna came out onto the porch in her bathrobe, a cup of coffee in one hand, a pensive smile widening her mouth.

"Not a word, Mom," Cheyenne warned, climbing the worn steps on spaghetti legs. "I've got to get ready for work."

Ayanna took another sip of coffee as she stepped aside to let Cheyenne pass. "Jesse?" she asked.

Cheyenne tossed a look over one shoulder. "I didn't plan it," she said. "It just—happened."

"These things usually *do* 'just happen,'" Ayanna observed, following Cheyenne into the house. "You might have called, you know. I suspected you were with Jesse, but I was pretty worried just the same."

Cheyenne sighed. "I'm sorry," she said, keeping her

voice down because Mitch was probably still asleep, and if he wasn't, she didn't want him to overhear. "I knew I ought to call, but I couldn't think what to say. I mean, you *are* my mother."

"And therefore a completely sexless person who bore two children by virgin birth?"

She laughed softly. "Point taken."

"Good," Ayanna said. "I'll make you some breakfast. And Cheyenne?"

Cheyenne waited.

"You're glowing. Unless you want everybody at McKettrickCo to know you spent the night with Jesse, you'd better turn down the dimmer switch a little."

Cheyenne laughed again, waved her mother away, and hurried down the hall to her room.

When she came out forty-five minutes later wearing a lightweight tweed pantsuit and sensible shoes—hair wound into the customary bun—Ayanna was dressed for another day at the supermarket. Jeans, a long-sleeved T-shirt and a blue vest embroidered with her name.

She handed Cheyenne a cup of hot coffee and some news.

"The leasing people just took your car away."

"Great," Cheyenne said, deflated. She'd known Nigel was canceling the lease, but she'd expected a little warning. After all, technically she was still working for him.

"Don't worry," Ayanna told her, patting her arm. "I'll drop you off in the van."

Just then Mitch wheeled out of his room all spruced up. "Bronwyn's picking me up in an hour," he announced. "We're going to Sedona to commune with red rocks."

Ayanna and Cheyenne looked at each other.

"When was this decided?" Ayanna asked moderately.

"Last night," Mitch answered. "She stopped by before you got home from the supermarket." His gaze flicked to Cheyenne and turned pensive. "Doesn't it hurt to pull your hair back like that?"

Cheyenne ignored him, heading for the kitchen. Normally she didn't eat much breakfast, but today she was ravenous. She and Jesse had never gotten around to having supper. Nor had they talked, as she'd intended.

She'd planned to tell him that she was still working for Nigel, but it hadn't happened.

Mitch buzzed along behind her. "How do you feel about nepotism?" he asked with a humorous, hopeful lilt in his voice.

Cheyenne laughed, refilled her coffee cup, then sat down at the table. Ayanna had made pancakes, eggs and sausage patties. If she consumed this much food on a regular basis, she'd have to replace her wardrobe.

"I mean it, Cheyenne," Mitch insisted. "You're the human resources person at McKettrickCo. I'm human. I want a job."

"I'll see what I can do," Cheyenne promised.

"Maybe I could buy a car. If I had a job, I mean. And I could get a really good computer, too. Shit-can that piece of junk I'm using now."

"Mitch," Cheyenne warned.

"If I get hired and I can find a car, will you co-sign for the loan?"

"Mitch," Ayanna said.

"We'll see," Cheyenne told him.

She continued her breakfast in relative peace.

"I need money," Mitch announced. "Bronwyn's driving us to Sedona. I can't expect her to pay for lunch, too."

Cheyenne gave him forty dollars.

"You clear the table and wash the dishes, then," Ayanna told him. "And don't give me any static. You can reach the sink just fine."

"Not a problem," Mitch said.

Ayanna glanced at the clock. "We'd better go, Cheyenne. I like to allow myself extra time, since the van gets temperamental once in a while."

Inwardly, Cheyenne sighed. Maybe no one would notice when she arrived for her first day on the job in a psychedelic vehicle lacking only a peace sign to look like a time machine freshly arrived from the 1960s.

Regretfully, she left her plate on the table, still half-filled, and followed Ayanna out to the minibus.

There was a spring popping through the passenger seat.

Ayanna pulled a fringed pillow from the back and set it in place, grinning as Cheyenne hauled herself up and sat down.

The ignition made a disturbing grinding sound when Ayanna turned the key, and the exhaust pipe belched so much smoke, Cheyenne thought the rig was on fire.

Ayanna laughed at the expression on her daughter's face.

"Mitch is right about your hair, you know," she said. "You look perpetually surprised, like somebody who's had one too many face-lifts."

"Thanks a lot, Mom. That's just what I needed to hear."

Ayanna cranked the van into Reverse. Her eyes shone with mischief. "Uh-oh," she said.

"What?" Cheyenne demanded, worried that the van was either going to blow up or fall apart on the spot.

"You've lost that lovin' feelin'," Ayanna chimed. "Whoa-oh, that lovin' feelin'."

"Very funny, Mother."

Ayanna threw back her head and laughed out loud.

It was a good sound, Cheyenne thought, smiling a little, even if it *was* at her expense.

CHAPTER THIRTEEN

JESSE GRINNED AS THE horses bolted through the corral gate, some of them kicking up their heels for sheer joy, others prancing and tossing their heads. He felt like joining them.

He'd awakened before Cheyenne that morning, and had lain for a long time just watching her sleep. Imagining what it would be like to wake up and find her beside him *every* morning. He'd even gone so far as to try and picture what their kids would look like—anybody's guess, he finally concluded.

He was fair, she was dark.

It was a genetic toss of the dice.

Whistling, he closed the gate and fastened the latch.

He'd tried to talk Cheyenne into staying for breakfast, but she'd been hell-bent on showing up on time for her first day at McKettrickCo. They'd showered together, though, and had made sweet, slick love before she'd toweled herself off and shimmied back into yesterday's clothes.

There'd been one awkward moment—just as she was leaving—a sort of hitch in the flow of events. She'd wanted to tell him something. Something that had sobered her expression and darkened her eyes. Probably that neither of them ought to put too much stock in how good the sex had been, because, after all, they were both consenting adults. Things happened.

He'd had similar thoughts himself—until Cheyenne had taken him to places he'd never dreamed existed. Shown him the landscape of his own spirit, with all its sunlight and shadow, all its canyons and mesas and shining creeks.

He wasn't prepared to call it love.

But it sure as hell wasn't casual sex, either.

He'd had plenty of that. Probably qualified as an expert. It was usually good; sometimes it even shook him up a little, made him want to reconsider some of the things he'd decided about his life. But *sex* was an inadequate word in this context; it didn't describe the kind of sacred communion he and Cheyenne had shared. He could search the dictionary from now till doomsday and never find a definition that suited the situation.

Leaning on the uppermost rail of the gate, he watched the horses frolic in the field for a while, delighting in their freedom, then turned and headed back toward the house.

He was hungry; he'd throw together an omelet or nuke something from the freezer, then drive into town. He needed a break from poker, but maybe he'd stop by McKettrickCo, show a little interest in the family business—now that Cheyenne was part of it.

She'd probably run him off with the verbal equivalent of a shotgun, but at least he could say howdy.

After that, he'd go on over to the Bridges place and work on the railings for Mitch's wheelchair ramp.

Sounded like a productive day to him.

Inside the house, he washed up at the kitchen sink, then got out the fixings for his omelet—a few green onions, some mushrooms, a little cheese would dress up the eggs just fine.

While the skillet was heating, Jesse remembered his mother's message the night before. Time to call her back. The familiar beep reminded him that he'd skipped right over Brandi's call. With a sigh, he punched in the appropriate numbers. Might as well get it over with.

"Jesse, this is Brandi," the recorded voice said. "It's—listen, I really need to talk to you, because this

guy came around, and he offered me a lot of money—
damn, I forgot to charge this thing—call me later, will
you?"

Frowning, Jesse thumbed the call-back sequence.

Another recording. "Hi, this is Brandi. I can't come
to the phone right now, but your call is important to
me. Leave your number and I'll get back to you as
soon as I can."

Annoyed, Jesse simply said, "It's me, calling back.
Bye."

What "guy" had come around, offering Brandi "a
lot" of money, he wondered, and what the hell did any
of that have to do with him?

The phone rang before he could replace the receiver.
"Brandi?"

Familiar laughter trilled in his ear. "Sorry, Jess. It's
only me—your mom. You remember—Callie McKettrick. Tall. Brown hair. A real sense of fashion. The
person who gave birth to you."

Jesse grinned, went back to the stove, stirred the
onion-and-mushroom mixture around with the end of a
spatula. "I have a vague recollection," he said with a
chuckle. As mothers went, he'd drawn a pretty good
one, all things considered. "What's up?"

"Nothing much." His mother sighed cheerfully.
Callie was a happy woman, for the most part, and she
described herself as *fulfilled,* whatever that meant.
She'd never been involved with the company, like his
dad was, and she spent most of her time socializing
and raising money for various charities, but she was no

airhead. Jesse had always been proud of her. "Your dad and I were just wondering how you are, that's all."

"Couldn't be better," Jesse said, remembering the night before.

Not that he intended to share any details.

"I wish we could have attended Sierra and Travis's engagement party," Callie said, "but your father had meetings, and we'll be in Europe on their wedding day. Eve is just over the moon, having Sierra back in her life, and Liam as a bonus. What's she like, Jesse?"

"Sierra?"

"Of course Sierra. I already know what *Eve* is like."

Jesse chuckled. "Sierra's a blood McKettrick. Proud. Stubborn."

"I've seen her picture, of course. She's very pretty."

"Yeah, Mom," Jesse said, wondering where this conversational train was headed. "She's a looker, all right."

"I wish *you* would meet a nice young woman, Jesse."

He should have seen that one coming.

"I meet all kinds of nice young women, Mom." *I slept with one last night, as a matter of fact.*

"What do you think about McKettrickCo going public?"

"No opinion," he said, whipping up the eggs, milk and cheese and pouring the concoction into the skillet, with the sizzling onions and mushrooms.

"You *should* have an opinion, Jesse. All the rest of us do."

"Okay. Tell me your opinion, and I'll throw in with your side."

"You really should be more interested."

Jesse chuckled. "How are you and Dad voting? For or against?"

"For," Callie said. "Your father works too hard. So does Eve. We'd all be rich."

"Mom," Jesse pointed out, "we're *already* rich."

"Exactly my point."

Jesse turned the omelet out onto a plate, grabbed some silverware and carried the whole shooting match to the table, along with the phone receiver, of course. "You know I'm not a big believer in twelve-hour workdays, pie charts, graphs and the rest of it. Keegan's going to fight you, though. He's in line for a stress-related triple bypass when he hits fifty, and by God, nobody's going to deprive him of it."

"He's not over that terrible divorce," Callie said sadly.

Jesse's good spirits dipped a little. "No," he agreed. "Shelley's giving him a lot of trouble over Devon. She wants to take the kid to live in Europe, with her and the new husband."

"The woman is a bimbo," Callie said. Since she rarely made remarks like that, Jesse was a little taken aback. "Furthermore, she's stupid."

He sat with his fork suspended midway between his mouth and the plate. Momentarily, he wondered if his folks had found out about the Brandi escapade somehow, and his mother was leading him along a meandering path to confession. "Shelley's not the brightest ball in the bowling alley," he said carefully, "but she's not stupid." *And neither is Brandi.*

Callie was silent for a beat or so. "No," she said, with a sigh. "I guess she isn't. I worry about Keegan, that's all. With his folks gone, he's all alone in the world."

Keegan's parents, Libby and John Henry McKettrick, had been killed in a hotel fire in Singapore when Keeg was fourteen. After that, he'd been shunted from one part of the family to another until he'd been old enough to leave for college. "He's not alone, Mom," Jesse said. "He's got all the rest of us."

"Just the same," Callie insisted, "Keegan is lonely. He needs a home and a family. Of his own."

"He's *got* a home—the main ranch house—and he's got Devon."

"A house and a home are not the same thing, and you know it," Callie said. "And he doesn't see Devon very often as it is. Just imagine if Shelley takes her to Europe."

Jesse went on eating his omelet, but it had all the flavor of shredded cardboard. "What's your point, Mom?" he asked. Callie might beat around the bush all day, if he let her. Like a lot of McKettricks, born or, as in her case, married, into the family, she was a lawyer.

"It's time the three of you settled down. That's all I'm saying. Rance runs all over the world taking over companies, and leaves those little girls with their grandmother. Cora is a good woman, but she's past the age when she should be raising children. Keegan works like a man possessed, and you—you're at the other end of the spectrum. You play poker. Your father and I didn't sign over that house on your twenty-fifth birthday just so you could rattle around in it like a pebble in the bottom of a coffee can."

"You want it back?"

"Jesse McKettrick, do *not* smart off at me."

"Okay. I'll rush out, marry the first woman I run across and get her pregnant by Tuesday. Or would Monday be better?"

"Jesse." Callie's tone carried a warning.

He laughed. "Mom. Take a breath. I'm the perennial bachelor in the family, remember?"

"I remember, all right. And I'd love to forget it. I want grandchildren."

"You *have* grandchildren, Mom. Two by Sarah, and three by Victoria."

She sputtered, and Jesse heard his father's voice in the background.

"Leave him alone, Callie," Martin McKettrick said.

"Your father says to leave you alone," Callie said, sniffing.

"Yeah," Jesse said. "I heard him. Is this conversation over, Mom? Because I've got to head into town. See how things are going with the family business."

"You mean you're going to ask for a—job?"

Jesse put his fork down, pushed his plate away, closed his eyes. He was a multimillionaire in his own right. Life was roiling all around them—trees and mountains on every side—it was like living in the mind of God. What did he need—what did *any* of them need—with a job? "Yeah, Mom," he said. "Maybe I

243

can run the copy machine. Or manage the mail room."

"Jesse, you have a college degree."

"I know, Mom," he replied. "I majored in girls and rodeo."

"You majored in pre-law. And you graduated with a 4.0 grade average."

Before Jesse could answer, he heard a brief scuffle on the other end of the line, then his father came on.

"Don't listen to her," he said. "About the job, I mean. But you really ought to get married."

"I'll see what I can do, Dad," Jesse promised.

Martin laughed. "Goodbye, Jesse."

"Later," Jesse said and hung up before his mother could get hold of the receiver again.

CHEYENNE SPENT HALF the morning in meetings with Rance and Keegan and Travis Reid, who was one of the company's dozens of lawyers, and half mapping out a preliminary plan for the work-study program.

At eleven-thirty, Keegan appeared in the doorway of her office and invited her to join him and Rance and Travis for lunch. They were driving out to the Roadhouse.

She declined graciously. Myrna had already offered to share the double-decker tuna on rye she was having sent over from Lucky's, in addition to presenting Cheyenne with a welcome gift of a potted bamboo shoot with a little stuffed panda clinging to its stalk and, anyway, she wanted to have some facts and figures in place by the end of the day.

Keegan hesitated, as though he wanted to say something more, then nodded, grinned and left.

Jesse showed up fifteen minutes later, with Chinese takeout from a place halfway to Flagstaff.

Cheyenne blushed when she saw him, remembering all the things they'd done together and, worse, wanting to do them again.

"Hey," she said lamely.

"Hey," he replied. "What's with the hair?"

She gave him a pretend glare, lowered her voice. Why did everybody seem to have such a problem with her hairstyle? She pinned it up because she didn't want it getting in her way when she worked. "This is an office, Jesse, not a bedroom."

He stepped inside, closed the office door and looked around speculatively. There was barely any furniture—just a credenza, bookshelf, and her desk and chair. No pictures on the walls. No coffee mug with something silly imprinted on it.

Cheyenne blushed harder. She was there to *work*. She hadn't had time to make any kind of personal imprint on the room and, besides, she'd read in one of the million and one self-help books she'd devoured over her lifetime that women shouldn't have cozy offices if they wanted to be taken seriously in the business world.

"You a betting woman, Cheyenne?" Jesse asked.

"Rhetorical question," she said, recovering a little from the initial shock of having to deal with Jesse on the morning after. "You know I am. At least, when it comes to poker."

He set the deliciously fragrant bags on the corner of her desk. Came around to place both hands on the arms of her chair and look straight into her eyes. "I'll bet we make love, right here in this office, before the month is out."

Cheyenne's temper flared, along with a visceral need to lose the bet, and devil take waiting a month. "You're on," she said.

Jesse's lips were a fraction of an inch from hers. "If I win," he said, "you've got to wear your hair down, like it was last night, every day for a year."

Heat surged through her.

She remembered a movie she'd rented, a long time ago.

9 1/2 Weeks was the title, and sexual obsession was the theme.

Her pelvis bones seemed to widen, even though her legs were clasped tightly together. "Yeah? Suppose I win? What do I get?"

"Anything you want."

"Anything?"

"Anything," Jesse drawled. He reached for her desk calendar, flipped ahead thirty days, picked up a pen and covered one whole page with an *X*.

She swallowed. "What if I want you to sell me that land you're so determined to hold on to?"

His cool blue eyes seemed to sizzle. His breath was warm on her mouth; she felt her pulse there.

Cheyenne figured she'd be lucky if she didn't lose the bet in the next five minutes, let alone in a month.

"I'm willing to take that chance," Jesse drawled, damnably confident.

Unsettled, Cheyenne tried to peer around him, afraid Myrna would come in with the tuna on rye and catch Jesse with his hands on either side of her chair and her trembling like Kim Basinger in that movie.

"We'd better agree on some terms, don't you think?" Jesse went on when she didn't speak.

"What kind of terms?"

"What constitutes making love, for one thing." He touched his mouth to hers. "You're a responsive woman, Cheyenne. I can think of at least half a dozen ways to bring you to a climax."

She couldn't deny that. He'd had her in every position in the *Kama Sutra* the night before, and her body was still singing at the memory.

"Say I were to kneel," Jesse went on, "and set your legs over the arms of this chair—"

Cheyenne suppressed a groan. Closed her eyes. "Jesse, *stop.*"

"Suppose I used my tongue—"

"Jesse."

"Would that count?"

Cheyenne trembled, just imagining the scene. "No," she said. "It wouldn't count. Making love is—"

"What?" He kissed her lightly. "What is making love, Cheyenne?"

"Damn you, Jesse. Get out of here. I have *work* to do, unlike some people I could name—"

He nibbled the length of her neck. Tasted her earlobe.

"What is making love, Cheyenne?" he repeated, murmuring the words. "Full penetration?"

"Yes," she said, breathless. Maybe if she went along with him, he'd leave and she could get back to the task at hand. "Full penetration."

"In this office."

She gulped, mortified at the prospect—and the depths of her own desire to indulge the fantasy in real time. "In this office," she agreed.

"It's a deal," he said.

A lusciously spicy scent wafted from the bags of Chinese food. "Do I smell sweet-and-sour chicken?" she asked, desperate to ground herself in the real world. Desperate to distract Jesse from seducing her.

"Yes," Jesse said, grinning as he pushed back. Then he opened the bags, took out a carton, and proceeded to feed her morsels of sugary, savory chicken, bite by bite.

By the time they got to the fortune cookies, Cheyenne was moist in places that should have been dry.

IF JESSE HADN'T KNOWN Rance and Keegan would have asked too many questions, he would have slipped into the gym for a cold shower before he left McKettrickCo.

As it was, he was as hard as petrified tamarack.

No relief in sight, either.

Cheyenne wouldn't be joining him on the ranch that night. She had a date to play poker with the girls at Sierra's place.

He got out of the truck in Cheyenne's front yard, or what passed for one, hauled his tool box from the back and approached the pile of lumber he'd unloaded the day before.

How exactly *did* a person build rails for a wheelchair ramp, anyhow?

He wished he'd asked his dad about it, while they'd been on the phone that morning. Woodworking was one of Martin's hobbies—he'd built the deck and all the bookshelves in the house with his own hands.

Jesse shoved a hand through his hair. He hadn't even picked up a hammer yet, and he was already sweating. A big part of him was still back in that office, feeding Cheyenne sweet-and-sour chicken.

Another big part of him hurt like all hell.

Maybe there was a garden hose around somewhere. He could turn on the spigot full blast and stand under the spray.

He laughed at the thought, glanced toward the house.

Cheyenne was at work, of course, and Ayanna, too. Maybe Mitch was around; he'd say hello and see if the kid wanted to hold nails or something.

He rapped on the door.

No answer.

Jesse frowned. Could be Mitch was sleeping, or playing a video game, or maybe he just wanted to be left alone.

He knocked again, a little harder.

The image of the tractor overturning flashed into his mind.

What if Mitch had fallen again? What if he was in some kind of trouble?

Jesse tried the knob, found the door unlocked. That wasn't unusual in Indian Rock—like most towns, it had its share of petty crime, but most folks had lost track of their house keys years before.

He stepped inside. Called out, "Mitch?"

Nothing. The place felt empty, as if it were waiting for its people to come home. Still, how many places could Mitch have gone, confined to a wheelchair and with no other visible form of transportation?

Jesse scanned the living room. Linoleum floors. Old furniture. Dust-free surfaces. A console TV with a channel knob, and aluminum frozen-food trays duct-taped to the antenna. Poor people, making the best of a tough situation.

He headed for the hallway. "Mitch?"

Nothing.

Get out of here, he thought. *You're trespassing.*

Then he heard the groan. It was distant, and so low that he almost missed it.

He raised his voice. "Mitch!"

The answer was more a feeling than a sound. A shift in the atmosphere, a silent grinding of gears, like when a poker game was about to turn sour.

Jesse opened the door of the first bedroom. Nothing.

The hall was dark, since there were no windows. He backtracked, found the light switch and flipped it.

Mitch was sprawled on the floor, his wheelchair out of reach.

"I tried to yell when Bronwyn came to the door," Mitch choked out. "I guess she didn't hear me—"

"It's okay, buddy," Jesse said, crouching beside Mitch. "What happened? Do you hurt anywhere?"

"I thought maybe it was all a mistake. My being crippled, I mean. Maybe I could walk if I just tried hard enough—"

Jesse wanted to look away from the despair he saw in Mitch's face, but he didn't because that would have added to the indignity. "That was a damn fool thing to do," he said.

"Help me up."

"I'm not sure I ought to move you."

"I'm *okay,* Jesse," Mitch said. His words came out evenly, but there was a plea in them. "Please—don't call anybody. Mom and Cheyenne will freak if we have to go through the whole ambulance thing."

Within himself, Jesse debated the matter. His instincts said Mitch was telling the truth—he was all right—but what if those instincts were wrong? What if there were internal injuries? What if the kid had broken a bone or something?

"Just get me back in the chair," Mitch said.

"We're taking a chance here, buddy."

"Just get me back in the chair."

Jesse sighed. "Okay," he said. He stood up, rolled the wheelchair within reach, then stooped to put both hands under Mitch's arms and lug him semi-upright, then backward, into the seat.

Mitch just sat there for a few moments, probably getting a grip. He was dressed up, wearing chinos and a polo shirt. He closed his eyes.

"You were going someplace with Bronwyn?" Jesse asked, to give Mitch a way out of the silence.

"Sedona," Mitch said bleakly. "I should have known it wasn't going to work out."

Jesse set a hand on his friend's shoulder. "You shouldn't have tried to stand up," he said. "But that's where the shoulds and shouldn'ts end. Bronwyn's a pretty girl. Of *course* you wanted to go to Sedona with her."

The look of sorrow in Mitch's gaze bruised something in Jesse. "I ought to accept reality," he said. "Face it. I'm never going to have a life."

"Bullshit," Jesse said with certainty. Then he got behind the chair, took hold of the handles and started pushing it back down the hallway, toward the living room. "Come on, cowboy. You're not dressed for a day on the range, but what the hell. The cattle don't care if you look like a dude."

Mitch looked back at him, and the hope Jesse saw in his expression was almost as hard to swallow as the sorrow had been. "A day on the—?"

"We'll saddle up and ride."

"Cheyenne will flip out," Mitch said, grinning tentatively at the prospect.

"I can handle Cheyenne."

Mitch went solemn again. "Can you, Jesse? Things—things aren't what they seem."

They'd reached the front door, and Jesse moved

ahead onto the porch, holding the screen open so Mitch could pass. "What do you mean, 'things aren't what they seem'?"

Mitch wouldn't meet his eyes. "They just aren't, that's all."

Jesse recalled that morning, back at the house, and the sense that Cheyenne wanted to tell him something, but couldn't quite bring herself to do it. It made him a little uneasy, but it wasn't his nature to dwell on things, especially when there wasn't squat he could do about them.

"Fair enough," he said.

Mitch flipped on the juice, and the chair whirred as he zipped down the ramp, heading for the truck. Jesse lingered only a second or two on the porch, watching him go and wondering.

"You hungry?" he asked after loading Mitch into the passenger seat and his chair into the back.

"I could use a burger," Mitch admitted.

They whipped through McDonald's and ate on the road.

Out at the ranch, Jesse reversed the loading process.

Mitch's mood had changed on the way out. Maybe it was the burger and fries. Maybe it was the chance to go somewhere, get out of the house.

"Bronwyn probably thinks I stood her up," Mitch mused, but he looked happy as he did a three-sixty in his chair, taking in the barn, the house and the scenery.

There was nothing like that scenery, Jesse reflected. It had the power to heal a man's soul, if not his body.

"You can call her from inside," Jesse said.

Mitch nodded, looking solemn again. "What do I tell her? I don't want to lie, but I'm not too thrilled with the idea of saying I tried to walk, either."

"Just tell her the truth," Jesse counseled.

Good advice, McKettrick, he thought. *Maybe you ought to follow it. Tell Cheyenne a thing or two.*

The voice ambushed him, gave him pause. He hadn't lied to her, had he?

Brandi? his conscience prompted.

Damn. He hated that voice.

"Let's go make that call," he said, feeling a little subdued. "Then I'll saddle a couple of horses."

Mitch's expression was luminous at the idea of riding a horse, of having legs again, even if they were borrowed. "Okay, Jesse," he said.

Okay, Jesse. The phrase rang with trust.

Why did that make him feel guilty?

CHAPTER FOURTEEN

KEEGAN STOOD IN THE doorway of Cheyenne's office, dangling a set of keys. There was something reminiscent of Jesse about him, she thought, even though the two men didn't resemble each other physically.

"Your car has been delivered," Keegan said. "And it's almost six o'clock. When were you planning on calling it a day?"

Cheyenne would have countered that she could have

asked the same question of him, if she'd known him better. As it was, she smiled and switched her computer to Standby. "My secret is out," she said. "I'm a workaholic. Six o'clock is the middle of the day to me."

Keegan approached, set the keys in the middle of her blotter. "Me, too," he said. "But sometimes I wonder if Jesse isn't right to spend his days playing poker, riding the range and just taking things as they come."

Cheyenne reddened a little. Jesse took things as they came, all right. Like her, for instance. She certainly didn't want to talk about him, at least in the office, because it reminded her of the bet. That X he'd drawn on her calendar? He might as well have tattooed it on her flesh.

"Workaholism is a noble addiction," she said.

"But still an addiction," Keegan reasoned thoughtfully. "Go home, Cheyenne. The project will still be here in the morning."

Cheyenne nodded. Swallowed. Echoed the question Mitch had put to her, concerning a job at McKettrickCo. "How do you feel about nepotism?"

Keegan laughed. Perched on the edge of her desk, he folded his arms. He was powerfully built, where Jesse was leaner, more—agile. Rance, in contrast to both his cousins, was built like a linebacker. Despite these dissimilarities, there was an indefinable similarity between the three of them, as though their souls had all been cut from the same cloth.

"I'm a McKettrick," he answered. "I eat, sleep and drink nepotism. Why?"

The look in his eyes told her he already *knew* why, but he wanted her to say it aloud. "I'm hoping there might be a place for my brother, Mitch. In the work-study program, I mean."

Was she hoping that?

Since when?

She lived to protect Mitch. To shelter him. Even a month ago, she'd have said he wasn't cut out for the business world. But the relationship was changing; the dynamics were different. Since Jesse.

She shook off that thought. The shift in her perception of Mitch had nothing to do with Jesse.

Did it?

She recalled the joy in Mitch's face, and the terror in her own heart, when he'd ridden that horse out at the Triple M, the night of the party. Then there was Bronwyn. Mitch obviously liked the girl. He didn't know—or was it that he didn't care?—how dangerous it was to hope for something you would probably never have.

"I talked with Mitch a little out at Sierra's place," Keegan said with a nod of recollection, as if he'd gone back there, in his mind, and had the whole conversation all over again. "He seems like a bright kid, and Jesse thinks highly of him."

"Is that a recommendation?" Cheyenne asked quietly, without weighing the words first. "Jesse's opinion, I mean?"

Keegan thrust out a sigh, ran a hand through his hair, the same way Jesse did. "Jesse," he said, "is Jesse.

Sometimes he frustrates me—I'd like to drag him away from the poker table, or off some horse, and beat the hell out of him. He likes to play the laid-back country boy, but he's got one of the finest minds I've ever run across. So, yeah, if he says your brother is a good bet, I'm inclined to take it seriously."

"Thanks," Cheyenne said and glanced down at the keys resting on her blotter. Thought of Nigel. Looked up. "Keegan, I—"

Just then, Myrna stuck her head in at the door.

"I'm leaving," she announced. "Shall I lock up?"

"I'll do it," Keegan said.

"You're not staying? Burning the midnight oil?"

Keegan sighed. "Not tonight," he said.

Myrna nodded her approval. "Maybe there's hope for you yet, *Mr.* McKettrick."

"That's *Keegan* to you," he replied lightly, in a way that made Cheyenne wonder what it was like to be part of a circle, a close community of friends and fellow workers, a member of a large extended family, sharing the same history.

She had grown up in Indian Rock.

Why did she feel as though she had no roots? No place where she truly belonged?

And what was with all this bloody introspection?

"Thanks for sharing your sandwich, Myrna," she said. Already full of the sweet-and-sour chicken Jesse had hand-fed her, Cheyenne hadn't had the heart to refuse the offer. The other woman's gesture, while ordinary, had meant a lot to her. So did the bamboo and the little panda bear, sitting prominently on the corner of her desk.

"No problem," Myrna said. "See you tomorrow." With that, she was gone, heels clicking a fading drumbeat on the floor as she walked down the corridor.

Cheyenne took her purse out of the big drawer in her desk, slipped the strap over one shoulder and stood. "Guess I'd better run," she said to Keegan. "I'm supposed to be at Sierra's in an hour or so."

Keegan led the way out of the office, along the corridor, to the front door. "That's yours," he said, pointing out the only remaining vehicle in the lot, besides his black Jaguar. A forest-green Escalade.

Thinking there must be some mistake, she looked around.

Following her gaze as he locked up, Keegan chuckled. "I know it's pretty showy," he said, "but it was all they had available."

"Hey," Cheyenne said, "I'll adjust."

Keegan laughed. Then looked solemn again. "Is it serious, between you and Jesse?"

"It's—something," she said, after a long time. "I'm not sure what."

"Then I won't ask you out to dinner," Keegan said. "Damn it."

He walked Cheyenne to the Escalade, opened the door for her.

She was glad she'd worn pants instead of her usual suit with a straight skirt. Long-legged as she was, it was a climb into that rig. She sat still behind the wheel for a few seconds, staring through the windshield, struggling with her conscience, feeling like a car thief about to go on a joyride.

She decided to bite the bullet. Risk it all. She turned. "Keegan—"

He was already getting into the Jag. After a brief wave, he shut the door and started the engine.

Cheyenne could have rolled down the window, called to him, spilled her guts about the contract with Nigel. But the time for bullet-biting was past—Keegan was backing out of his parking space.

Her purse rang.

Muttering, she rummaged for the phone—Nigel's phone—and answered with a brisk, "What do you want?"

"Still charming," Nigel sang.

"Go to hell, Nigel," she said.

"Did you find out anything? Within the hallowed halls of McKettrickCo, I mean?"

"Yes." Cheyenne stuck the key in the ignition, studied the controls and fired up the Escalade. Wait until her mother and Mitch saw it. They'd want to go for a spin. "I found out what it means to have a *real* job. With an office and a desk. You're suffering by contrast, Nigel."

Nigel laughed. "I generally do," he said.

"I'm not going to spy," Cheyenne insisted, hitting the speaker button and laying the phone in the console, so she could drive with both hands. "You might as well know that I'm going to bank my paychecks and give them back to you when my contract expires. If you have any decency at all, you'll fire me and be done with it."

Jesse crept back into her mind. He was betting a lot—the land—on her being unable to resist his charms over the next thirty days. Surely he hadn't been serious, though.

Nigel interrupted her thoughts. "Fortunately," he said, "decency is not one of my shortcomings. *I need that land,* Cheyenne. My grandmother is calling in the loans, and if I—we—don't pull this deal together, my slice of the American dream is going down the swirler. I will do whatever I have to do to make this happen, and I'm counting on you to help."

"Maybe you should be talking to your grandmother," Cheyenne reasoned, testy, looking both ways before she pulled out onto the highway fronting McKettrickCo's Indian Rock offices. "Not me."

"My grandmother is in Knightsbridge, thinking of ways to cut off my balls and cauterize the wound. I am most definitely talking to *you.*"

"How many times do I have to tell you? I'm not doing this. I'm not digging up dirt on Jesse McKettrick so you can force him into selling you the land. There *isn't* any dirt, Nigel. Get that through your head."

"Don't be so sure," Nigel retorted slyly. "Get that through *your* head. If you do anything to blow this deal, I'll keep you tied up in court until the next ice age."

"It's not going to happen," she said.

"See that it does," Nigel warned. "I've been getting a lot of calls from the investors. They've seen the plans for the condos. They love them. They're wondering when we can get this thing rolling. With every day that passes, they're a little less convinced that I'm Wonder Boy."

"Build the development somewhere else," Cheyenne said. It wasn't the first time she'd made the suggestion, and she knew Nigel wouldn't listen. She felt like the lone voice of reason, calling in the wilderness. And her throat was getting raw.

"They want that property. *I* want that property."

She'd reached the turnoff to home without being aware of the drive from work, which was disturbing. She signaled, bumped over the railroad tracks. "Do you know what your problem is, Nigel? You're spoiled. The land belongs to Jesse. He loves it. He's not giving it up, okay? Let this go."

Let me go.

"He owns a third of the Triple M," Nigel argued. "He doesn't need that five-hundred acres."

"There's a spring up there," Cheyenne said. "It feeds the creek that flows through the middle of the ranch. They depend on the water, at least part of the year."

"Promise him the rights to it, then."

"I tried that. Jesse's not stupid, Nigel. He knows a promise like that isn't worth the proverbial paper it's written on."

Her purse rang again. She remembered the second cell phone, the one Keegan had given her that morning.

Most likely, nobody else had the number yet. "Gotta go," she said. "My boss is calling."

"*I'm* your boss!"

Cheyenne brought the Escalade to a stop in the yard, thumbed Nigel into satellite-oblivion and fumbled for the other phone.

"Hello?"

There was a smile in Keegan's voice. "Just checking to see if the phone works," he said. "Hope I'm not interrupting anything."

Cheyenne swallowed. Something popped and she looked into the rearview mirror to see Ayanna chortling in behind her in the van. "I'm glad you called, Keegan. I really need to talk to you."

"So talk."

"Not on the phone."

"Okay," Keegan said. "We can meet somewhere. Back at the office? Your place? Mine?"

"I promised to play poker at Sierra's tonight."

"I could stop by there."

"It isn't something I want anybody else to know about. Just you and Rance."

"I'll be in the office early tomorrow morning," Keegan said. "Around eight? I'll bring breakfast."

Ayanna was out of the van and reacting to the Escalade with humorous exaggeration, like a mime.

"Eight," Cheyenne agreed.

Ayanna tapped on the driver's-side window.

"Gotta go," Cheyenne said.

"See you tomorrow," Keegan replied.

They disconnected.

"I'm in big trouble," Cheyenne told her mother after shutting off the engine and climbing down from the SUV.

Ayanna widened her eyes. "Oh, I can see that," she teased. "You're driving a Cadillac, on McKettrickCo's dime. Things just seem to go from bad to worse."

Cheyenne sighed. "You know what I mean," she said, starting toward the house. She was due at Sierra's in a little under an hour, and she wanted to switch out the pantsuit for jeans and a T-shirt, loosen up her hair, find out how Mitch's day had gone.

Her mother fell into step beside her. "I take it you didn't tell Keegan the truth today."

Probably because she knew she was in the wrong, the remark stung. "I wouldn't be driving an Escalade if I had," she said, with her voice drawn back as tautly as her hair. "I'd have had to hitchhike home."

"Telling the truth is *important,* Cheyenne."

The tension was too much; the recoil came. "The way *you* told the truth, Mom? All those times you lied for Dad? Lied to his creditors—his employers, on the rare occasions when he had a job? When you told the police you hadn't seen him? When you told a court of law that he was with you the night he robbed a convenience store in Phoenix to feed his gambling habit? Is *that* what you're preaching, Mom?"

Ayanna paled, and tears filled her eyes. "Cash *was* with me that night," she said.

"Mother, they had the whole thing on tape,

remember? Security cameras don't lie."

"It was a mistake. There was something wrong with the camera, or the film, or something—"

"Stop lying to me, Mother. Stop lying to *yourself.* If you were with Dad when that store was robbed, then you must have been driving the getaway car!"

Ayanna had never struck Cheyenne before, but in that moment, she lost it. The flat of her hand smacked Cheyenne's cheek, hard.

The two women stared at each other, mother and daughter, each on one side of a wide chasm that might never close.

The shock took Cheyenne's breath away. She started up the porch steps, but the sound of an arriving car made her turn around.

Jesse's truck was coming up the driveway.

No, Cheyenne thought.

Ayanna, still standing in the yard, glanced up at her, and there were tears in her eyes.

Jesse brought the truck to a stop, and Cheyenne saw Mitch's wheelchair in the back. Spotted her brother next, sitting on the passenger side, grinning at her through the windshield.

"I thought Mitch went to Sedona with Bronwyn," Cheyenne mused.

"So did I," Ayanna said stiffly. "Apparently we were wrong."

Jesse jumped down from the truck, walked back and opened the tailgate, hauled the wheelchair out and set it on the ground. A stray thought rustled through the underbrush in Cheyenne's mind, poked its head up like a gopher. The chair was heavy, and though both she and Ayanna could manage it, it always took a lot of maneuvering, dragging and sweaty effort.

Jesse handled the thing as easily as he would a lawn chair.

And then there was Mitch. He had to weigh as much as Jesse did, and yet Jesse carried him without any sign of strain.

He set Mitch in the chair, and Cheyenne really looked at her brother's face. He seemed windblown, as though he'd spent the day riding in a convertible with the top down, and he was smiling from ear to ear.

"Ask me what I did today!" he shouted.

"What did you do today?" Ayanna asked, very softly.

Mitch punched the air with his fist. "I rode a horse. Not just around and around in a corral, either. *On the range.* Jesse and I went clear up on top of the ridge."

Cheyenne looked at Jesse, then back at Mitch. "You're kidding, right?" she asked. "*Tell me* you didn't take a chance like that—"

"He did fine," Jesse said quietly.

"Leave it alone, Cheyenne," Ayanna added.

Didn't *any* of them understand? Another spinal injury could *kill* Mitch, or render his arms as useless as his legs, which, for him, would probably be even worse than dying.

Not trusting herself to say another word, Cheyenne turned, wrenched open the screen door and went inside. The rusted spring pulled the door shut with a crash.

· · ·

"Damn it," Jesse muttered, watching Cheyenne vanish into the house, flinching when the screen door slammed.

Hard to believe she was the same woman he'd made love to the night before.

Ayanna approached, laid a hand on his arm. "Thanks, Jesse," she said quietly as Mitch rolled up the ramp to the porch. "For taking my boy out riding, I mean."

Ayanna was grateful. Mitch was grateful. But the Bridges vote clearly wasn't unanimous.

Jesse sighed. "You're welcome," he answered dismally.

She smiled. "Cheyenne's been through a lot," she said. "She's not used to things going well. Always waiting for the other shoe to drop—the next terrible thing to happen. Give her a little time, Jesse. And then ask her about Nigel."

The uneasiness was back, with a wallop. Jesse had managed to elude it all day because he could escape just about anything on horseback, but now he was on foot again. "Nigel?" he repeated. "Her old boss?"

"Ask her," Ayanna said. She paused, staring at the house for a long, long time. When she turned back to Jesse, her eyes were full of ancient sorrows. "I'd invite you in," she told him, "but right now, things are a little awkward."

"*Awkward* doesn't cover it," he said. "Anyway, I've got a game in Flag."

Ayanna nodded.

266

Jesse said goodbye, turned and went back to his truck.

There was no game in Flag.

But he'd find one if he looked.

He drove out onto the highway, headed for Indian Rock. Passed through town, saw Keegan's Jag and Rance's SUV parked outside the Roadhouse.

On an impulse, and because for some curious reason he didn't want to play poker with a bunch of strangers, or even back at Lucky's with the usual suspects, he stopped, parked and went inside.

His cousins sat at a corner table, deep in some earnest discussion.

Jesse waved off Roselle's offer to escort him, with a grin meant to soften the rejection, and joined the party.

"Is this a private argument," Jesse asked, dragging back a chair, "or can anybody join in?"

Rance leaned back abruptly.

Keegan looked as if he were going to slam his palms down on top of the table. "Sit right down," he drawled ironically, since Jesse was already sitting.

"What's going on?" Jesse asked, reaching for a menu.

"Nothing," Rance snapped.

"Try again," Jesse said. Sirloin steak? Fried chicken? He sighed. What he wanted wasn't on any menu. He closed the vinyl-clad folder and set it back in its customary place between the napkin holder and the salt and pepper. "The two of you are about ready to tear each other's ears off."

Rance and Keegan exchanged glares.

"It's none of your damn business how I raise my kids," Rance told Keegan. "Mr. Divorced Father."

"And I thought it was about going public," Jesse said moderately. "Just goes to show I'm out of touch."

"You've been out of touch since high school," Keegan told him.

"Nice to be in the bosom of my family," Jesse replied. "I can always depend on you two for a warm welcome."

Both of them turned to him, still glaring.

"What?" he asked, spreading his hands.

"Don't you have a poker game or something?" Rance asked.

Jesse pretended to be hurt. "Are you trying to get rid of me?"

Keegan huffed out a sigh. Ignored Jesse and focused on Rance. "Look, maybe I shouldn't have said anything. But it can't be good, your leaving Rianna and Maeve with Cora so much."

"Cora is their grandmother," Rance said, but there wasn't much steam behind the words. "She loves them."

"You're their father," Keegan answered. "They need you."

Rance looked away. There was something bleak in the way he held his head and the set of his shoulders.

Jesse scooted his chair back. "Maybe I'll go find a game after all," he said.

"Stay," Keegan said huskily.

Jesse pulled up close to the table again. "Are we through with the heavy stuff?"

"It's *family* stuff," Rance pointed out.

"Speaking of family stuff," Keegan said, eyeing Jesse's jeans and cotton shirt, "Travis and Sierra are getting married Saturday after next. You picked up your tux yet?"

"No," Jesse replied. He'd sent the suit to the cleaner's after his last trip to New York, about six months back, and had forgotten all about it.

"You're the best man," Keegan reminded him.

Jesse grinned. "Jealous?"

Keegan laughed. "Hell, no," he said. "But if you show up at that wedding looking as though you've been herding cattle, like you do right now, I wouldn't give a plugged nickel for your hide."

Rance signaled the waitress, ordered three draft beers and a double order of nachos with everything. The steaks would come later, if at all.

"How did Cheyenne's first day go?" Jesse asked. He'd intended to put that question to Cheyenne herself, but she wasn't speaking to him.

"She's settling in," Keegan said.

"Something wrong there," Rance reflected, after downing half his beer.

"Like what?" Jesse asked.

"Yeah," Keegan agreed. "Like what?"

Rance shrugged his big shoulders. "She's a beauty," he said, staring off into space. "Really brightens up the office. But she's up to something."

Since Rance wasn't known for his people skills, the remark seemed odd.

"Cheyenne has a degree in business and plenty of experience," Keegan said, as if it were *his* place to defend Cheyenne. "She does one hell of a lot more than 'brighten up the office'!"

"Take a breath," Rance said, sounding bored. "I was just making a comment."

"You know what you are?" Keegan demanded. "You're a *chauvinist*."

Rance laughed. "You just figuring that out?"

The nachos arrived. Jesse helped himself. "You ought to spring for some furniture," he said to Keegan. "For Cheyenne's office, I mean. The place looks like a monk's cell."

"When did you see it?" Keegan asked. "Or a monk's cell, for that matter."

"Today. I would have said hello, but neither of you were around."

"She has a desk, a credenza, all that," Keegan said. "What else does she need?"

"Maybe a couch," Jesse said, snagging a few extra jalapeño slices off the nachos to sprinkle over his own portion.

Rance grinned.

Keegan went red in the neck. "A *couch?*"

Jesse munched for a while. "You have one in your office. So does Rance. What's the big deal?"

Rance gave a chuckle.

"Jesse," Keegan warned. "What the hell do you care

if Cheyenne has a couch in her office or not?"

"And you think *I've* been alone too long," Rance said, rolling his eyes.

Keegan narrowed his. "Jesse?"

"Oh, get a grip, Keegan," Rance put in. "He's already sleeping with the woman."

"What makes you think that?" Jesse asked, sounding as innocent as he could.

"I met her on the road this morning," Rance answered. "The sun was barely up. Since Keegan's place is across the creek from mine, I'd have noticed an extra car over there. She sure didn't spend the night with me, so, by process of elimination, she must have been at your place. Add that to the way you two were dancing at Travis and Sierra's shindig, and the books balance to the penny."

"Damn it," Keegan said.

"I know you like her, Keeg," Rance reasoned, sounding mellow and wise, like some visiting therapist on a radio talk show, "but she's obviously fallen for the cowboy, here. Do yourself a favor and stop hoping the cards are going to turn."

Keegan and Jesse did some glaring of their own across the plate of nachos.

"And while I'm giving out sage advice," Rance went on, focusing on Jesse now, and as full of shit as ever, "you'd do well to watch your step. Something's not right. You're in over your head."

"Is that right?" Jesse asked with deceptive mildness. One more beer and they'd have all the ingredients for good old-fashioned fisticuffs in the parking lot. He loved his cousins like brothers, but it might feel good to throw a few punches, the way they used to do out at the ranch, behind the old barn.

"I'm not saying she's bad, Jesse," Rance said, and this time, he sounded damnably sincere. Even concerned. "There are folks around here who would remind you that she's Cash Bridges's daughter and the huckleberry doesn't fall far from the bush, but I'm not one of them. All I'm telling you is, I've got the same feeling I did just before I stepped on that rattler, down by the creek, when I was a kid."

Jesse remembered the incident. He and Keegan had been there when it had happened. Rance, nine or ten at the time, had been rushed to a hospital in Flagstaff, and he'd nearly died on the way. He'd had to have surgery, once the doctors had pumped him full of antivenom and stabilized him and, ever since then, he'd been proud of the scar.

"Now you're psychic," Keegan scoffed. "You didn't have a premonition that day. You were trying to run off with the mess of trout *I* caught. You jumped over a log and stepped on the snake."

The waitress came back. They ordered another round of beer and T-bone steaks.

"We keep drinking like this," Keegan said, being the practical one, "and we're going to need a designated driver."

Rance belched copiously. "And who are we going to designate, genius?"

"You could call Cora. She's right down the street."

"Sure," Rance said. "I'm going to get my mother-in-law on the horn and tell her I'm too drunk to drive."

"Better than calling her from jail," Keegan said.

"Or," Jesse suggested, "we could stay sober."

Keegan and Rance considered the idea.

"Naaahhh," they said in chorus.

It was all downhill from there.

CHAPTER FIFTEEN

"I PAID OUR ENTRANCE FEES for the tournament," Elaine announced when the ladies' poker club convened on the screened sunporch running alongside Sierra's family home. For party leftovers, the spread was pretty fancy—barbecued spareribs, coleslaw, cold chicken and about nine kinds of dessert. "We're in!"

Cheyenne, who had been thinking about whether or not the house was haunted, when she wasn't wishing she hadn't been so quick to cut Jesse off at the pockets when he'd brought Mitch home, snapped back to the here and now in an instant. "When *is* the tournament?"

"The preliminary round is next Saturday afternoon," Elaine answered. "At the casino down the road." She held out her hand, palm up. "Fifty bucks from each of you. Fork it over."

Sierra, Janice and Cheyenne all paid up.

"This was a crazy idea," Sierra said. She was probably thinking about her wedding, which was scheduled for the Saturday following the tournament. "We're all terrible at this, except for Cheyenne."

"You're not terrible," Cheyenne lied.

"Yes, we are," Janice said, resigned.

"Do you think everybody on the World Poker Tour is a seasoned pro?" Elaine asked, separating twenties from tens and tucking the bills into her wallet. "Why, some of those people are rank amateurs. And they win *big bucks.*"

"*Rank* is the word for us." Janice sighed.

"We've paid our entrance fee and told half the town we're going to help pay for the in-patient wing on the clinic," Elaine said. "Now you want to just forget it?"

Please, God, Cheyenne prayed silently.

"No!" Elaine cried, with all the verve of an old-time preacher rallying a revival crowd to seek salvation. "We're going to follow through. And one of us is going all the way, too!"

"Don't mind her," Janice whispered loudly behind one hand. "Elaine's in sales, so she listens to a lot of motivational CDs in her car. She goes to seminars, too."

"It wouldn't hurt you," Elaine complained indignantly, "to think about something besides soap operas and feeding the cows."

"Time out," Sierra said. "We started this. We might as well finish. And it's not as if any of us are *really* going to end up at the final table in Vegas."

She was right about that, Cheyenne thought. What was the harm in playing in a local tournament? They'd be aced out in the first few hands of cards anyway. Then they could all go back to their regular lives— Sierra to being a bride, Elaine to selling houses, Janice to feeding cows and watching soap operas.

And what was *her* regular life? Cheyenne asked herself.

She had her new job—and, regrettably, her *old* one, too. She had her family.

She had screaming orgasms with Jesse.

Provided he hadn't written her off.

"Thoughts," Elaine lectured, shaking her finger at one and all, "are *things*. If you don't *believe* you'll succeed, you won't."

Everybody nodded, tacitly promising to believe.

Believing, hopeless as it was, was easier than arguing with Elaine.

The evening went by rapidly, probably because Cheyenne was having fun, and she had absolutely nothing to look forward to when it was over. At least there had been some comic relief while they were playing.

Janice had gone all in on a seven and a three, off-suit.

Elaine was as serious as a kidney stone, the whole time, studying her cards like holy writ.

Sierra bet on a king and queen, figuring that made a marriage.

Oh, yeah, Cheyenne thought. *Dolly Brunson, eat your heart out.*

After Elaine and Janice left, Cheyenne stayed to help Sierra clean up. Liam had already gone to bed, and there was no sign of Travis. The house was quiet, in an expectant sort of way.

"You promised to tell me about the ghosts," Cheyenne said shyly, as they stood side by side at the sink, Cheyenne rinsing plates, glasses and silverware, and Sierra sticking them in the dishwasher.

Sierra smiled. "They're not ghosts," she said. "Not really."

"What, then?" Cheyenne asked. She was being nosy, but she couldn't help it. Anything supernatural gave her delicious shivers.

"It's hard to explain," Sierra told her. "But have you ever thought about how time might not be linear—you know, past, present, future—but all of it happening simultaneously instead?"

"I've considered it," Cheyenne said. "You're talking about different dimensions, existing side by side?"

Sierra nodded. "And sometimes intersecting," she added. "Liam sees Tobias on a regular basis. Once, I saw Hannah—Hannah McKettrick, that is—she was an ancestor of mine, and lived—lives—in this house."

Cheyenne shut off the faucet, groped for a dish towel and dried her hands. "But you don't think she's a ghost?"

"I think she's as real—and as alive—as we are."

"Wow," Cheyenne marveled.

Sierra bit her lower lip, then looked directly into Cheyenne's eyes. "I don't talk about this a lot," she said carefully. "I mean, there have been rumors about this house for years, according to my mother and a few other people who would be in a position to know. But I don't want to stir up talk. It could be hard on Liam, at school."

"I understand," Cheyenne said. "I won't say anything to anyone else."

Sierra's smile was sudden and dazzling. "Thanks," she said.

Twenty minutes later, driving toward town, Cheyenne considered taking a detour. Pictured herself heading up Jesse's long driveway, knocking on his door.

When he answered—if he answered—she'd apologize for the way she'd acted when he'd brought Mitch home earlier in the evening. Try to explain that sometimes the fear of seeing her brother get hurt again just surged up out of her psyche, like a banshee, and possessed her.

On the other hand, what Jesse had done *was* reckless. Mitch was normal, and it was good of Jesse to treat him that way, but he was also vulnerable. Another injury would not only crush his body; it would crush his spirit, too.

He'd almost given up the first time, Mitch had.

Cheyenne and Ayanna had simply refused to let him go.

They'd kept vigils by his bedside, even when he'd been unconscious, holding his hand. Whispering to him. Telling him to hold on, to fight with everything he had, to *come back.*

Weeks after he'd regained consciousness, Mitch had

admitted that he'd heard them. Followed their voices home to his body. Back to the pain, and the limitations.

Once or twice, Cheyenne had seen a reproachful question in his eyes.

Why didn't you let me go?

Cheyenne drove past Jesse's road.

He wouldn't understand.

WYATT TERP AMBLED into the Roadhouse on about the umpteenth round of microbrews. With the unerring instincts of his almost-namesake, he zeroed right in on the McKettrick table.

"I *know* you boys aren't planning to drive," he said amiably.

Rance gave him a bleary once-over. "Did somebody call you?" he asked and cast a suspicious glance around the restaurant.

"Nobody called me," Wyatt answered, leaning in and bracing his hands against the table edge. "I stop by the Roadhouse three or four times on every shift. You know that. Now, is this a celebration, or a wake?"

"Something in between," Keegan said. He probably hadn't been this drunk since college, and Jesse could see, even in his own profound state of inebriation, that his cousin's regular, buttoned-down self was wondering what the hell had hit him.

Wyatt's gaze moved to Jesse. "I bet you couldn't touch the floor with your hat right about now," he observed. "By the way, those rounders from Lucky's haven't been back since I gave them a speeding ticket and told them to keep moving."

"Good work, Wyatt," Jesse said with a salute.

"John," Wyatt said.

"Wyatt's a proud name," Keegan put in. "I don't know why you don't want to use it."

"John's a good name, too," Wyatt told him. "And it goes a lot better with Terp."

"That," Rance said, with an accompanying belch that sounded as if it came from someplace around his ankles, "is a matter of opinion."

"Well," Wyatt said reasonably, "here's *my* opinion. The three of you are drunk as squirrels rolling in corn mash. My advice would be, settle up your bill, and I'll drive you as far as Cora's. I haven't got time to go all the way out to the Triple M."

"I can't let my kids see me like this," Rance said.

"Like what?" Jesse asked.

"Drunk," Keegan explained.

"Oh," Jesse said.

Wyatt sighed. "Let's go," he said. "If you don't want to go to Cora's, I'll drop you off at the motel on the other end of town."

Jesse got about half-sober when he stepped outside and the fresh air hit him. Unfortunately, half wasn't enough to suit Wyatt. "I'd rather sleep in my truck," he said.

"Fine," Wyatt agreed. "Let's have your keys."

"People are going to think we've been arrested," Rance fretted, looking around as if he expected to see that a crowd of spectators had gathered. Given that Indian Rock would have a hard time coming up with a crowd for anything less than the Second Coming, Jesse was amused.

"We ought to call a cab instead of riding in the squad car," Rance said.

"There *aren't* any cabs," Keegan pointed out.

"Get in the squad car," Wyatt said.

A tour bus, making a pit stop on the way to Sedona or the Cliffcastle casino, pulled in and disgorged a flock of gapers.

"These people," Wyatt told them, "are not under arrest."

"Oh, that was great, Wyatt," Rance protested.

"John," Wyatt corrected, beginning to sound testy.

"Whatever," Rance said.

In the end, Jesse surrendered his keys to Wyatt and slept in his truck.

God only knew where Keegan and Rance wound up.

"YOU LOOK TERRIBLE," Cheyenne was emboldened to say at eight the next morning when she arrived at Keegan's office for the meeting they'd agreed upon. She'd fully intended to tell him about the pickle she was in with Nigel but she'd lost her courage. When she'd arrived home from Sierra's the night before, she'd found Mitch and Bronwyn sitting on the front porch, sharing their dreams. Mitch's was a shot at a job at McKettrickCo.

If she got fired, he probably wouldn't have a chance.

Keegan was swilling strong coffee, and Cheyenne would have sworn he was wearing the same clothes he'd had on the day before. He was clearly *not* in the mood to hear confession—or grant absolution.

"I had a very bad night," he said grimly.

"I can see that. Maybe you should go home. Eat chicken soup or something."

Keegan paled. "Please," he said, setting the coffee down to rub his temples, "do not mention food again."

"Okay," Cheyenne said uncertainly.

"Doughnuts, anybody?" Myrna chimed from the doorway of Keegan's office. "I got the goopy ones, with lots of frosting and sprinkles—"

"Excuse me," Keegan said and bolted past them.

"What's the matter with him?" Cheyenne asked.

"He's cracking under the pressure," Myrna said cheerfully.

"What pressure?"

"He works too hard. He's just been through a nasty divorce. If he had any sense at all—which he doesn't, because he's a boneheaded McKettrick, through and through—he'd take a vacation." Myrna spoke with great affection, and a sort of blithe fretfulness, oddly juxtaposed to her actual words.

"We were supposed to have a meeting," Cheyenne confided.

"Ain't gonna happen," Myrna replied, shoving a pink bakery box at her. "Doughnut?"

JESSE'S HEAD WAS about to split wide open.

He sat up in the driver's seat of his truck with a groan.

As luck would have it, the Roadhouse was doing a brisk breakfast trade. He tried to smile when the preacher walked by and gave him a happy little wave.

Had he been in a fight? It felt as if somebody had kicked in his ribs.

No, he realized, as his brain began to clear a little. He'd probably fallen asleep with the knob on the gearshift poking into his side.

Real bright, McKettrick.

He dug in both front pants pockets, looking for his keys, before he remembered that Wyatt had taken them. On his worst day, Jesse wouldn't have driven drunk, but Wyatt, of course, wouldn't have taken that chance.

Now, he was stuck, sitting there in his truck like a damn fool while half the town paraded by.

This was what he got for being the one person in North America who didn't carry a cell phone.

On top of it all, he needed to piss like a racehorse.

No way was he walking the length of the Roadhouse, passing by every jam-packed table in the place, to get to the men's room.

He glanced speculatively toward the alley.

Not a good day for taking chances.

"Hell," he said, closing his eyes, hoping that would make the headache let up a little.

A rap on the window made him turn.

Travis was standing on the running board, grinning in at him. Holding up his keys.

Jesse pushed the door open, forcing Travis to jump

clear or be knocked to the asphalt.

"Wyatt sent me," Travis said with mock seriousness. "As an officer of the court, I can't let you have these keys until I know for sure that you're sober."

Jesse was sober, all right. And he cut loose with a blue streak to make his point.

Travis handed over the keys. "Rance ended up at the motel. Keegan spent the night at the office. What the hell happened here?"

"I don't have time to discuss it," Jesse said, having cooled off a little. His bladder was screaming and, short of risking arrest on charges of indecent exposure by whipping it out behind the Dumpster, he was out of choices.

He headed for the nearest gas station.

Travis was waiting when he came out of the john.

"Maybe you ought to let me take you home," he said. "Sierra and I could pick up your truck later. Drop it off at your place."

"I'm *fine,*" Jesse said.

"You don't sound fine. You don't *look* fine, either."

Jesse ignored him. Got back into the truck and went straight for the Triple M. When he got there, the horses were still out in the pasture, from the day before, having a good old time.

Jesse swore off booze forever.

Climbed over the corral fence, opened the gate and whistled for the herd.

The sound sliced between the right and left sides of his brain like a sharp ax, swung hard.

The horses galloped toward him.

He stepped back, watched as they thundered into the corral, then the barn.

They were *horses,* he reminded himself. One night in a grassy pasture, with plenty of water, did not amount to animal abuse. But he felt guilty, just the same.

He gave them each a handful of grain, a rare treat, since too much of it wasn't healthy for most horses, then brushed them all down for good measure. It was a kind of personal penance.

By the time he went inside the house, not even stopping to make coffee, he wanted nothing but a hot shower, a couple of aspirin and about twenty hours of sleep.

That was probably why he didn't realize he wasn't alone until it was way too late.

KEEGAN DID SOMETHING unprecedented that day. At least, it was unprecedented according to Myrna. He took the day off. Rance didn't come in at all. The staff, which consisted of a few people in the mail room and several secretaries, worked diligently behind the scenes.

Cheyenne made phone calls to various junior colleges in the area and continued mapping out the plan Keegan had hired her to develop and execute.

On her lunch hour, she drove over to the supermarket, bought a sandwich in the deli and offered Ayanna half as a peace offering.

"I'm sorry," she said.

Ayanna looked small and forlorn, hunched at the table outside the employee's lunch room, in her jeans and her perky blue vest. "Me, too," she replied. "I shouldn't have hit you." She stopped, clapped her hand over her mouth for a moment, her eyes filling with tears. "Oh, Cheyenne. I actually *hit* you."

"It's okay, Mom."

"It *isn't* okay!"

"You're right. It isn't. But it's over." Cheyenne took her mother's hand, squeezed gently. "I'm sorry," she repeated.

"I'm not a liar!" Ayanna whispered. Fortunately, the few other workers taking their lunch break at the same time as Ayanna had chosen to stay inside.

"I know," Cheyenne said.

"No, you don't. You think I lied for your father. In court. *Under oath!* Okay—I did lie to his bosses a few times, and people he owed money to, because we didn't *have* any money to pay them with, Cheyenne— but he *was* with me the night that store was robbed. We were across the street, at Denny's."

Cheyenne sighed. On television, there would have been a lengthy trial, with lots of witnesses. In real life, Cash Bridges's case was just one of many. He'd been arrested, charged and convicted. Ayanna had testified on his behalf. There hadn't been a jury. An assistant D.A. had played back the film from the security camera, and Cash had been sentenced to five years in prison.

He'd died in a fight between inmates, eighteen months later.

"He *did* leave the table to buy cigarettes," Ayanna said miserably.

Cheyenne stared at her. "How long was he gone?"

"Long enough," Ayanna said.

"Did you tell the police that?"

"Of course not. I was young, I was stupid. I had a daughter to raise. Useless as he was, I didn't want Cash to go to jail."

"You knew he was guilty."

"No," Ayanna protested. "I know he left the table for five minutes or so."

"Mom, what about the tape?"

"It was just somebody who looked like him."

"Okay, stay in denial."

"If you saw that tape, you'd know it wasn't your dad."

"It's long gone by now, Mom." She sighed, feeling inexpressibly weary. "Maybe you're right. Maybe it wasn't Dad." *Maybe if I hold my arms out, a flock of cartoon birds will flutter down and light on my dainty little Snow White wrists.* "The point is, we're never going to get anywhere talking about this."

"You're right."

Cheyenne hugged her. "Eat your hoagie," she said.

"I've tried to be a good mother," Ayanna told her.

"You *are* a good mother."

Ayanna sniffled. Her eyes shone behind a film of tears. "You ought to eat this sandwich," she said. "You're too skinny."

286

"I wish," Cheyenne said. She hugged Ayanna again. "I'd better go, Mom. I've got lots to do back at the office."

Ayanna caught hold of her hand when she would have walked away. "Tell Jesse the truth," she said. "Tell him *the truth,* Cheyenne, before it's too late."

Cheyenne bit her lower lip, nodded.

"Promise?"

"Promise."

"Today?"

"Today."

Ayanna approached, kissed Cheyenne on the cheek and dashed back into the store to bag groceries.

CHEYENNE LEFT THE OFFICE promptly at five that afternoon, called home from the car to make sure Mitch was all right. He answered on the second ring.

"Hey," Cheyenne said.

"Hey," Mitch responded.

"You doing okay?"

He bristled. "I'm not helpless, you know."

"I know," Cheyenne answered. She didn't ask if Ayanna was home yet because she'd seen the van in the lot when she'd driven past the supermarket. "Anything you'd like me to pick up?"

"Bronwyn's bringing pizza," Mitch said. "Feel free to stay gone for a while. Mom's staying after work for a union meeting or something."

"The coast is clear, then," Cheyenne told him. "I'm on my way out to Jesse's place, and I don't know when I'll be back. Tell Mom, okay?"

"Okay," Mitch promised. "Chey?"

"What?"

"Did you ask your boss about—?"

"Yes," Cheyenne said carefully. She'd wanted to have this conversation in person, *after* she knew how Jesse in particular and the McKettricks in general would react to the news that she hadn't been completely honest with them. Now, she was on dangerous emotional ground. If she went down in flames, most likely so would Mitch and all his hopes of getting into the training program. "I mentioned that you'd like to participate in the project. Keegan didn't give me a definitive answer, Mitch. That's the bottom line."

"You're going to tell Jesse about Nigel?"

Cheyenne swallowed hard. "Yes."

Mitch's response surprised her, though she realized, immediately after the fact, that it shouldn't have. "Jesse's a good man, Chey. He might be mad at first, but he'll understand."

"I hope you're right," Cheyenne said, but she was doubtful, and she knew Mitch could hear it in her voice.

"I'm right," Mitch told her confidently.

"See you later," she said.

"I'm betting on sometime tomorrow," Mitch replied.

Cheyenne said goodbye and hung up.

Jesse's house was rimmed by the fiery golds and crimsons of a sunset that would flare brightly and then dim by degrees of lavender and purple as the twilight crept in. In all the time the earth had existed, there had never been a sky show exactly like this, and there would never be one again.

The glare almost blinded her, even with her sunglasses. She made out the distinctive shape of Jesse's truck, parked at an odd angle near the barn, but that was about all.

She parked at the top of the driveway, spent a few moments working up her courage before she got out of the Escalade.

There was no answer when she knocked at the kitchen door, but she could hear the faint, smoky strains of jazz coming from somewhere inside. She considered looking for the front entrance and ringing the bell, or going around to the back.

Instead, she opened door number one, stepped nervously over the threshold.

"Jesse?" she called.

Nothing, but she thought the jazz went softer.

She took a few more feet of ground. "Jesse?"

The stereo went off.

A premonition of inexplicable doom overtook Cheyenne.

"Jesse!" she called again, but her voice shook. Anybody listening would know it was pure bravado.

Cheyenne thought of the two men at Lucky's. An icy chill trickled down her spine.

They would have attended to business—beaten Jesse to a pulp or even killed him—and left—wouldn't they? Not stuck around, listening to jazz.

On the other hand, some criminals delighted in doing that kind of thing.

Heart pounding, Cheyenne fished her cell phone out of her handbag, clasped it in one sweaty palm and listened hard. She shouldn't have called out—now, if there *was* someone else in the house, besides Jesse, they knew she was about to discover them.

Should she call 911?

And say what? *Hello. My name is Cheyenne Bridges, and I'm trespassing, and I think someone else is, too?*

When the cops showed up, she'd probably be arrested, and she'd feel like a fool.

She slipped out of her shoes and moved cautiously through the dining room. The windows faced east, so there wasn't much light.

The living room was empty, too.

Terrified of what she'd find when she got there, equally afraid of never making it that far in the first place, Cheyenne headed for Jesse's bedroom.

The double doors stood partially open.

Cheyenne peeked through.

Another woman peeked back.

Both of them shrieked.

In the dazzling light of the same sunset she'd admired earlier, now pouring through the windows arching around Jesse's bed, Cheyenne saw him sit up.

Meanwhile, the woman on the other side of the threshold stood with one hand pressed to her heart. She was a stunningly beautiful blonde, as tall as Jesse, clad in a white T-shirt, probably one of his, and nothing else.

Finally, the pieces fell into place.

Cheyenne backed up a few steps.

"Shit," she heard Jesse say.

Cheyenne turned to run.

Jesse must have pushed past the blonde because there was no sign of her when he caught up to Cheyenne in the living room, made her stop and face him.

"Cheyenne," he said, "listen to me—"

"No," Cheyenne said, praying she wouldn't cry. "*You* listen to *me,* Jesse McKettrick. I came here to tell you that I still work for Nigel Meerland. He wanted me to spy on you, dig up some dirt, so you'd have to sell us the land—"

Jesse's face went still. The blue of his eyes, usually like a summer sky, was glacial. He'd been gripping Cheyenne's shoulders, and he let go so suddenly that she almost fell.

The blonde appeared behind him. "Hi," she said, putting out a hand. "My name is Brandi and I'm—"

"She's my wife," Jesse said.

Brandi must have been an actress because she looked confused, and she was damn convincing, too. "I'm your *ex*-wife—"

Jesse's gaze bored into Cheyenne. "You lied to me," he said.

"You lied to *me,*" Cheyenne replied.

"Will somebody listen?" Brandi asked, sounding plaintive.

"No," Cheyenne said.

"No," Jesse said, at precisely the same moment.

"Oh, *crap,*" Brandi said. "This is all—"

Cheyenne bolted.

CHAPTER SIXTEEN

LIKE A MAN WAKING UP in the middle of a nightmare, Jesse turned to stare at Brandi, standing there in his living room, wearing one of his T-shirts and nothing else, as far as he could tell.

"What the *fuck* are you doing here?" he demanded.

Brandi's plump lower lip wobbled, but her huge eyes were defiant. "If you'd carry a cell phone, like everybody *else* on the planet, or just check your voice mail once in a blue moon, you'd *know* what I'm doing here!"

Jesse sighed. Some of the stunned fury subsided.

He ought to go after Cheyenne, he knew that. She'd blown out of the house like a hurricane wind, and he felt a twinge of fear to think of her driving the dark, crooked miles from his house to Indian Rock in that state. But his bare feet seemed glued to the floor, and he didn't know what he'd say to her, anyway. "I heard your message, Brandi," he said, with an equanimity that cost him plenty. "Something about a guy and a lot of money. I called you back, and I got *your* voice mail."

Brandi was in a huff. She looked around, found the phone resting on an end table, grabbed up the receiver

292

and shoved it at him. "*Listen,* if you don't believe me."

Jesse sighed again. Sank onto the edge of the nine-foot leather sofa his mother had ordered up on one of her furniture-buying sprees. "Talk to me," he said warily, well aware that he was letting himself in for something.

"I can't. You're almost naked."

"Shit," Jesse said. It was true. He'd pulled on a pair of briefs after his shower and fallen into bed, facefirst. The next thing he knew, there were two women shrieking in fright in the doorway of his bedroom.

Never a good sign.

Calmer now, he got up off the sofa, went into his room and pulled on yesterday's jeans. Dragged a T-shirt on over his head. When he got back, Brandi was curled up in his father's big leather chair, swathed in an afghan one of his sisters had knit during an earth-mother phase.

Her blond hair was rumpled, her eyes and mouth pouty.

"What were you doing in my room?" Jesse demanded, taking his former place on the sofa.

"This is a big house," Brandi said. "I was scared. I was tired from driving all the way here from California, and you weren't home, so I stretched out on that little couch in your bedroom. I must have fallen asleep."

The couch in question faced away from the bed, toward the fireplace, and Jesse rarely used it, except as a depository for dirty laundry.

"I came in," he said carefully. "I took a shower. Don't tell me you slept through that."

Brandi's lip started wobbling again. "I didn't. But I thought I might scare you to death if I just popped up and said 'hello,' or you might shoot me or something, so I decided to wait until you woke up. I fell asleep again, and when I woke up, I was hungry. I raided the fridge and put some music on the stereo, thinking that might bring you around—you know—gently. *Then,* I think I hear somebody moving around in the house. This place is *big,* and it's old. I figured it might even be a ghost. So I went back to your room to wake you up, but you were practically comatose—"

That much was true, Jesse thought ruefully.

"Okay, okay," he said. "I'm up to speed on the arrival part. Now, if you'll just explain the unexpected pleasure of your company?"

"The guy I wanted to tell you about—*on the phone,* so I wouldn't have to take time off from work and school—is named Nigel Meerland. He wanted me to put the squeeze on you, so you'd sell him a tract of land for a development. He said there might be as much as four and a half million dollars in it for me— *four and a half million dollars,* Jesse—so I couldn't just ignore him."

"Right," Jesse said, after willing his clamped jaw to release. Nigel Meerland. Cheyenne's boss.

What a damn fool he'd been. All the evidence had been right there in front of him, like cursive on a giant blackboard. He'd ignored it. Skirted around it.

294

Why?

Because he'd wanted Cheyenne Bridges.

Wanted her body.

Wanted her mind.

Even wanted her spirit.

He'd *wanted* to believe her. So he had.

And all the while, she'd been jacking him around. Setting him up.

Her deception wasn't the worst part, though. Oh, no. The worst part was that he'd bought in, in spite of everything.

I came here to tell you that I still work for Nigel Meerland, she'd said, in a fury of indignant conviction. *He wanted me to spy on you, dig up some dirt, so you'd have to sell us the land. . . .*

In that moment, the bottom had dropped out of Jesse's personal universe.

Now, remembering, he closed his eyes.

Sucker, he thought.

"What are we going to do now?" Brandi asked.

Jesse opened his eyes. Sighed again. "The ball's in your court," he countered quietly. "You can't force me to sell the land, Brandi. You're almost a lawyer, so you know that. All you could do is keep me tied up in court for a long time, and trust me, my resources would last a lot longer than yours."

Brandi looked as though he'd slapped her. "I'm not stupid, Jesse. And I'm not mean. *I tried to warn you, remember?* Does that sound like somebody who wanted to make trouble?"

"No," Jesse admitted. "But the prospect of making four and a half million dollars obviously caught your attention."

"It would catch *anybody's* attention, Jesse," Brandi said, smiling for the first time since the whole boulder of a disaster had rolled down on him from out of nowhere. "Maybe not yours. But to the rest of us, that's a chunk of change."

Jesse spared a grin, even though he felt dead inside. In the end, everything came down to money. With Brandi. With Cheyenne.

It was all about money.

The idea depressed him so much that he almost couldn't stand it.

"What do you want?" he asked, after suffering in silence for a while.

"A settlement?"

"Brandi, we were married for a week."

She blushed. "But we *were* married."

Jesse pondered that, staring at the floor. At his naked, ugly feet. "Okay," he said. "You'll hear from my lawyer. His name is Travis Reid. Just in case you're wondering—*no,* I'm not giving you four and a half million dollars—but it will be enough to set you up. In return, you'll have to sign off on any claims, past, present or future. No more phone calls. No more 'loans.' Especially no more showing up at my house, stripping to the skin, and helping yourself to my shirts. Understood?"

Brandi looked both ashamed and encouraged. "Understood," she said.

"Good. Now, put your clothes on and get out of here."

She nodded, but she didn't move from the chair. Tears glazed her eyes.

"How come I didn't see your car when I came in?" Jesse asked, as an afterthought. His mind was still reeling, sorting and sifting, struggling to make sense of things that seemed obvious in retrospect, but weren't. He had a lot of catching up to do, a lot of squaring away.

Only a couple of weeks ago, his life had been so simple. The next step? Always obvious. Keep on keeping on.

Then Cheyenne had come back to Indian Rock and turned the whole works upside down.

Nothing about his relationship with Cheyenne Bridges was obvious. Or simple. She'd played Delilah to his Sampson, and that infuriated him. But there was something else coursing beneath that rage, an underground river of emotions he couldn't readily define.

"I parked behind the house," Brandi said.

"Why?"

"Because everything about that Meerland guy creeped me out, that's why. I felt like he was following me. *Watching* me. He looked me up on the Internet, Jesse. He knew all about Dan, and my dad getting shot in that robbery, and us being married. I'm not a famous person—I sell shoes and go to night school. It's not like there are a bunch of Web sites dedicated to me. But Meerland *knew* so much."

Jesse shook his head. Ah, the wonders of mega search engines. "Nobody's going to hurt you, Brandi," he said. "I'll deal with Meerland. You go back to California and do your thing."

"You're not mad at me?"

"I'm not mad at you," Jesse confirmed.

"Couldn't I just stay the night? Sleep in one of your sisters' rooms? I'm not scared, now that you're awake."

Now that you're awake.

Was he? If so, then why did he still feel as though he were stuck in the middle of a bad dream?

"No," he said. "I'll follow you back to town. Get you a room. In the morning, you're out of here, Brandi. For good. That's part of the deal."

She sighed. "Okay," she said, unfolding her long legs and standing up, keeping herself cosseted in the afghan, like a small child with a favorite blanket. "No hard feelings?"

"No hard feelings," Jesse agreed.

Not where Brandi was concerned, anyway.

"I KNEW IT," RANCE SAID, the next morning in the meeting room when Cheyenne spilled the whole story to him and Keegan. Turning to his cousin, who looked grim, he added, "Didn't I tell you something was rotten?"

Cheyenne sat up very straight, fighting tears. All she had left was her dignity, and precious little of that. It was over with Jesse—if indeed "it" had ever really begun—and now her job was gone, too. She'd already left a message for Nigel on his voice mail.

"Sue me," she'd said. "I'm telling them everything."

With that, she'd hung up, and when the inevitable callback had come, a few minutes later, she'd shut off the phone instead of answering.

"Now what?" Keegan asked, focusing on Cheyenne with disturbing intensity.

"I guess that's up to you," Cheyenne said. "I know you probably won't want me around, so—"

Keegan frowned. "Hold it," he interrupted. "I need some time to think about this."

"What's to think about?" Rance asked.

Cheyenne braced herself. What, indeed, was there to think about? She'd committed the unpardonable sin. She'd deceived people who had placed their trust in her.

Tears threatened again. She was going to lose ever so much more than her job. When the word got out, nobody in Indian Rock would want her around.

Not Jesse, certainly.

Not Rance and Keegan.

Not even Sierra and Janice and Elaine.

She'd be left without a single friend.

"She came to us and told us the truth," Rance went on. "That's worth something to me."

The words so startled Cheyenne that, for a long moment, she didn't believe she'd actually heard them. She'd made them up, surely.

"Me, too," Keegan agreed, but only after a gusty

sigh. "It took a lot of ba—er—courage, considering."

Cheyenne blinked, confused. Were they—? Did she dare hope—?

"Nobody," Rance said, "messes with a McKettrick."

Forget hope. She was toast.

"Come off it," Keegan argued wearily. "*Plenty* of people mess with us. Shelley, for instance."

Cheyenne fished in her purse, brought out the keys to the leased Escalade and the McKettrickCo cell phone. Laid them on the conference table.

"I'll just go now," she said.

"Go?" Keegan asked, looking blank.

"I'm fired, aren't I?"

Rance and Keegan exchanged glances.

"Is she?" Rance asked.

"I don't think so," Keegan answered.

Cheyenne swallowed. "But—"

"Everybody makes mistakes," Keegan said. "*Especially* the McKettricks. You're allowed, Cheyenne."

"Of course, if you hadn't made it right—" Rance ventured.

Cheyenne risked a faltering smile. "You might as well know that Nigel intends to sue me for breach of contract, and that will mean some legal wrangling. And Jesse—well—Jesse is never going to forgive me."

"Never is a long time," Keegan told her, gruffly gentle. "Jesse's a hothead. Once he's had a chance to cool down—"

Cheyenne shook her head, and the smile fell away, dropping like a stone into a bottomless abyss. Jesse had turned white when she'd told him why she was there, in his house, the night before. His eyes had turned so cold that she'd felt embalmed. Frozen.

And there was the matter of the woman.

The leggy blonde.

The wife.

Ex or current—it didn't matter.

Jesse had asked, early on, if she'd ever been married. She'd answered honestly, with a no. He, on the other hand, had told an out-and-out lie. And, worse, it had been an *unnecessary* lie. He could have told her about—what was her name?—Brandi.

But he hadn't, probably because he was still involved with her. She'd been in his bedroom, after all. Clad in a T-shirt, the uniform of women who have just made love with a man.

Yes, it was definitely over with Jesse.

He'd never trust her again, and she felt the same way about him.

"I met his wife," she said numbly.

"Jesse has a *wife?*" Keegan answered.

"No way," Rance said.

"I *met* her," Cheyenne said, miserable. Now, inadvertently, she'd opened another can of worms. How could Rance and Keegan, of all people, not have known Jesse was married? It only went to show just how deep his capacity for deception really went. "Her name is Brandi. She's drop-dead gorgeous."

Rance closed one hand into a loose fist and tapped the conference table with it once, sharply. *"Damn."*

"I'll kill him if it's true," Keegan vowed. "The legal ramifications—"

"It's true," Cheyenne confirmed. She wasn't certain of many things, but she *did* know that Jesse either was or had been married. And her insides were scraped raw by the knowledge, by the incessant mental pictures of Jesse and Brandi making love.

She had no claims on Jesse, she reminded herself. Never had.

And he had no claims on her.

Rance's secretary rapped at the door. He had a phone call from Hong Kong. He knuckled the table again, in parting, and left to take care of business.

"Have dinner with me tonight?" Keegan asked when he and Cheyenne were alone.

She sighed. Shook her head. She'd already tried to play in the McKettricks' league once, and she'd been trampled. Besides, Keegan was her boss. "I don't go out with men I work for," she said.

Keegan flashed a grin. "Then maybe I should have fired you."

"I am beyond glad you didn't," Cheyenne admitted.

He reached across the table, touched her hand. Keegan McKettrick was as handsome as any man she'd ever met, including Jesse, but there was no charge. "Okay, then," he said. "We'll be friends. Would that be all right with you?"

"It would be wonderful."

"Good." Keegan stood, looked down at her for a few moments in thoughtful silence. "Let's get back to work, Ms. Bridges. I'd like to talk with your brother about joining the company, on a provisional basis, of course. Can he make it in today, or should I go to him?"

Cheyenne's heart wedged itself into her throat, and she had to swallow it before she could answer.

"I'll get him here," she said.

"You can handle the chair?"

Jesse had been loading and unloading Mitch's wheelchair lately. She'd gotten used to it. Grown complacent. Time for that to change.

"Yes," she answered.

Keegan took in her white linen suit. She'd put it on that morning, along with the usual panty hose and makeup, thinking she was dressing for her own funeral. Expecting to be thrown on the pyre.

"Let me help," he said.

Cheyenne started to protest, then swallowed her pride and nodded. Then, standing shakily, she spoke again. "Could you excuse me for just a few moments?"

"Sure," Keegan replied.

Cheyenne got up, walked past him, traversed the hallway and entered the women's restroom.

There, after checking the stalls for feet, she cried.

She cried until her mascara ran.

She cried until her throat hurt.

She cried until she was empty.

Then she scrubbed her face with a wet paper towel, sucked in a restorative breath and rejoined the real world.

· · ·

TWO HOURS LATER, MITCH ROLLED into McKettrickCo as if he meant to own it one day. He and Keegan had talked for forty-five minutes back at the house, on the front porch, while Cheyenne had stayed inside, giving them space, repairing her makeup, putting a load of laundry in the washer, washing up the breakfast dishes piled in the sink.

Miraculously, Nigel hadn't called on the landline.

*Un*miraculously, Jesse hadn't called, either.

Best not to hold her breath waiting for *that* to happen.

It was the last thing she wanted, anyway.

Wasn't it?

After the porch conference, Mitch had wheeled inside, beaming, to get into his best clothes.

Now, as Mitch toured his cubicle, already outfitted with a serious computer, Cheyenne retreated to her office, trying to look busy. In truth, all ability to concentrate had deserted her. She was a person going through the motions.

At lunchtime, Myrna popped in, like the mother on *Bewitched.* "Jesse-alert," she said, waggling her perfectly plucked eyebrows. "He just walked in with Travis."

Cheyenne stiffened. "And I'm supposed to care because . . . ?"

Myrna grinned. "I know about the Chinese food," she said.

Cheyenne, who had been standing, sank into her chair, stricken.

"Shall I tell him you're out of the office?" Myrna asked in a conspiratorial whisper.

"I can't imagine why he'd ask," Cheyenne answered, having recovered a little. "How did you know about the—the Chinese food?"

"I know everything." It wasn't a boast. Myrna was a woman stating a fact.

Cheyenne's gaze strayed to the desk calendar, where Jesse had marked a big *X* on the deadline for full penetration. "Everything?"

Myrna's grin widened. "Everything," she said.

Cheyenne blushed. "Oh, God," she murmured.

Myrna laughed. "I was young once, you know," she confided. "If I were you, that's one bet I'd be determined to *lose.*"

"I can't believe you said that."

"Believe it," Myrna said.

"If you know 'everything,' then you must have known—"

"About Brandi?" Myrna gave a dismissive wave. "That was just sex."

"How could you possibly—"

"Nothing gets by me," Myrna said. "Zip. Nada. There are no secrets in Myrna-world."

"Then—"

"Yes," Myrna interrupted, pausing to peer down the hallway. "They're coming," she whispered. Then, as a parting shot, she added, "So you're really not moonlighting for Meerland anymore?"

Cheyenne almost swallowed her tongue.

Myrna chuckled. "Incoming," she warned, before stepping out into the hallway and shutting the door.

Cheyenne laid her head down on her desk and practiced deep breathing.

"DAMN, JESSE," Travis marveled when the two of them were shut up in his office. "I can see why you'd want to come to terms with Brandi, but a *million dollars?* Isn't that a little excessive?"

"Cheap at twice the price," Jesse said. He tried to make his tone light, but the fact was, he felt dried up and hollowed out. It was as though his soul had hit the trail and left the rest of him in the dust for good.

"Good God," Travis exclaimed. "It was a week of monkey sex in a Vegas hotel suite, Jesse, not a real marriage."

"Do it," Jesse bit out. "It won't make a dent, anyhow."

"That isn't the point." Travis was a lawyer, after all. He could be expected to argue, Jesse supposed.

He sighed. Rested one booted foot on the opposite knee. He'd dressed up for the visit to McKettrickCo, but not because he expected to run into Cheyenne.

Definitely not because of that.

"What *is* the point, then?" he asked.

"It *wasn't a real marriage,*" Travis reiterated.

"It was real enough to Brandi," Jesse reasoned. "She's not a bad person, Trav. She works hard, selling shoes. She's in law school. She's getting married after graduation. For real."

"All of which has *what* to do with her backing a semitruck into your bank accounts?"

"She could have pressed for a lot more money than I'm offering. She could have played along with Cheyenne and that Meerland yahoo. But she drove all the way from L.A. to Indian Rock to clue me in. The way I see it, she saved me a lot more trouble than she's causing."

Now, it was Travis's turn to sigh. "You realize that you're going against the advice of your attorney, who also happens to be your best friend?"

"I get that, Trav," Jesse said. "Just write it up, will you? So I can get out of here?"

"And go where?"

"Not to jump off a bridge, if that's what you're thinking," Jesse answered. He was headed up onto the ridge, once he was through putting *paid* to the Brandi epic. He planned to assemble some gear, saddle up his favorite horse, gather the others like a pack string and ride for the high country.

No telling when he'd be back.

The land had patched up his soul before. It would do it again.

Travis fixed him with a look that said he wanted an answer, and he wouldn't give up until he got it.

"I'll be on the ridge," Jesse said, willing to give up that much because Travis was his friend, but no more.

Travis nodded to show he understood and pulled a pen from the inside pocket of his spiffy suit coat and reached for a legal pad. "You'd better be back in time for the wedding," he said.

Jesse grinned. "I'll be there."

"Good," Travis replied. His jawline looked a little tight, but he seemed to be coming around to Jesse's way of thinking. "Now, we've got a figure for the settlement. What's Brandi's side of the agreement?"

CHEYENNE WAS JUST SHUTTING down her computer when Mitch came in to get a look at her office.

He gave a low whistle. "Pretty bodacious," he said.

Cheyenne smiled. "I like it," she answered.

Mitch turned to shut the door, then scanned the room again. His gaze snagged on the bamboo-shoot-with-panda on her desk, and a small frown creased his forehead.

"What's this?" he asked rhetorically.

"Myrna gave it to me," Cheyenne said, skipping the obvious answer, distracted now, rifling through a desk drawer for a file she'd downloaded and printed out earlier. "Welcome-aboard kind of thing."

"Nanny-cam," Mitch said.

Cheyenne laughed. "Right," she scoffed. Where was that file? She was sure she'd put it in her desk drawer.

"I mean it," Mitch insisted. "See for yourself."

Cheyenne looked up, saw that Mitch had pulled the panda off the bamboo shoot. Fishing into a little slit in the stuffed animal's back with his fingers, he brought out a tiny technological wonder with an infinitesimal lens on the front.

"So *that's* how she knew."

"Who?" Mitch asked, frowning. "That's how who knew what?"

Cheyenne snatched the camera out of her brother's hand, held it in front of her face and looked into the little glass eye staring back at her. "The game is up, Myrna," she said. "And if you've got any other bugs planted around here, you'd *better* tell me, because I'm going to take this little piece of equipment straight to Keegan if you don't."

"Wow," Mitch said, full of apparent admiration. "That Myrna is really something."

"She sure is," Cheyenne agreed.

A quick, nervous tap sounded at the door.

"Come in, Myrna," Cheyenne called.

Myrna slunk in, red-faced. "I need twenty-four hours," she said. "To gather up the surveillance equipment, I mean."

"Twenty-four hours," Cheyenne agreed, feeling implacable. "Not one second more."

Myrna nodded and vanished again, shutting the door behind her.

Cheyenne blew on the Lilliputian camera, like a gunfighter blowing the smoke from the barrel of a pistol, and dropped the thing into a desk drawer.

"Where could she have gotten something like that?" she whispered.

Mitch grinned. "On the Internet, of course," he said. "$19.95 plus postage and handling. Are you really going to report her to Keegan?"

Cheyenne sighed, deflated. "I don't know," she replied.

"You don't have to whisper," Mitch told her. "The mic was attached to the camera."

"Why would anybody want to spy on me?" She didn't care if Myrna overheard that one, through some bug they hadn't discovered yet. She intended to ask her about it straight out, when they got a private moment.

"For fun?" Mitch suggested.

Cheyenne remembered Jesse feeding her morsels of sweet-and-sour chicken. Remembered the wager they'd made, and all the talk about full penetration.

"Yikes," she muttered, wincing.

Mitch changed the subject with abrupt good cheer. "Keegan's having the Escalade fitted for a lift," he told her. "That way, we can ride to work together."

"Sounds good," Cheyenne said, feeling better in spite of discovering the camera in the panda bear and losing Jesse and all the rest of it. "Ready to go home?"

Mitch nodded. "Rance said to back the Escalade up to the loading dock under the building. That way, we can just roll the chair inside."

"Great idea," Cheyenne replied. "I guess that's why they pay him the big bucks." It still left the problem of hoisting Mitch up into the passenger seat, but with her help, he could probably manage.

"That and because he's part owner," Mitch said. "Let's get a move on, sis. I have a hot date with Bronwyn tonight. We're going to a drive-in movie."

Cheyenne laughed. "Well, I wouldn't want to interfere with your social life or anything."

As she closed her office door a couple of minutes later, she noticed that Travis's was still shut, and low voices came from inside. Jesse was still with him, then. For a moment, Cheyenne devoutly wished she'd planted a few panda-cams of her own, à la Myrna, so she'd know what was going on.

Myrna gave her a guilty glance as she passed the reception desk with Mitch, headed for the elevator.

Mitch pushed the button, and while they waited, Cheyenne approached Myrna, meaning to ask the burning question.

She didn't get the chance because the elevator arrived and because Myrna cut her off with an urgent whisper. "Jesse's paying that woman a million dollars," she said, "and he's going camping on the ridge for who knows how long."

CHAPTER SEVENTEEN

BEFORE CHEYENNE COULD respond to Myrna's announcement about the million dollars and the camping trip, she heard Jesse and Travis talking in the hallway.

Unable to face Jesse and endure being freeze-dried again, Cheyenne dashed to the elevator, where Mitch was waiting, impatiently holding it open. She jabbed at the close button with her thumb. As the doors shut, Jesse appeared and their gazes collided, like a pair of heat-seeking missiles over a war zone.

"Sooner or later," Mitch said looking up at her, "you're going to have to work this out."

"No, I'm not," Cheyenne argued. "Why is this thing so slow?"

They reached the loading dock, finally, and the doors whisked open.

Jesse was standing squarely in front of them, his eyes as glacial as ever—until they dropped to Mitch's upturned face.

"Hey, buddy," he said.

"Hey," Mitch replied.

"I thought you might need a little help getting into the Escalade," Jesse told Mitch. Cheyenne might have been invisible, for all the notice he gave her.

"He doesn't need—" Cheyenne began.

Mitch nudged her. "That'd be great, Jesse," he said.

Cheyenne suppressed a sigh, produced her keys and rushed off to get the Escalade from the parking lot. A couple of minutes later, she was backing up to the waist-high concrete slab where trucks unloaded office supplies, equipment and the like.

Meanwhile, Mitch descended the ramp alongside the stairs and reached to open the door of the Escalade on the passenger side.

"Watch this, Jesse," he said.

Jesse folded his arms, one side of his mouth quirking in a wan grin. "I'm watching," he answered.

Mitch strained, got hold of the inside door handle and hauled himself up into the seat. He was sweating, and he'd gone pale, but he looked so pleased with the accomplishment that Cheyenne's heart threatened to split right down the middle.

It occurred to her that the sensation might have more to do with Jesse being there than Mitch's newfound ability to get into a big SUV without help, but she instantly dismissed the idea. Hurried up the stairs onto the dock to raise the hatch on the back of the Escalade.

"Excellent," Jesse said. Again, his attention was solely for Mitch. "I hear you signed on with the outfit."

Mitch nodded proudly. "Thanks for putting in a good word with Keegan and Rance," he said.

Cheyenne went still to the very core of her being. He was thanking *Jesse? She* was the one who'd stuck her neck out.

"Not a problem," Jesse answered.

He was taking the credit.

Cheyenne simmered, tapped one foot in suppressed exasperation. The sound echoed in the empty chamber like a series of gunshots.

"Guess we'd better go," Mitch said, suddenly uncomfortable.

Jesse nodded, pushed the chair back up the ramp to the loading dock, elbowed Cheyenne aside, still without the slightest acknowledgment of her presence, and shoved it into the back.

Cheyenne fully intended never to speak to Jesse again. Two could play at the freeze-out game, after all.

"Jesse," she said instead.

He wouldn't look at her.

She repeated his name.

He slammed the hatch down, turned and walked away, without so much as a glance in her direction. She might have been a disembodied spirit, a dead person, caught between heaven and earth, trying in vain to communicate with a living one.

That was certainly how she felt.

She would not go after him.

She *would not.*

Oh, but she wanted to. She wanted to pound on his back with her fists. She wanted to yell. Make him turn around and look at her. Make him—

What?

She drew a deep breath, squared her shoulders and walked down the ramp. Got inside the Escalade and started the engine.

"What did you *do* to him?" Mitch asked.

Cheyenne shoved the SUV into gear and peeled out with a screech of tires. "What did *I* do to *him?*"

"It's got to be more than the Nigel thing. He is *seriously* pissed."

Cheyenne slammed on the brakes at the exit leading up into the parking lot and onto the street. "Now, you listen to me, Mitch Bridges! I don't want to hear another *word* about Jesse *or* Nigel! Not *another word!*"

"Whoa," Mitch said, awed.

Cheyenne laid her forehead against the steering wheel, fighting another attack of tears. "I'm sorry, Mitch," she whispered. "I'm sorry."

He reached out, patted her back in a tentative, little-brother way. "You know why he's so mad, Chey?" he asked. "I just figured it out. It's because he cares so much."

Cheyenne sniffled. Lifted her head. Drove on.

"Chey?" Mitch persisted.

"I heard what you said, Mitch. I'm simply choosing to ignore it."

"Why?"

"Because it isn't true."

"That's what you think," Mitch replied, very quietly. "When Jesse and I went riding, all he talked about was you. He wanted to know what your favorite color was, and whether or not you liked horror movies. That kind of stuff."

"He was just making conversation. Being polite. And besides, I thought we weren't going to talk about Jess—him."

Mitch sighed, and it was such a sad sound that Cheyenne turned to look at him. "Except for Mom," he said, "Jesse's the first person in a long time who believed I could do something besides play video games on my laptop."

"Mitch, I didn't mean—"

"Yes, you did. And I just want to go home, okay? I've already stood Bronwyn up once. She won't understand if I do it again."

Cheyenne glanced into the rearview mirror, saw Jesse's truck behind her. An overwhelming loneliness rose up inside her, swelling, threatening to tear her apart.

"I wouldn't want to interfere with your love life," she said stiffly.

"At least I have one," Mitch countered.

Cheyenne let the remark pass.

Drove down the main street of Indian Rock, Arizona, as if she didn't have a care in the world. All the while, though, she was painfully conscious of Jesse, following at a distance.

Maybe he was having second thoughts.

Maybe he would be willing to talk things over, like a rational human being. They could go their separate ways afterward, that was inevitable, but at least there would be some closure.

Cheyenne was desperate for closure.

There had been too many loose ends in her life.

She turned off when she came to her road.

Jesse went right on by.

CHAPTER EIGHTEEN

CHEYENNE HATED CASINOS.

Hated the noise, the sense of underlying desperation. The greed.

Most of all, she hated poker.

Now, here she was on a Saturday afternoon in June, set to play in a tournament. Her friends, Sierra, Elaine and Janice, were all counting on her to win. Run this gauntlet and carry the torch to Las Vegas.

She closed her eyes for a moment.

Elaine moved close, whispered, "You can do this, Cheyenne. For the clinic."

"For us," Janice added.

Only Sierra seemed uncertain. Little wonder, given that her wedding was one week away. She was probably wondering why she'd ever gotten involved in something this hopeless.

Cheyenne was wondering the very same thing—about herself.

She took a wary step toward the thirty or so preliminary tables, set up in a corner of the busy casino and officially roped off.

Was Jesse around?

God, she hoped not. Hoped he was still on the ridge, where Myrna had said he'd gone, doing whatever it was he did up there. Hoped he *wasn't*, too, because it had rained every night since the last time she'd seen him, on the loading dock at McKettrickCo. A man could come down with pneumonia, getting drenched like that.

Raining outside. Raining *inside*.

Cheyenne felt saturated, sodden through to the center of her heart.

"Just do your best," Sierra whispered

Cheyenne nodded.

Her best wasn't going to be good enough, that was the problem. Sure, she knew the game, but mostly as an observer. She had a passion for it, equal and entirely opposite to Jesse's.

She despised it. Wished it had never been invented.

Just one more reason why she'd been a complete idiot to fall for Jesse McKettrick.

She'd come to terms with that much, at least. She'd played with fire, and she'd been burned. She was in love with Jesse, had been since she was a kid, tacking pictures to the wall of her bedroom.

It was just as hopeless now as it had been back then. End of story.

She and the others signed in at the registration desk, pinned on their name tags, found their widely separated tables, moving between other milling dreamers. Cheyenne had hoped to sit with Sierra. Instead, she found herself among strangers.

She ignored the others at her table—they all seemed to know each other—and sat looking down at her interlaced fingers, longing to get through this day. Put it behind her, along with all the other days she wanted to forget.

Her dad's voice spoke suddenly inside her head. *Things are never so bad they can't get worse, kiddo.*

Startled, Cheyenne looked up.

Jesse was sitting directly across from her. His eyes burned into hers.

Instinct said, *Run!*

Pride said, *Stay.*

What did she really have to lose? She was zero-for-nothing as it was.

So she went with pride. Lifted her chin, straightened her spine. Waited out the first deal.

Jesse took the hand, with pocket aces. It didn't seem

to please him, though. He looked grim, like some lesser, scruffier version of his old self, sitting there in a baseball cap and a plain navy-blue sweatshirt. His face was gaunt and he needed a shave.

Cheyenne shook off the impressions, along with the tenderness those stirred in her.

He was the enemy.

Jesse didn't need to play in the early rounds to enter the Vegas tournament; he was the defending champion, which meant he was comped in, with his entry fees paid, a free suite and God only knew what other perks. There was only one reason for him to be here, in a local casino, on a rainy Saturday afternoon, and that was to bring her down. Knock her out of the running, just to prove he could.

Adrenaline surged through Cheyenne's system. *Damn* him, if he thought she was going to slink away like a kicked dog. Most likely, he'd beat her—he was, after all, a shark—but not without a fight.

Her focus intensified. Everything she knew about poker came back in a rush of dizzying clarity.

She met and held his gaze.

Bring it on, she told him silently.

He gave a semblance of a grin, as if he'd heard the thought. Then he nodded.

Cheyenne survived the first round.

So did Jesse.

She hung in through the second, too, with a back-to-the-wall determination to stay alive.

Jesse came with her.

319

All afternoon, it went that way. Players fell away, including Elaine, Janice and Sierra, who were now clustered together on the other side of the fat velvet rope marking off the battleground. Mitch and Ayanna were somewhere in the crowd, too. Ayanna didn't approve of poker any more than Cheyenne did, but she wanted to lend moral support.

The games wore on.

Finally, at seven o'clock in the evening, they were down to the final table.

Cheyenne. A man who looked like a truck driver. An old woman with blue hair. A biker, with a bald head and tattoos up both arms.

And Jesse.

Cheyenne began to sweat, on the inside, where it didn't show.

She figured she could take the truck driver. He was nervous, despite an outward pretense of calm. The tells were there, in the tick under his right eye and the way he tapped his fingertips on the table between hands.

The old woman was harder to read. She wore wire-rimmed glasses and a cotton print dress, and looked as though she might have left a pot of jelly simmering on the stove at home.

The biker cared too much. He leaned slightly forward in his chair and constantly fiddled with his dwindling stack of chips.

And then there was Jesse.

Cool.

Quiet.

Totally in control.

God, how she wanted to beat him.

The biker went broke first, then the truck driver.

The old woman held on, then went all in on a bluff.

Jesse called.

Granny went down.

Cheyenne waited for her cards. Internally, she was a jabbering mess, and Jesse might have been picking up on that, but she'd learned a few things from her dad. One of them was never to reveal any emotion at all, not at the poker table, anyway.

She got a two and a four, off-suit.

The flop was three queens.

She was screwed, unless another two and four came up. Then she'd have a full house.

She could fold, but then Jesse, being the only other player still in the game, would take the pot by default. He had three times as many chips as she did as it was, and another win would put him in an unassailable position. The blinds were steep by then, and the next one would clean her out.

She shoved in a small stack of chips. Out of the corner of one eye, she caught sight of Mitch and her mother, watching from the sidelines. Ayanna put one hand to her mouth.

The turn came down, and it was a four of clubs.

Cheyenne didn't move a muscle, but her heart was pounding.

Jesse raised the stakes, quietly relentless. There was

blood in the water, and he knew it. He was circling in for the kill.

Cheyenne matched his bet.

The river, the fifth card, was a jack of spades, useless to Cheyenne.

Jesse sat back in his chair. Smiled a little.

Damn him. He had the other queen.

He went all in.

Cheyenne did the same, knowing there was no way in hell she could take the pot, unless Jesse was bluffing. Even if he was and she won, she'd have to surrender most of the chips to make up for the disparity in their bets.

He wasn't bluffing. He had the fourth queen.

Cheyenne left her cards facedown, which was her prerogative, and pushed back her chair to stand.

Jesse stood, too, seemingly oblivious to the applause, and the exuberant man who appeared at his side with a microphone.

After all, Jesse McKettrick was used to winning.

No big deal.

Calling on all the dignity she possessed, Cheyenne turned and walked away. As she passed Sierra, Elaine and Janice, who were staring at her in awe, as though she'd just parted the Red Sea, as though she'd *won,* she shook her head.

She didn't want them to follow her.

Didn't want *anyone* to follow her.

All she wanted was a few minutes alone.

She spotted a side exit and headed for it. Stepped

outside into a drizzling, chilly rain. It was dark, and the lights on the side of the building seemed muted.

The door opened behind her.

"Cheyenne?"

She didn't have to turn around. It was Jesse. He'd come to gloat, of course.

"Go away," she said without looking at him. "You won. You're a better player than I am."

He stepped in front of her, hooked a finger under her chin, so she had to look at him. "Is that why you think I came? To take you down?"

She swallowed. "Why else would you do it?"

"Because I love the game. Maybe because I love—"

Cheyenne's heart stopped. "Don't," she whispered.

"Cheyenne, will you listen to me?"

"No."

He kissed her, lightly. Cheyenne was electrified.

"I figured out one thing, while I was up there on the ridge feeling sorry for myself, Cheyenne," he said. "I love you. I think you love me. So what if we start over? Play with a new deck?"

"You *lied* to me."

"That makes us even," Jesse said.

"You could have told me about Brandi."

"I know," he answered. "I'm sorry."

She blinked. "You are?"

"Yes." He waited.

"I tried to tell you about Nigel."

Jesse nodded. "I know," he repeated. "I guess I just didn't want to hear it."

Stubbornly, Cheyenne folded her arms. It was cold out and, besides, she had a dangerous impulse to throw them around Jesse's neck and hang off him like a groupie at a rock concert. "I still don't understand why you didn't mention a little thing like *being married.*"

"I didn't think of it as a marriage, Cheyenne," Jesse answered. "Brandi and I were together for a week. It's not as if we had any kind of a history together, or kids. It was a sexcapade."

"Very colorful. Is that supposed to make me feel better?"

He grinned. "No. But I can think of a couple of other things that might do the trick."

Cheyenne opened her mouth to speak, but before a word came out, she saw a shadow move behind Jesse. There was another flash of motion, then a sickening thunk. Jesse's eyes went blank, and he crumpled at her feet.

"CHEATING BASTARD," said one of the two men Cheyenne had seen in the back room at Lucky's, when Jesse had signaled her, with a single look, that things were about to go south in a hurry.

The assailant was holding a crowbar, and the other man had a knife.

Cheyenne stepped between them and Jesse, who was bleeding at the back of his head and groaning. She had no weapons, nothing but rage.

"Step aside," Crowbar man said. "We're not through with him yet."

"Security!" a woman's voice screamed in the thrumming void that buzzed around Cheyenne like a swarm of invisible bees. "Somebody get security!"

Ayanna.

"Like we're afraid of a bunch of casino cops," scoffed Crowbar man. He shoved Cheyenne aside, sending her crashing against a Dumpster, and raised the steel bar over Jesse with both hands.

Acting on primitive instinct, and nothing else, Cheyenne scrambled toward Jesse's prone form, intending to cover him, absorb the blow herself, anything.

She was nearly run over in the process.

By Mitch's wheelchair.

He zoomed into Crowbar man, mowed him down, screaming like a warrior in the midst of battle.

Crowbar man shrieked in pain and terror, and his buddy dropped his knife, whirled and ran.

Mitch probably would have backed over Crowbar man if Ayanna hadn't stopped him. Meanwhile, Jesse sat up, dazed, bloody and grinning like an idiot.

Security swarmed around them, radios crackling.

Cheyenne crawled to Jesse, threw her arms around him.

Sobbed with relief.

"Your brother is a good man to have around in a fight," Jesse said, close to her ear. With one hand, he plucked the pins from her hair, so it fell down around her shoulders.

She rested her forehead against his.

The rain came down harder.

Medics closed in.

Somebody pulled Cheyenne to her feet, and she was surprised to discover that it was Mitch. Ayanna wrapped her in a tight embrace.

"Oh, honey. Are you all right?"

Cheyenne nodded, sniffling.

An ambulance arrived, and Jesse, protesting the whole time, was strapped to a gurney and loaded into the back, right alongside the man who had attacked him. Cheyenne wanted to go with Jesse, but it wasn't in the cards. A policeman scrambled in, the doors closed, and the ambulance sped away.

Cheyenne was led back into the casino, by security, examined by a staff medic, and questioned extensively. Ayanna and Mitch stayed with her until she was finally, blessedly, allowed to leave.

Her mother and brother had come to the tournament in the van, but they left in Cheyenne's company Escalade, with Ayanna at the wheel. Mitch rode shotgun, his chest swelled with pride because he'd been able to help Jesse when it had mattered.

Cheyenne, dazed with exhaustion and relief, was content to sit in the backseat.

When they got home, she was content to let her mother and brother fuss over her. She sat on the front porch, with Mitch, watching the rain fall, while Ayanna made tea.

"You were great, Mitch," she said, when she thought she could trust herself to speak.

"You think Jesse's okay?" Mitch fretted.

"I know he is," Cheyenne said, reaching over to squeeze her brother's hand. "It takes more than a crowbar to crack that hard McKettrick skull of his."

"You came so close—at the tournament, I mean."

Cheyenne smiled.

"You know, don't you," Mitch went on, "that you get the seat in Vegas? Jesse's already in. I heard him tell one of the casino officials, during the last break, that he was forfeiting the prize. That means it goes to you."

Cheyenne didn't have time to absorb that bit of information.

The phone rang, the sound muffled by the walls of the house and the rain.

Cheyenne rose out of the ancient lawn chair she'd been sitting in and rushed inside to answer.

Ayanna, with a tea bag in one hand and an empty cup in the other, stood staring at the jangling black antique affixed to the kitchen wall.

Cheyenne grabbed the receiver. Her heart pounded and she couldn't seem to catch her breath. It had to be Jesse. It had to be.

It was.

"Hello?" he said when she didn't speak.

"Jesse." The name whooshed out of Cheyenne, like a sigh of relief. She'd been putting on a brave front, for Mitch's sake, mostly, but now she could cry. "Are you—are you okay?"

"I don't know," Jesse said. "Did I dream the part where I told you I loved you?"

She laughed, but she was crying at the same time. "No," she said. "You didn't dream it."

"I don't recall getting an answer."

She drew in her breath. Let it out, slow and moist. "I love you, Jesse," she said.

"Good," he answered. "Good."

"Are you all right, Jesse? What did the doctors say?"

"They stitched up the back of my head and plastered on a bandage. I have to have a CAT scan, and if that's clear, I can come home. Or, at least, I could—if I had a ride."

"I'll come and get you," Cheyenne said.

"I'll be the guy in the gauze hat," Jesse answered.

She laughed.

"Drive carefully, Cheyenne. The roads are slick and Arizona drivers aren't used to rain."

"I'll be careful," she promised.

He gave her the name of the hospital and said goodbye.

Ayanna watched as she hung up the phone, a tentative smile playing on her lips. "Will you drop me off at the casino, Chey? So I can pick up the van? I need it for work tomorrow."

Cheyenne nodded.

Ayanna didn't move. "This can be good, Cheyenne. You and Jesse, I mean. Let it be good. Just relax and let it be good."

"I will, Mom," Cheyenne said softly. She took the cup and the tea bag from her mother's hands and set them aside. Hugged her hard.

Forty-five minutes later, Cheyenne rushed into the waiting room at the hospital in Flagstaff.

Jesse was waiting, seated in a wheelchair.

She went to him, cupped her hands on either side of his beard-stubbled face. "The scan?" she asked, and everything inside her, every cell of every organ, went still, waiting, reaching for the answer.

"Nothing in there but a few rocks," Jesse said, tapping his head.

She kissed him. "Let's get out of here."

"I was thinking we could play poker," Jesse told her as a nurse wheeled him outside, over to the parked Escalade.

"Poker?" Cheyenne marveled when the two of them were alone, Jesse buckled into the passenger seat and her behind the wheel.

"Strip," Jesse said. "Winner take all."

Cheyenne laughed. "You're on, buddy," she replied.

They played sitting cross-legged in the middle of Jesse's bed, and Cheyenne was on a losing streak. Every time Jesse won a hand, she had to take off another article of clothing, and he celebrated the victory by kissing and caressing every newly uncovered part of her anatomy.

She was down to her panties, her nipples wet and hard from Jesse's tongue, when she finally protested.

Grinning, he got up, pulled his sweatshirt off over his head. Unbuttoned his jeans, tossed them aside, along with his boxer briefs. Except for the wad of gauze at the back of his head, he looked like his deliciously usual self.

Cheyenne swallowed, her gaze traveling from his impressive erection to his face, then back down again. She took off her panties.

He laughed at her expression, stretched out on the bed and reached for her.

Cheyenne gasped with anticipation, thinking he was going to set her astraddle of him, and take her in a single, soul-splintering thrust. She loved riding him like that, loved having him so deep inside her.

Instead, he scooted down until his head was between her legs. He nuzzled through, took her into his mouth and sucked, gently at first, and then with a hunger that set her blood on fire.

Clasping her hips, he stayed with her until she threw back her head, shouting with ecstatic surrender, her body buckling helplessly in the throes of a blazing release.

When it was over, she fell onto the mattress beside him, delectably spent.

He moved up, took her into his arms. Kissed her temple.

She crooned with contentment and cuddled against his side. "Maybe you should be resting," she said. "After all, you just got out of the hospital."

"Like hell I'm going to rest," Jesse replied. "And you're not, either."

She ran a hand slowly down over his chest and belly, closed it around his erection. Stroked him.

He groaned.

She went down on him.

And when he shattered, she was there to pick up the pieces.

One week later . . .

EXCEPT FOR THE BANDAGE, Jesse looked like any other member of the wedding party. He stood proudly beside Travis at the front of church in his fancy tuxedo.

Travis, of course, had eyes only for Sierra.

She made a beautiful bride, in her voluminous white dress and pearl-studded veil. Liam, precious in a miniature tux of his own, stood next to her, holding a pillow with Travis's and Sierra's wedding bands shimmering on top of it.

Cheyenne watched, stricken with love for Jesse and happiness for her friends, from the third pew. Ayanna sat beside her, and Mitch was on the aisle, in his chair.

"See?" Ayanna whispered, squeezing Cheyenne's hand. "There *is* such a thing as a happy ending."

Cheyenne nodded, but she didn't take her gaze off Jesse.

As if he felt her eyes on him, he turned his head slightly and winked.

"Dearly beloved," the minister began, to a chorus of female sniffles rising from the congregation, "we are gathered here—"

We are gathered here, Cheyenne thought.

Family.

Friends.

A whole community.

Gathered together as one, in celebration.

Somehow, Cheyenne reflected, her heart had found its way back to this place, and these people, and she had followed it, never dreaming what was in store for her here.

She had come home.

Home to Indian Rock.

Home to herself.

Home to Jesse.

At long, long last, Cheyenne Bridges had come home.

After the wedding, there was a reception in the hall adjacent to the sanctuary. Jesse, as best man, lifted a glass of champagne, gave a toast to the bride and groom.

Then came the cutting of the cake, and the band struck up a waltz.

Travis and Sierra took the floor first, alone, surrounded by a golden glow of love and summer sunlight. Cheyenne blinked away tears, watching them.

Jesse stepped up behind her, wrapped her loosely in his arms.

She turned to look up into his eyes.

"I love you, Cheyenne," he said, very quietly.

"I love you," she replied.

"Good," he told her, "because that guy is outside, asking for you. Nigel."

Cheyenne frowned. "Nigel is here?"

Jesse took her hand, led her out of the church hall, into the sunshine.

Sure enough, Nigel was waiting on the sidewalk, looking winsomely apologetic. He wore a sports shirt and slacks, and Cheyenne saw his passport peeking out of one shirt pocket.

"If you came to serve papers on me," Cheyenne told him, in an angry whisper, "you picked a *really* lousy time to do it!"

Nigel glanced at Jesse, then looked back at Cheyenne. "I'm not going to sue you," he said.

Cheyenne, who had advanced like a storm trooper, backpedaled a little. "You're not?"

"Of course I'm not," Nigel said. "I was only trying to scare you into doing what I wanted."

"And you're here—in the middle of our friends' wedding celebration because—?"

"Because I didn't know there was a wedding until I got here," Nigel said. "I came to apologize. Wipe the slate clean."

"Did the company collapse?"

Nigel sighed, nodded. "My grandmother is waiting in England to welcome me back to the fold with open arms." He paused, smiled sadly. "And a meat cleaver."

Jesse's grip tightened on Cheyenne's hand.

"Forgive me?" Nigel wheedled.

"I forgive you," Cheyenne replied. "Which does *not* mean I ever want to lay eyes on you again, as long as I live."

Nigel grinned. "So long, Pocahontas," he said. Then

he leaned forward, kissed Cheyenne's cheek lightly and turned to walk away.

Jesse and Cheyenne stood on the church steps, watching him go.

"Should I be jealous of that guy?" Jesse asked speculatively, after a long moment.

"No," Cheyenne replied, turning from her past and looking up into the face of her future.

"Are you sure?"

"I'm positive."

"Why?"

"Because Nigel is gay. And that's just *one* of the reasons."

Jesse laughed. Then he pulled Cheyenne against him. Kissed her thoroughly—as thoroughly as if they were playing strip poker in his bedroom instead of standing in front of a church.

"What was that for?" she asked, once she caught her breath.

"Practice," Jesse said.

"Practice?"

"Kissing. Churches. I'm kind of getting into the spirit of the thing." He looked down at her, his eyes serious and soft. "Will you marry me, Cheyenne?"

She swallowed. "M-Marry you?"

He nodded.

"When?"

"When you're ready. I don't care how long it takes. I'll wait."

She smiled, slipped her arms around his neck.

The night before, she'd moved in with him.

She'd hoped for a proposal, but she hadn't expected it to come this soon. "My mother was right," she said.

Jesse looked puzzled. "About what?"

"There *is* such a thing as a happy ending. That's what she said. Inside, a few minutes ago, when Travis and Sierra were exchanging vows."

Jesse's mouth turned up at the corner, in the way she loved. "Is this one of them? A happy ending, I mean?"

"More like a happy beginning," Cheyenne said. "And happy beginnings always start with a yes."

"Yes?" Jesse echoed.

Cheyenne kissed him again.

"Yes."

Center Point Publishing
600 Brooks Road ● PO Box 1
Thorndike ME 04986-0001 USA

(207) 568-3717

US & Canada:
1 800 929-9108